Praise for *[The Wrong Callahan]*

'For romance lovers, this is [   ]
you!' –*Australian Women's Weekly*

'I loved this book ... *The Wrong Callahan* is a well-paced tale of love, betrayal, family, PTSD and small town communities. Another five-star read from me!' –Beauty and Lace

'I enjoyed this book immensely ... I don't have words to describe exactly how excited I am to read the second book in this trilogy next year. I loved being on Stringybark Creek with the Callahan family and just want to dive back into it.' –Noveltea Corner

'Just in time for Christmas, Karly Lane returns with another winning read ... Although *The Wrong Callahan* is here to entertain rural romance readers, Karly Lane would love the audience to take away a small sense of appreciation of the work our agricultural workers commit to, day in day out. It truly is tremendous and worthy of our attention in this current challenging environment for our Aussie farmers.' –Mrs B's Book Reviews

Praise for *Mr Right Now*

'To say that I've been waiting for the sequel to *The Wrong Callahan* might be understating just how excited I've been to read this book! Karly Lane has a wonderful way of creating a sense of place; and the characters leap off the page. These are books I know I can fall into time and time again and still be transported.' –Noveltea Corner

'*Mr Right Now* is another delightful read from one of my favourite authors, Karly Lane ... Lane's stories have depth and explore many themes that are relevant to relationships in all forms, exploring father/son relationships and the old-ways versus the new-ways, farming accidents, diversity on the land, droughts, storms, community support, family and friendships ... I simply can't wait for book 3.' –Beauty and Lace

Karly Lane lives on the mid north coast of New South Wales. Proud mum to four children and wife of one very patient mechanic, she is lucky enough to spend her day doing the two things she loves most—being a mum and writing stories set in beautiful rural Australia.

Also by Karly Lane

North Star
Morgan's Law
Bridie's Choice
Poppy's Dilemma
Gemma's Bluff
Tallowood Bound
Second Chance Town
Third Time Lucky
If Wishes Were Horses
Six Ways to Sunday
Someone Like You
The Wrong Callahan
Mr Right Now
Fool Me Once
Something Like This

KARLY LANE

Return to *Stringybark Creek*

Book 3 of the
Callahans of Stringybark Creek series

ALLEN&UNWIN
SYDNEY·MELBOURNE·AUCKLAND·LONDON

Allen & Unwin
83 Alexander Street
Crows Nest NSW 2065
Australia
Phone: (61 2) 8425 0100
Email: info@allenandunwin.com
Web: www.allenandunwin.com

A catalogue record for this
book is available from the
National Library of Australia

ISBN 978 1 76087 861 0

Set in 12.4/18.2 pt Sabon LT Pro by Bookhouse, Sydney
Printed in Australia by McPherson's Printing Group

10 9 8 7 6 5

The paper in this book is FSC® certified.
FSC® promotes environmentally responsible,
socially beneficial and economically viable
management of the world's forests.

To my children, Jessica, Kaitlin, Rourke and Milly

One

Hadley felt the weariness of the long hours in the car fade away and a sense of homecoming fill her. *Stringybark Station*. It was good to be back. She pulled up in the driveway and climbed out of the car, stretching her cramped legs and aching shoulders. There was nothing like the smell of wide-open spaces—and nothing as peaceful as the stillness and quiet of simply stopping and allowing yourself to listen to . . . nothing. She closed her eyes and tipped back her head, feeling the warmth of the sun on her face and letting herself enjoy the instant serenity that always came with being home.

Her phone began to ring inside the car, breaking the moment, and with a reluctant sigh Hadley opened her eyes and got back in. She glanced at the name on the screen and then turned off the phone. Another reporter wanting a quote . . . or, better yet, a story. Hadley gave a harsh snort at that—there was a special kind of irony in the fact that she made a living roaming the world in search of a good story, and now she was the source of mindless entertainment for local tabloids and cheap gossip magazines.

Maybe as a lowly war correspondent, she'd have been able to fly under the radar, but unfortunately when a lowly overseas correspondent marries a national media celebrity, it was always going to be impossible to keep their divorce out of the spotlight.

She pulled back out onto the dirt driveway, the tranquillity shattered. She'd been dreading this part for months.

Hadley might be a grown woman with a successful career in breaking news from all around the world, but when it came to telling her parents that the marriage she'd been leading them to believe was fine was actually over . . . well, she might as well be thirteen years old again and about to tell them the principal would be calling with unpleasant news.

The house loomed ahead and Hadley smiled despite the anxiety she was feeling. She knew her parents wouldn't disown her over this, but she hated disappointing them. She hated being a failure, and that's what she felt like—a big fat failure. How hard was it to stay married, for goodness sake? She hadn't even been able to do that. Worse still—her family had always had doubts about Mitch, but she'd been so determined to prove everyone wrong that she'd ignored all the warning signs that she was making a huge mistake.

She'd stupidly believed she had to be more like her perfect older sister, Harmony. She'd grown up in her sister's shadow at school, the teachers perplexed that two children from the same family could be so different. Harmony had never been more aptly named. She was the perfect student. The perfect daughter, the perfect wife. She left school and married into a perfectly respectable family from Griffith, then went on to have two perfect children—one boy and one girl. She had a beautiful house and an expensive car. She was on all the important committees and volunteered in her spare time. The woman was a walking advertisement for the perfect life. Hadley gave a small, bitter snort. Until she wasn't.

Her perfect sister was now divorced, but even that didn't seem to have dimmed the light of her halo. She was now the perfect single mother . . . another failing Hadley felt keenly after she'd had a miscarriage only a handful of months earlier. But she wasn't going there. Focus on the anger, she reminded herself. That's what had got her through the past few months. It was far more empowering to be angry.

Hadley still couldn't quite believe it. Harmony had been having an affair with her husband.

Hadley blinked away a sting in her eyes but she'd managed to plaster a bright smile on her face by the time her mother appeared on the verandah upstairs and give a surprised yelp of delight at seeing her daughter.

'Robert!' Lavinia Callahan yelled. 'Robert, come and see who just arrived!'

God, she loved her parents. Married over forty years, they were still as in love as they had been back when they first met. And they were absolutely devoted to each and every one of their four children. They were her anchor.

Hadley quickly climbed the front stairs of the sprawling, low-set Queenslander she'd grown up in and was immediately wrapped in her mother's arms. For a split second she could imagine she was six years old again and safe from all the troubles in the world.

'Why didn't you tell us you were coming?'

'I wanted to surprise you,' she said, grateful that her father chose that moment to wander outside and see what all the fuss was about.

'Well, I'll be! Look what the cat dragged in,' her father grinned, opening his arms wide at her approach.

'Hi, Dad.' Hadley breathed in the smell of his freshly washed shirt as he hugged her tight.

'*Wanted to surprise us*, she says,' Lavinia admonished from behind them. 'You and your brother have a lot in common,' she added. 'This is something Linc would do.'

'We just like to keep you on your toes.'

'How long are you here for? What are you doing? Where's Mitch?' Lavinia shot off the questions in rapid succession, her gaze moving to scan her daughter's car.

'Give the girl time to breathe, woman,' Bob chuckled.

'Ah, Mitch is . . .' Hadley hesitated as her mother looked back at her expectantly. *Tell her*, a voice inside pressed. '. . . not here,' she finished.

'Well, I can see that. Is he coming out later?'

'No. He's working,' she said slowly.

'Oh. That's a shame,' Lavinia said, patting her daughter's arm. 'I guess that means we get you all to ourselves then.'

Hadley smiled weakly. She had to tell them, but surely there was some kind of protocol with things like this? You couldn't very well be expected to announce your divorce within the first five minutes. Her parents both stood there beaming at her. No, it would be better if she broached it gently later on.

Two

Oliver Dawson grabbed his dog, Diesel, by the scruff of the neck and rubbed him vigorously in their daily greeting ritual. 'You wanna go for a drive?' he asked, roughing the animal lightly in a show of affection. 'Go on then, get in,' he said and watched as the dog turned in happy circles and then headed over to the farm ute.

Ollie opened the cabin door and the red-coated heeler leaped gracefully up onto the passenger seat and waited patiently for his owner to start the car.

The sound of Ollie's ringtone made him pause and he pulled the phone from his pocket. 'Hey, loser,' he greeted his best friend and neighbour, Griffin Callahan, in lieu of a more traditional hello. 'Ready to get your butt kicked tonight?'

'Whatever, tosser,' Griff scoffed. 'That's what I'm calling about. I can't make darts tonight.'

'What? You really are scared, aren't ya?' Ollie added in a gleeful tone.

'Yeah, right.'

'So what's your excuse?'

'We've got a surprise visitor. Hadley's come home. Mum wants us all at dinner tonight.'

Ollie felt something kick in his chest briefly at the mention of his mate's sister, but he cleared his throat and forced his attention back to the conversation. 'I guess I could let you off this once. I'm gonna tell the guys that you were only using your sister as an excuse 'cause you were scared, though,' he added.

'Yeah, yeah,' Griffin drawled. 'Enjoy your moment. Next week you won't have anything to gloat about. Hey,' he added before they hung up, 'drop by and say g'day to Hads when you get a chance.'

'Yeah. Sure. I'll do that,' Ollie said before disconnecting the call and staring out through the front window in an attempt to get his disjointed thoughts under control.

Hadley Callahan had always managed to throw him off guard, even as kids. He and his twin sister, Olivia, had grown up with the Callahan kids, and for a long time they'd been more like cousins than neighbours, until one day they weren't . . . or, more to the point, Hadley wasn't. Seemingly out of the blue, Ollie had started having different feelings towards his best friend's little sister and everything changed.

He'd never acted on any of these impulses, though. He wasn't game. Griffin would probably have killed him if he'd told him he liked his sister as he'd always been protective of her. And then there was Hadley herself—she'd been no stranger to throwing a punch if she had to, and he hadn't been too keen on being on the end of one if she didn't feel the same way about him. But that had been when they were in high school. They'd just been kids.

Diesel gave a soft whine beside him and tilted his head. 'Yeah, all right,' Ollie said, reaching over to turn on the engine. 'I'm goin'.'

Drop by and say g'day, Griff had said. Ollie clenched his jaw as he drove down the paddock to where he'd left his tractor yesterday afternoon. He wished it was that easy. It should be that easy—only every time Hadley came home it stirred up this restlessness and regret inside him.

Once he had thought maybe he could take a chance and tell Hadley how he felt, but something had stopped him. What was the point? It couldn't work. She travelled all over the world and had a career she wasn't likely to give up in order to live back here. He was a farmer. It was what he knew and, after his dad's accident, it was his responsibility to keep things running on the farm. It was doubtful his father would ever go back to full-time farming again—his mother wanted him to retire, go travelling—but the new paddock-to-plate venture they'd started as something to give their old man an interest had really taken off, much more than any of them had anticipated.

There was no way Ollie could leave the place even if he wanted to.

And, yet, there were times when he couldn't shake the feeling that Hadley Callahan was the woman he was meant to be with. Of course, her wedding had been a bit of a setback...

He gripped the steering wheel tighter as he remembered watching her walk down the aisle towards the moron she'd married. He'd always thought it was a bit of a joke when movies got to the part in a wedding ceremony when anyone in the congregation who had reason to object to the marriage was told to speak now or forever hold their peace, but he'd found he was somewhat disappointed that Hadley's ceremony hadn't included it. Okay, so he probably wouldn't have actually stood up and objected. After all, what would he say? 'You're making a mistake, Hadley. You can't marry a tosser like Mitch Samuals.'

Ever since she'd announced her engagement, her whole family had tried to delicately point this out. He was pretty sure she wouldn't have thanked him for an interruption to her picture-perfect bloody wedding. So instead he'd sat there, feeling like his insides had been ripped out and struggling to look like the happy childhood friend from next door. He'd made sure he dulled the pain at the reception by drinking more than he'd drunk in a long time—or since, for that matter—but it hadn't really helped.

He'd even convinced himself that he'd moved on from whatever this lingering feeling was. Now that Hadley was married, the sane part of his brain told him, it really was time to forget her. And then, during last harvest, Hadley's dick of a husband had been caught out, with Hadley's older sister of all people. Of course, Ollie wasn't supposed to know anything about it, only he'd found out from his sister, Olivia, who'd been the one to stumble upon the little rendezvous and had confided in him. For a lot of reasons, he wished he hadn't heard about the betrayal—mostly because it was damn hard not to act on his compulsion to beat the crap out of Mitch for hurting Hadley, but running a close second was the fact that ever since he'd found out, his hopes had been reignited and they were currently raging like an out-of-control bushfire.

It hadn't been hard to keep the secret around Hadley, given she was never here, but it had been tough knowing that Griff, Hadley's older brother, knew about it but that he still couldn't talk it over with him. Ollie had given Griff plenty of chances to bring it up, asking if there was something on his mind when he'd clearly been distracted, but Griff was the loyal kind and he'd never mentioned it. He and Griff were a lot alike that way, Ollie thought. But it would have been a hell of a lot easier over these past few months if he could have vented a bit of his frustration alongside his best friend.

And now Hadley was home.

∽

Ollie looked up at the troop carrier that came rolling towards the tractor and gave a weary sigh. For a guy who'd been so hard to win over to the idea of this damn business venture, Bill Dawson sure looked like he was enjoying himself. Ollie watched as his father pulled up in the paddock nearby, climbing out of the driver's seat slowly and standing in front of a small group of students and their teacher.

Ollie gave a wave as he passed by them on his next run. Although he'd never admit it aloud to anyone, he actually got a bit of a kick out of the excited waves he always got back from the kids. It didn't matter if they were a kindergarten group or a TAFE class—they all waved. It seemed every age group loved a big tractor.

He played a minimal role in his family's paddock-to-plate business. This was his parents' and sister's project, and he was happy to let them deal with it, allowing him to concentrate on the farming side. Initially he hadn't been as optimistic as his sister about the new venture. In fact, he'd never thought she'd get their old man to go for it in the first place. But he'd underestimated his sister's powers of persuasion. He'd also underestimated how popular this thing would turn out to be. He had to hand it to her, when Olivia got an idea in her head she threw herself into it one hundred per cent. His father had also surprised him by just how motivated he was. He really seemed to enjoy having a bunch of kids traipsing about after him, asking questions all day. Ollie couldn't remember him ever being that patient with him. Then again, he supposed, his dad wasn't trying to teach a headstrong son how to do something, while also racing against the clock to get all the farm jobs done. They hadn't had the luxury of time when he had been growing up—his father had been trying to run the place with the help of Ollie and only a few hired contractors, so things had been tough.

The troop carrier moved on to check out the next stop on the tour, and Ollie sent them another wave and gave a short chuckle as he caught a glimpse of his father's face through the driver's window, a smile from ear to ear. It was good to see him happy again. He hadn't been sure they ever would after his accident on the farm had left him so debilitated, but this idea of his sister's had made his dad feel useful once again. It also didn't hurt that the venture kept father and son out of each other's pockets throughout the day. A farmer who was unable to farm was a disaster waiting to happen. No one liked to feel useless when there was work to be done—least of all a man who'd been farming all his life and wasn't ready to retire.

Three

Hadley sank onto the lounge in her brother's house with a weary sigh. Her best friend Olivia, soon to be sister-in-law, watched from the couch with a sympathetic smile.

'When are you going to tell them?' Olivia asked.

The question had been weighing heavily on her mind and as usual, in times of doubt, her big brother's voice was always there whispering, or sometimes shouting, what she needed to hear. She knew what Linc would say: 'Just do it.'

'I don't know, Liv. The whole drive home, I played it out in my head, you know?' she said, and her friend nodded. 'I thought, tell them straightaway—like ripping off a bandaid. But then they were both so happy to see me and I just couldn't make myself do it.'

'Do you want me to come with you?'

'No.' Hadley blew out a long breath. 'I just have to stop being such a baby and tell them.'

'It's a pretty big deal,' Olivia said, eyeing her friend with a gentle look. 'You've been through a lot lately. And I can understand why you're reluctant to do this, but it isn't your fault, Had. You aren't the one who broke up your marriage, Harmony and Mitch are the guilty ones.'

'How am I supposed to tell them that?' Hadley searched her friend's eyes, feeling almost frantic at the thought. 'This is going to kill Mum and Dad.'

'Let's just calm down and think it through,' Olivia said in her steady tone. 'This will not kill your parents. Yes, it'll upset them and, yes,' she continued when Hadley opened her mouth to protest, 'things are going to get pretty messy for a while but, like you said yourself, it's only a matter of time before they find out through the media. You can't allow that to happen,' she said seriously. 'They need to hear it from you now. Before they find out along with everyone else in town.'

'You're right. As usual,' she added dryly. 'Why are you always the voice of reason?'

'Because I'm a lawyer and because it's easy for me to be reasonable when I'm not the one having to tell your folks,' she said with a lopsided smile. 'Griff and I can be there if that helps. We could have dinner here or something?'

'No. I think I need to do it alone . . . but thank you,' she said, managing a smile. Hadley knew they wanted to help and, in truth, she wasn't sure how she would have got through the past few months without her best friend and brother to talk her down when she felt like she was losing her grip on everything. But this she felt she needed to do alone.

Fortified with strong coffee and a pep talk, Hadley left her friend and headed back towards the main house, determination in every step. *Just sit them down and tell them*, she repeated.

'Hello, darling. That was a quick visit. I didn't expect to see you again until dinnertime. I know what you and Liv are like once you get yacking,' her mother said as she placed a roast in the oven.

'Mum, I need to talk to you and Dad about something. It's important.' There, she'd said it. Seeing the concern on her mother's face, she knew there was no way she could back out of this now.

'Your father's in the office. Why don't you go get him and I'll put the jug on.'

Hadley smiled gratefully, before turning to head down the long hallway towards the office. Chewing her lip anxiously, she paused outside the doorway before knocking and sticking her head inside the room. 'Mum said to get you. She's got the jug on.' *Chicken*, a little voice taunted inside her head. She didn't care, she'd made the first step and now she needed to prepare for the next one.

'Hadley's got some news,' Lavinia said as Bob came into the kitchen. She saw the small look that passed between her parents and felt a sting in her eyes. She'd wanted that. She'd wanted to have that bond married couples had—the one where a single look could say everything that needed saying. She wouldn't experience that now.

15

As her mother placed their cups in front of them on the kitchen table, Hadley swallowed nervously and stared down into the murky depths of the coffee, praying that the right words would come.

'Mum, Dad . . .' she started, before looking up reluctantly. 'There's something I need to tell you, before you hear it . . . somewhere else. It's about Mitch and me.' She swallowed hard and took a deep breath. 'He's left me.'

'What!' Bob practically roared.

'Well, it was kind of mutual. He's moved out and we're getting a divorce.'

'Oh, darling,' her mother breathed, placing a smooth hand on Hadley's wrist. 'Why? What happened?'

Here it was. The why. 'He was having an affair.'

'That bastard,' her father snarled.

'Now, Robert,' her mother cautioned—although Hadley could see it was taking a great effort of will to control her own emotions—'we need to remain calm. When did all this happen?'

'We actually broke up not long after I left here last time.'

'I knew something was wrong. You weren't yourself at all during that visit, and then you left so suddenly—I knew it wasn't because of work.' A frown creased between her mother's brows and she squeezed Hadley's wrist comfortingly. 'I should have made you tell me what was wrong then.'

'I'd only just found out . . . I needed some space to deal with it.' She'd also been dealing with a miscarriage, which only Olivia had known about, and then she'd been hit with her husband cheating on her with her sister. She'd needed more than a little space. Lately her life felt like a bad daytime talk show.

'I had more faith in Mitch,' her mother said with a disappointed shake of her head. 'I really did.'

'I suppose it was one of those window-shopped women off TV,' her father said, narrowing his eyes.

'I believe the term you're looking for is *photoshopped*, dear,' Lavinia put in gently, but then turned her gaze upon Hadley for an answer.

Say it.

The house phone rang, and her mother gave a long-suffering sigh before getting up to answer it.

Hadley bit back her own frustration. So help her God, if that was someone calling about a committee matter and rambling on forever, she'd hang up the phone herself.

'Oh, Harmony, I'm so glad you called, sweetheart. Guess who has just arrived home for a surprise visit?'

Hadley froze and could feel the blood draining from her face. The room wobbled a little, but she took a deep breath and fought for some control.

'Hadley!' her mother supplied when her sister was obviously at a loss. 'Darling? Hello? Are you still there?'

Hadley clenched her jaw as she pictured her sister's shock on the other end of the line. She watched as her mother's face slowly changed from delight to deep concentration. 'Oh, I see. Well, that's a shame, but it can't be helped. All right, you enjoy yourself and take care. Bye, love.'

'What's Harmony up to?' Bob asked as his wife came back to the table.

'She's on her way to a girls' weekend,' she said, pulling a small surprised face.

'That came out of the blue, didn't it?' her father said, eyeing his wife.

'She certainly didn't mention anything to me about it the other day when I popped in to see her. Still,' her mother conceded, 'she's been doing it really hard lately with the kids being a bit of a handful and on her own too. It can't be easy for her, poor love,' Lavinia said with a touch of sadness in her tone. 'She deserves a bit of a getaway.'

Hadley was surprised she couldn't taste blood in her mouth, she was biting her tongue that hard. Part of her wanted to scream that Harmony didn't deserve anything, that she was a cheating home-wrecker. But another, saner part sent herself a sideways glance that made her hesitate. Deep down she knew that she was reacting more out of wounded pride and betrayal than genuine heartbreak. The truth was that her sister couldn't really be a home-wrecker if there was never really a home to wreck in the first place.

She hated admitting it, but it was true. She and Mitch both worked jobs that either took them from home for weeks at a time or had them working weird hours. When Hadley was at home between assignments, Mitch was usually buried in work commitments, and his new TV program meant late nights and early mornings. They'd barely spent any quality time together since their wedding.

No, she didn't blame her sister for her failed marriage. It was probably over before it even started. She wasn't sure why they'd both let it go so far. Their relationship was familiar and comfortable, she supposed. They were suited to each other—both fiercely independent workaholics, happy to have someone at home when they needed a little downtime.

She'd first met Mitch on assignment and they'd briefly been friends before becoming lovers. Things only started falling apart once Mitch left the field and found his niche as a TV celebrity. He always did love preening for the camera, whereas Hadley's passion had always been the story. She loved writing, researching and digging around until she found answers. For her, the thrill was never about being in front of the camera, it was being able to bring people the truth about what was really happening in places few people ever went to—or had a desire to go to. These were the stories people needed to know about. How would change come around if people weren't even aware of what was happening to their fellow human beings?

Harmony might not be responsible for breaking up the marriage, but she was completely responsible for being the woman her husband had cheated with. At some point the thought must have run through her head that this was wrong. Hadley couldn't have cared less if her sister had had a sordid affair with someone else, married or not. Hadley wasn't about to judge her, but what she could never forgive was that she chose *her* husband. They hadn't been close over the past few years, mainly due to Hadley rarely being home, but they still shared the bond of being sisters. Surely that had to count for something?

'Sorry about that, darling. Now, where were we?' Her mother broke into her hectic thoughts.

'That was pretty much it,' Hadley said, trying for a forced joviality. 'I think that's more than enough drama to deal with for one day.' She pushed away from the table and hoped they didn't see that her hands were shaking. 'I'm really tired. Do you mind if I go and lie down for a little bit? It's been a long day.'

'Of course,' her mother said, concern furrowing her brow. 'You go and have a rest.'

Hadley didn't wait for a second invitation, she needed to escape any further questions. Harmony's unexpected call had shaken her more than she cared to admit. Not once had she called to try to justify her actions to Hadley. Mitch had tried briefly to explain the situation, but Hadley had refused to listen—she'd been too upset and shocked to even try to wrap her head around the reasons. In all honestly, she didn't care about Mitch's explanations; the only person she wanted to hear an explanation from was her sister, and Harmony had refused to return her calls.

Part of her felt a childish need to tell her parents exactly what their poor Harmony had actually done—make them open their eyes to how *un*-perfect she really was. She wanted her sister to feel the scorn of her parents' disappointment and outrage. Although Hadley couldn't imagine what that would even look like. She'd never once heard her parents say they were disappointed in any of their children.

Going away for a girls' weekend, she thought bitterly. How lovely for her. She pictured her sister sitting in a day spa surrounded by her minions from the P&C or whatever damn committee she was president of nowadays, all reassuring her how wonderfully she was handling the scandal of her own husband having had an affair and leaving her for his secretary earlier in the year.

That was the part Hadley couldn't understand. How could a woman who had been cheated on go ahead and do the same thing to someone else? She got that maybe Harmony's pride had been stung and she felt a need to retaliate in kind . . . but why with a married man? Her own sister's married man at that? Why the hell couldn't she have found some unattached toy boy somewhere?

She hadn't intended to actually lie down, she'd just needed an excuse to stop the interrogation, but now that she'd sunk onto her bed, she realised just how exhausted she really was. Hadley kicked off her shoes then curled up on the bed and hugged the pillow to her securely. Maybe if she just closed her eyes for a few minutes, when she opened them again she'd find that somehow the last few months had all been a bad dream.

Four

Ollie walked into the pub and greeted the three other men standing around the pool table. He nodded to Ashley behind the bar, holding up three fingers to indicate how many beers he needed. This was their weekly social event—mainly an excuse to drink midweek but, still, it was a great way to blow off some steam after a hard day.

'I heard Hadley's back in town,' said Josh, one of Ollie's old schoolfriends, as he selected a pool cue and rubbed chalk on the end.

Ollie gave a noncommittal grunt and busied himself paying for the drinks that Ashley had brought over. The last thing he wanted to do was get involved in a conversation about Hadley.

'Heard she's home without that knob she married. Maybe she got sick of guys in suits and realised she wanted a real man after all,' added Aidan, their other regular player, wiggling his eyebrows at Ashley.

'Well, she'd be hard-pressed to find one of them around here, wouldn't she?' Ashley commented, walking away without a backwards glance, a chorus of grumbling following her.

Ollie observed the third man, Luke Patterson, better known as Patto to his mates, staring down into his glass of beer. He was usually the first to come back with a smart-alec reply, but he'd let this opportunity pass by, which was strange.

'What's up with you tonight?' Ollie asked.

'He's sookin' because he can't score himself a girlfriend,' Josh cut in, in their usual derogatory style. 'Told ya, mate, with a mug like yours, you'll be lucky if ya dog even wants to stay faithful.'

Usually Luke, or any of the others who were on the receiving end of a particularly colourful insult, would laugh and give back something even more insulting, but not tonight. Tonight Luke just gave a half-hearted chuckle and said nothing.

'Come on, tosser, you going to play your shot or what?' Ollie said pointedly to Josh, who hadn't picked up on the fact their mate wasn't in his usual jovial form.

Later, when Josh went to the gents and Aidan headed to the bar for another round, Ollie took the opportunity to pin Luke down for a chat. 'What's goin' on?'

Luke glanced over, a little surprised by the question, but gave an offhand kind of shrug. 'Broke up with Jade over the weekend.'

'That sucks, mate. Sorry to hear.' He didn't know Jade very well. She lived up around Hilston way, but he knew Luke had been into her for the last few months.

'Yeah, well, shit happens.'

'Maybe things will sort themselves out?'

'Nah. She's found some other bloke already.'

'Her loss, mate.'

Luke gave a small twist of a smile but it didn't reach his eyes.

'How's work goin'?'

'Haven't had any. Got put off a couple of weeks ago.'

Ollie was shocked by that bit of news. 'I didn't know. What happened?'

'Had a fight with the boss. Told him off. He sent me packin'.'

Luke had been working for Arnie Stokes for the past three years and, as far as Ollie knew, the two had always got along. It must have been a doozy of an argument for the laidback Arnie to get so worked up. 'That's pretty rough. You lookin' for work?'

'Why? You hiring?' he shot back with a lopsided smile.

'Nothing full-time, I'm afraid, but I could scrounge up a couple of days here and there if you're interested.'

'Thanks, mate, but I'll be right.'

'You sure? I can ask around and find some more.'

'Nah. All good,' Luke said with a dismissive shake of his head. 'Thanks though. You're a good mate,' he added quietly. 'Anyway, I'm gonna head out.'

'But the game's not over yet,' Ollie said.

Luke's subdued mood was more than a little out of character. He was usually the life of the party. 'I'm pretty beat. I'll see ya round,' he said, getting to his feet and walking away with a wave of his hand.

Ollie found himself staring after him, feeling bad. He was a nice guy—funny as hell usually. Still, he'd broken up with his girlfriend and lost his job, so it wasn't like he had too much to be laughing about right now. Ollie made a note to drop by later in the week and offer him a few shifts on Moorbrook again. In the meantime, he'd ask around and see if anyone had an opening. There was always plenty of work going for guys with the kind of farming experience Luke had.

Something would turn up.

∽

Ollie pulled up outside the Callahans' house and stared at the warm light spilling from the windows. He'd tried to get out of coming over, but it was impossible to do so without having to explain to his parents why.

It wasn't that he wanted to get out of seeing Hadley—if anything, it was the opposite. He'd spent so long trying to accept Hadley would never be his, and now suddenly the possibility, slim as it was, was raising its head again. It was playing havoc with his state of mind. Of course, even though Hadley might unofficially be back on the market, it didn't mean she would be remotely interested in him. So basically there was absolutely nothing for him to peg any of his hopes on. Only, he was.

It would be so much easier if he could do what he'd always done—stay away from her. Then he couldn't be tempted to do or say something stupid that might jeopardise whatever kind of friendship they had. With a sigh, he pushed open the door and climbed out of the ute.

Griffin came across to shake his hand as he stepped onto the verandah, handing him a cold can of beer and then slapping him on the shoulder. 'It's about time. Couldn't you decide what to wear?'

'Yeah. Right. Denim or denim.'

'Seriously, if women just stuck to jeans and T-shirts, they wouldn't take two hours to get ready,' Griffin moaned, giving a startled *oomph,* as Olivia came up beside him and slapped at his midriff.

'Was that directed at me by any chance?'

'No, dear,' he said with forced meekness.

'I don't know why people say it's so hard to train a potential husband,' Olivia shrugged, smiling sweetly at her fiancé.

Ollie shook his head at his best friend woefully. 'Dude, you're a disgrace to men everywhere. Don't let her get away with that.'

Griffin slid his arms around Olivia and grinned over her head at him. 'I'll be sure to show her who the boss is later . . .' He winked.

'Oh, gross. That's my sister you're talkin' about.'

'Are they being nauseatingly happy again?'

Ollie turned and felt his mouth dry up as his gaze fell on the small woman with shining golden hair. When his eyes met hers, his heart gave a lurch. *An honest to God lurch.* Christ. He was such a goner. He forced himself to snap out of it as she leaned in and hugged him, and for the briefest of moments his eyes closed as he caught the clean, sweet scent of the perfume she wore. On second thoughts, it could just be her. Whatever its origins, it was uniquely Hadley and it never failed to send him into hyperdrive.

'Hey, Hads. How are you?'

'I'm great,' she said with a bright smile. 'Couldn't be better.'

Ollie frowned a little as he caught the slight slur of her words and, from the corner of his eye, saw his sister and Griff exchange a look.

'Who do I have to sleep with around here to get a drink?' she said a little too loudly and giggled when a few conversations nearby paused. 'Oops, I probably shouldn't have said that.'

'Come on, Hads, let's see if your mum needs any help,' Olivia said, smoothly crossing to her friend's side.

'I thought this was a party,' Hadley complained.

From across the verandah Ollie spotted Harmony sitting rigidly in her chair, watching them, and he groaned inwardly. He had a very bad feeling about tonight. What was Harmony even doing here? He supposed she'd had as little say about it as he had. If she wanted to play things cool, she couldn't very well not turn up to a family function ... and yet, Jesus, she had some kind of hide.

He didn't really have a relationship with Harmony—never had. She was older than the rest of them and had pretty much left home when he was still a kid. He couldn't believe she'd gone and had an affair with her own sister's husband though. That took a certain kind of self-centred arrogance. Maybe if it'd been only the once, he could possibly have understood it. A drunken, bad decision—God knows he'd made his share of those over the years—but from all accounts that wasn't the case here.

Maybe she deserved to be happy too. The thought seemed to come from nowhere and it shocked him. No. He didn't even feel a little bit happy that Harmony had played a part in Mitch and Hadley's break-up. That would be ... well, like betraying Hadley, and yet was it really such a terrible thing if it put an end to something even Blind Freddy could see was a disaster waiting to happen?

Lavinia called everyone to the table and Ollie breathed a sigh of relief that a potential crisis had been averted.

There was a clatter of cutlery and chairs moving across the timber floorboards as people settled themselves in seats around the long tables that had been joined together to fit everyone in.

'Sit beside me, Ollie,' Hadley said, taking his hand and leading him to a pair of free chairs.

Ollie hoped his eyes hadn't popped out of his head, cartoon-like, at this uncharacteristic request. 'Everything okay, Hads?' he asked quietly as they sat down.

'Absolutely,' she beamed up at him, but he could see the tension around her eyes.

He wanted to tell her that he understood. That he knew why it was all so weird, but it wasn't the right place or time. Why was it that there was always some kind of drama unfolding lately? He took a long drink from his can of beer and wished that *just once* the Dawsons and Callahans could have a normal and uneventful get-together.

'Everyone, I have an announcement to make,' Hadley said, tapping the side of her wineglass.

Apparently tonight was not going to be that night.

He glanced across the table where Olivia and Griff were watching Hadley warily, then moved on to Harmony and saw her sitting stiffly, eyes fixed on her plate. He almost felt sorry for her. Almost.

'Before we start, I want to clear the air once and for all, because I know everyone's been walking around on eggshells and I don't want that. Yes, it's true, Mitch and I are getting a divorce. There will probably be some reporters trying to contact you for an inside story. Feel free to make up some great gossip for them,' she grinned. 'Maybe it'll make entertaining reading that way.'

'Ah, actually,' Griff said, cutting in, 'Hadley's joking. It's probably best not to say anything,' he said, sending his younger sister a serious look across the table. 'If it's too entertaining they may never give up.'

Hadley waved her hand dismissively and took another sip of her wine. 'Whatever! I really couldn't care less at this point. Anyway, let's make a toast,' she said, holding up her glass quickly, making the contents slosh alarmingly. 'To family,' she said, smiling widely, her gaze travelling around the table, coming to rest on her older sister's pinched face. 'And loyalty and love,' she finished, without taking her hardening gaze from Harmony, who managed to mould her mouth into something resembling a smile.

'To family,' Ollie said loudly, taking a large gulp of his beer, relieved when the rest of the table followed suit, thankfully diverting attention away from the two women and the obvious tension between them.

'Eat, everyone, before it gets cold,' Lavinia called out, probably as anxious as he was to head off any potential awkwardness. Drunken speeches were a sore point. Olivia still held the crown for most awkward drunken speech, at Hadley's wedding reception, and would probably be grateful if Hadley took the title from her.

'You're a smart man, Ollie,' Hadley said, tucking into her meal with surprising gusto. Maybe it was the alcohol talking, or maybe she was just putting on a brave face for everyone, either way he could see through it. He knew she was hurting.

'You think?' he said, somewhat cautiously. He wasn't quite sure where she was headed with the conversation.

'Absolutely. You're the only one of us who's stayed single,' she said, pointing her fork at him as she chewed her roast. 'That's smart.'

'Yeah, that's me. It's been my plan from the start. Stay single,' he said, although she seemed to miss the sarcasm, nodding earnestly in agreement.

'Marriage is a joke. It's all a lie told to little girls to make them believe there's this big, happy-ever-after waiting in the future. It's like Santa Claus and the Easter Bunny,' she said almost mournfully.

'Not all marriages are like that. Look at your parents. And mine,' he added, nodding his head towards the other end of the long table.

'They're from another era. It doesn't count.'

'I don't know,' Ollie said. 'I think it's the person not the era that's the problem. You just have to find the right person.'

Hadley gave a scoff that was a little too loud, causing a few eyes to swing her way. 'That's like playing Russian roulette. You just can't trust anyone anymore.'

She had him there. He didn't believe that personally, but he could understand how her faith in humanity may have taken a pretty hard knock after finding out *who* her husband had been cheating with. She had a right to be angry for a while.

'I know that you know, Ollie,' she said, breaking the silence between them.

'Know what?' he said, genuinely confused.

'Who Mitch was cheating with,' she said quietly, holding his startled gaze.

He opened his mouth to deny it, but she just shook her head slowly, before lowering her gaze to the plate. 'Liv already told me she told you.'

So much for his sister threatening to do him bodily harm if he spilled. Thanks, Liv.

'Thank you.'

31

He eyed her warily. 'I didn't do anything.'

'You always could keep a secret,' she said, sending him a small smile.

She had no idea just how well. 'It'll get easier, Hads,' he said softly.

Hadley stopped eating to look up at him, and for the first time all evening the fight had gone out of her eyes. Ollie felt a tightening in his chest as he looked down into the sad face beside him.

'When, Ollie? When does it get easier?'

He couldn't answer that and, if he were honest, he knew no one could. 'How long are you home on holidays for?' he asked, hoping to change the topic and distract her.

'It's not exactly holidays. I was sent home to make sure I didn't say anything I wasn't supposed to say,' she scoffed, returning her attention to the meal before her. 'We wouldn't want any rumours getting spread about the wholesome Mitch Samuals,' she said, raising her voice pointedly. While she didn't look at her sister, Ollie noticed Harmony's grip on her cutlery had tightened and her mouth was a taut line.

'I know Liv's glad you're here,' he said, and his smile slipped a little when she turned her blue eyes up to his expectantly. 'She could really use some help with her wedding planning.' As soon as he said it, he wished he could pull the words back, but to his surprise and immense relief, she just nodded and continued eating.

Across the table he saw Gran elbowing Griffin and hid a grin as his friend poured something from a small flask into his grandmother's tea. Catching his eye, Gran sent him a wink and mischievous smile, before gleefully taking a sip from her cup.

'I hope I'm as outrageous as Gran when I'm her age,' Hadley said with a chuckle.

'I thought your mum said she wasn't supposed to be drinking whisky anymore,' Ollie said, trying to keep a straight face.

'You seriously think anyone's going to tell Gran what she can and can't do?'

She had a point.

'Mum only half-heartedly protests to keep Gran's doctor happy.'

After the main course was finished, they moved away from the table to sit and chat and let the meal settle before dessert. Ollie made a cup of coffee and took it across to Hadley. 'Here, I thought you might be able to use this,' he said.

'I don't remember you being this much of a killjoy, Ollie,' she muttered. 'I'm pretty sure if ever there was a time to get drunk, this would be it, don't you think?'

'You're probably right,' he agreed lightly. 'But maybe not the right place.'

She gave an unimpressed grunt at that, which he took as reluctant acknowledgement.

'But no one said you can't find a better place, right?' he added, and she looked up from her cup hopefully.

'Now you're talkin'. I'll meet you out the back. Do you remember where we went that time we tried to smoke?'

Remember? He often wished he could forget. They'd been barely ten when the four of them—Hadley, Griff, Olivia and he—had snuck away from a party and decided to make their own cigarettes from newspaper and hay.

'Give it five minutes before you leave. And make sure no one sees you go,' she whispered.

'Roger that, 007,' he said, adding a sloppy salute.

He managed to keep a straight face as she attempted to unobtrusively take a bottle of wine and hide it under her shirt before leaving the party. He hoped to God her career never required her to do anything remotely undercover.

He gave her three minutes' head start, not sure he trusted her to make it five minutes in the dark alone. She was waiting in the back of the shed, seated on an old dray left over from when the Callahans had used a horse before tractors came on the scene.

'I can't believe we didn't burn this place down that night,' he said, running his hand over the back of the aged timber cart and shaking his head at the memory of them huddled around a lit piece of newspaper rolled into a cigarette.

'I don't think I've ever coughed that much in my life since,' she added, a triumphant smile appearing as she popped the cork from the bottle she'd been working on when he came in.

'We should have invited Griff and Liv down here to relive our youth,' he said.

'Nah. They're too happy.' She took a swig of wine and grimaced. 'Not that that's a bad thing, mind you,' she said, searching Ollie's eyes. 'Do you think I'm a bad person, Ollie?'

'Of course not,' he said, taking the bottle from her. 'Why would you think that?'

'Because I wanted a tiny minute alone without seeing their goofy smiles and love-sick looks and that's why I'm going to hell.'

Ollie bit back a chuckle, knowing she was deadly, if drunkenly, serious. 'You're not going to hell for that.'

'See, I knew you'd understand,' she said, looking at him. Where she sat put her pretty much on eye level with him and he took a small step closer. 'You always got me.'

'It's not that hard to understand, Hads. You've been through a really shitty time. It's natural you wouldn't want to be around people in love.'

'Exactly,' she said with a baffled shake of her head as she searched his eyes. 'This is why I love you, Ollie,' she said, and Ollie froze. 'You're my best friend . . . other than Liv, of course, because, you know, she's Liv . . . but you're my second-best friend and I love you,' she said with a huge sigh and reached out towards him, almost falling forwards. Ollie reached out and took hold of her before she lost her balance completely, and she pulled him close.

Ollie's mind short-circuited for a split second as his body registered that he was standing very close to her; he felt her jean-clad thighs either side of his hips and the warmth from her body pressed against his stomach.

Just as he was trying to untangle the battle raging between his wayward arousal and a pretty pathetic attempt to be chivalrous, he felt her body start shaking against him as huge sobs racked her. His arousal all but curled up and died as he felt her tears seeping through his shirt. He felt like the worst kind of arsehole. She was in pain and here he was allowing himself to get his hopes up, not to mention other things, when he should have realised that she was in no state to know what she was doing.

'It's going to be okay,' he said, rubbing her back gently.

'I feel like such a loser,' she said between sobs.

'You're not a loser. You're the furthest thing from a loser that I know of. You're brave and you're smart and you're beautiful,' he said, gently easing away from her so he could look down into her face, but then he lost track of what he'd been saying as the sadness in her eyes tore at his chest.

'How could he do it? How could *she* do it?' she demanded, looking at him helplessly.

'I don't know,' Ollie said sadly as she rested her head back on his shoulder. How could Samuals just throw away this woman like that? Why couldn't he see what he had? Clearly he didn't deserve her. Ollie had known that the first time he'd met the idiot.

After a while he noticed her sobs had stopped and he realised she'd fallen asleep. With a reluctant sigh, Ollie gently roused her enough to walk her back to the main house.

'Get some sleep,' he said, holding open her bedroom door for her. He turned to walk away but stopped when he heard his name being called softly.

Hadley leaned against her doorframe, her head tilted slightly. 'Thank you for being here.'

'I wouldn't want to be anywhere else,' he said and meant it. There was nowhere else he'd rather be. The irony, though, was that he knew she meant she was glad he was here . . . as a friend.

Sometimes it really sucked to be the good guy.

Five

Ollie heard his phone ringing and, after he'd made the sweep at the end of the row, he grabbed it and answered.

'Have you heard?' Josh said without a hello.

Ollie frowned.

'About Patto,' Josh added.

He couldn't explain it, but before Josh even filled him in, he knew it was something bad.

Josh took his silence as a no and gave a long sigh. 'He's dead,' he said without preamble.

Ollie felt his mouth open but was sure he'd misheard. 'What?'

'Topped himself sometime last night. His old man found him this morning.'

'Bullshit,' Ollie snapped. This wasn't funny. His temper erupted at the thought of anyone making up something so stupid.

''Fraid not, mate. Mum's over at the Pattersons' now with his parents. They're a bloody mess.'

Ollie couldn't remember if he said goodbye to Josh before the call ended. He stared down at the phone numbly. It couldn't be right. Luke dead? He'd only just seen him at the pub the other day.

His phone let out a burst of music, making him start slightly, and he saw Griff's name flash.

'Hey, mate. I take it Josh has called?'

'It's bullshit. He's spinnin' shit. What have you heard?'

He heard Griff's long sigh and felt his gut clench. 'Same thing you heard. I wish it was Josh being a dickhead, but not this time. Mum's just left to take over some food and help out.'

Ollie couldn't believe it. It couldn't be true. Why would Luke kill himself? Sure, he'd been having some hard times lately, but to kill himself? How the hell was that even an option? 'Are you sure he . . . it wasn't some kind of accident?'

'Apparently it's pretty clear-cut. They found him out in the shed. Gun still by his side.'

This was so messed up.

'We're meeting down at the pub in a few hours. I'll see you down there. You want me to come and pick you up?'

'No . . . I'll . . . nah, it's right.' He couldn't even think straight. Luke *shot himself*? He disconnected the call and put his phone down slowly, still in shock. It couldn't be right. He finished the run and pulled up. He sat for a while in the silence, his thoughts racing. When he eventually dragged himself down from the harvester, he felt as if the ground was shifting beneath him.

∽

Ollie walked inside the house and saw his mother standing by the kitchen sink, staring out through the window. When the screen door shut, she gave a small start, quickly wiping her eyes before turning around to face him. He caught the devastation on her face and felt his throat tighten automatically in response.

'Have you heard?' Her voice cracked slightly, and Ollie managed a brief nod.

'Poor Alice,' she whispered and tears began to fall once more. 'To lose her son like that.'

He crossed the kitchen and took his mum in his arms, feeling her shoulders shake. It took all his strength not to let his own tears fall. He couldn't. He was still holding out some kind of desperate hope that someone, somewhere, had got the story all wrong.

His mother pulled away from him slightly, dabbing at her eyes, 'Are you okay, darling?'

'Yeah,' he said, swallowing hard. 'I'm fine.'

'You aren't,' she told him bluntly. 'He was your friend. But it's come as a shock—to everyone. Go sit down, I was just making tea.'

'I'm right, thanks. I was just coming back to get the ute. I'm heading into town with a few of the boys.'

Sue nodded quickly, giving a small sniff. 'That's probably a good idea. It's been a big shock.'

'I'm heading over to the Pattersons' a little later,' she said, sniffling once more at the thought of seeing her friend who'd just lost her son.

Ollie couldn't stand here any longer, he needed to get outside before he lost it. How could this happen?

∽

Hadley heard the phone ring in the house and smiled as her mother answered with that familiar warm greeting she used with everyone from family to the petrol station attendant. It was good to be home.

She stared at the screen of her computer and frowned again. She'd been sitting out on the verandah working her way through her email inbox, trying to sort through all the media requests for interviews to find her genuine work-related messages. Unfortunately, this damn divorce—not yet officially public—was probably one of the worst kept secrets in the business, at least where the media was concerned anyway. Thankfully it hadn't spilled out into mainstream Australia just yet, but it was only a matter of time. Journalists would keep digging until they uncovered the whole story and when they did . . . She looked up quickly at the sound of her mother's sharp intake of breath, followed by a mournful exclamation.

Hadley shut her computer lid and hurried to the kitchen door to find her mother leaning against the counter, her eyes shut and one hand over her mouth as she listened to whoever was on the other end of the phone. 'I can't believe it,' Lavinia was saying sadly. 'Yes, all right, thanks. Yes. Absolutely. Bye for now.'

'Mum?' Hadley said as her mother replaced the phone slowly. 'What's wrong?'

'Oh, Hadley, it's just terrible,' she said, shaking her head. 'It's young Luke Patterson. He's passed away.'

'Passed away,' Hadley echoed with a frown. 'Was he sick?'

'No,' Lavinia said slowly. 'It was suicide,' she said in a voice that shook. 'I can't believe it.'

Hadley held her mother's shocked gaze and felt a similar denial swirl through her. Suicide? Why? When? She'd gone to school with Luke. She'd had a crush on him back in primary school. They'd even joked about it last Christmas when she'd seen him in the pub after carols by candlelight. How could he be dead?

'I have to get over to see Alice,' Lavinia said, wiping her eyes and instantly switching to crisis mode. 'Darling, can you go downstairs to the big freezer and grab out a shepherd's pie, please. I need to make some calls before I go.'

Hadley went out the back door and headed down the wide stairs that led to the rooms under the house. She loved her old home. The large verandahs that surrounded the top of the house made an enormous spacious area beneath. Half of it had been converted into rooms that were self-contained with a kitchen and bathroom and three guestrooms, while the other half stored two massive freezers where the meat they grew on the property was stored in bulk, along with the many meals her mother always had on hand for emergencies—like today.

Comfort food. In times of crisis, there was always food on hand—bushfires, floods and death. Hadley had often wondered why food was the first thing everyone brought around when there was a death in the community but, after Mitch had left, she'd realised she'd gone days without eating a proper meal—her desire to cook was non-existent while she mourned the end of her marriage. If she had had a family, children to care for, the last thing she would have felt like doing was cooking dinner, so it made sense. All these years she hadn't understood. Now she did.

She opened the freezer lid and perused the contents, locating a stack of neatly labelled foil trays wrapped in plastic. Lasagne, curry chicken, savoury mince, shepherd's pie. She pulled out the tray and shut the lid, heading back upstairs. Poor Luke. She felt sad. How could a guy with so much of his life still left to live decide that killing himself was the answer to whatever problem he had? What kind of problem could be so bad that a person thought that was the only alternative? Didn't he have anyone to talk it over with? Instantly she dismissed the question. He had plenty of mates. Ollie and Griff were two of his closest. She knew her brother would have dropped everything to lend a hand had Luke asked. Ollie too. Ollie. Instantly she reached for her phone in her back pocket of her jeans. He'd

43

be devastated. She scrolled through her phone and located Ollie's number, pressing call, but it rang out.

She rang Griff, knowing that by now her brother would have probably already heard the news. News travelled faster than broadband out here. Always had.

∞

The pub was already packed. People sat in groups, tables dragged together and chairs stacked around the outside. Everyone gathered in times of need. It was outback grief counselling at its finest. The beer flowed, and echoes of stunned disbelief quickly turned to speculation. Why had he done it? How could he do it? Why hadn't he said something if things were so bad? The questions kept being asked despite the fact they'd been asked, and not answered, over and over.

Ollie sat quietly. He didn't have anything useful to contribute—he had no answers either, just questions and guilt. He should have checked up on Luke sooner. He'd been meaning to ever since pool the other night. He hadn't. He'd got busy with harvest and kept forgetting to do it. If he'd made time, maybe he could have talked Luke out of it. Had he missed the signs that night? He knew Luke had been miserable, but it was understandable—the guy'd broken up with his girlfriend, that was enough to depress anyone, but should he have seen that it was more than that? Luke had also been out of work . . . again, understandable that Luke had been down . . . but *that* down? He should have followed up on that work offer. He'd been meaning to. If he'd found work for him, would that have changed Luke's mind? Ollie felt sick. He'd promised the guy he'd find him some work and hadn't done anything about it. If only he had. . .

'Dawson,' Aidan called, breaking into his troubled thoughts.

Ollie glanced up.

'You want a beer?' Aidan repeated.

'Nah, thanks,' he added. 'I've gotta get going.' He stood up and pushed his chair under the table.

'Hey,' Griff said, standing up as well, 'you right?'

'Yeah,' Ollie said quickly. 'I just have to get home and . . . I'll catch up later.' He knew Griff wasn't convinced, but he didn't have the mindset to talk about anything right now.

He started to pull his door open, pausing when he heard his name being called.

Hadley came to a stop in front of him, her gaze searching his gently. 'You doing okay?'

He opened his mouth to answer but, to his horror, nothing came out. Part of him hoped it was his imagination—that it was just a delayed reaction between his mouth and his brain, but when her eyes welled up and her face softened he knew it wasn't his imagination.

'Give me your keys,' she said, taking them from his numb hands before he could protest. 'Come on.' She led him around to the passenger side and opened the door. He didn't protest, he really couldn't be bothered. He heard her get in and shut the door, the engine start, and felt the ute move, but he didn't know where they were headed.

When the car pulled to a stop, Ollie sat up straighter. He wanted to ask why they were here, but he didn't want to break the silence in the cabin. It was nice. After the noise of the pub and the stuff going on inside his head, he craved peace and quiet.

Hadley wound down her window and the gentle hum of insects provided a soothing background. Warm air carried the scent of the bush and filled him with calm.

'This was a good idea,' he said after a while.

'It's been a long time since I've been up here,' Hadley said without turning to look in his direction. 'We used to come here a lot.'

'Yeah,' he agreed. Many a night they'd use this place to drink and get away from the town's prying eyes. That was when they'd all been younger. Hadley, Griff, Olivia and him. There'd been others who'd come too, and some-times impromptu parties would happen, other times—his favourite times—it was just the four of them, lying under the stars and talking about their futures. He rolled his head sideways so he could see her. 'You got everything you wanted back then,' he said quietly.

He saw her sad smile and felt a matching sadness inside him unfurl. All he'd ever wanted was . . . he shut down that train of thought. There was no point going there.

'Why do I feel like that old saying "Be careful what you wish for" is particularly ironic right now?'

'You haven't had a bad run,' he said lightly.

'No,' she agreed with a sigh. 'No, I haven't. I was just feeling sorry for myself. I've been doing that a lot lately. Too much actually. It's time to stop.'

'In all fairness, you've earned the right to wallow a little.'

'It's so not me, though,' she admitted. 'I hate being miserable.'

'Me too,' he said, tipping his head back and staring at the view before them.

'Why do you think he did it?' she asked a little while later, voicing the thoughts that were swirling about in his own head. She'd always had a habit of doing that—thinking what he was thinking . . . it was weird.

'Who knows? I can't work it out. He'd broken up with his girlfriend and lost his job, but who hasn't been through that before? Doesn't seem drastic enough to warrant . . . that.'

'No, it doesn't,' she agreed. 'But depression and mental illness are things no one really talks about, so how can we hope to understand them when they're kept quiet? I mean, look at what happened last year with Linc? He was the toughest guy I knew—the things he'd been through . . . seen . . . done . . .' She let her voice trail off for a moment before continuing. 'And he completely lost it. I mean, I guess it's not the same thing—he didn't get to the point where he'd decided to kill himself, but he hid what was going on from everyone. When I think back, it scares me how well he'd managed to function before it all came to a head.'

It *had* been scary. Ollie had been there to witness Hadley's older brother succumb to his demons after her wedding and beat Griff into unconsciousness. No one had seen it coming, or at least he hadn't. 'I should have seen it,' he said, his thoughts returning to Luke.

'How?' she protested gently.

'I knew he wasn't his usual self.'

'Like you said, he'd just broken up with his girlfriend . . . of course he wouldn't be his usual self. That shouldn't have been an automatic reason to suspect he'd do something like this.'

Ollie shook his head slowly. 'I told him I'd give him a few days' work and put the word out about more, but I didn't get around to calling him. I said I would, but I didn't.'

He looked down at Hadley's hand as she put it on his arm and gave it a small squeeze. 'Ollie, this didn't happen because you didn't call him.'

'How do you know?' he asked, searching her concerned gaze. 'What if I'd made that call and got him some work? Maybe he'd see there was some kind of bright horizon . . . or, I don't know, maybe he'd have been too busy working to think about killin' himself,' he said, hearing his voice catch slightly. He pushed open the door and climbed out of the ute, walking around to the front of the vehicle to rest on the bonnet. The view spread out before him, but he saw none of it. The sting in his eyes began to blur out everything as guilt and remorse washed over him.

'Ollie, you tried to help him out, but this was not on you. He could have just as easily called you to follow it up. This was his decision.'

'*Decision?* Who makes the decision to shoot themself? It doesn't even make sense,' he said, beyond caring that he could feel wetness on his cheeks.

'It doesn't,' he heard her say softly before she stepped in front of him and wrapped her arms around him tightly.

He wanted to fight against the tears that came, but the moment he felt her arms around him, the last of his strength faded away. His arms went around Hadley, and her solid warmth against his chest grounded him as pain washed through him. It hurt so bad. He couldn't bear to think how alone his mate must have been as he sat out in that cold, dark shed, contemplating what he was about to do.

He'd failed him. The thought echoed emptily. Why hadn't he called? Why hadn't he reached out? He could have talked him down. Instead Luke had decided there was no other way out.

He wasn't sure how long they stood there for, but he suddenly became aware that Hadley was still holding him tightly and he felt ashamed. He eased her back from him so he could straighten against the bonnet of the ute.

He scrubbed his hands across his face and took a deep breath. He couldn't risk a glance at Hadley. He couldn't bear to see her reaction. The woman had been to war zones all around the world and reported on more natural disasters and human suffering than he could imagine. She must think he was pathetic.

'I should get back,' he said more gruffly than he'd intended.

'There's no hurry. No one's getting anything done today.'

'Yeah, well, harvest doesn't stop. I want to get it finished.'

'You're allowed to grieve, Ollie. It's normal. Hey,' she said, coming over to stand in front of him once more and forcing him to look at her, 'it's okay.'

'Nothing about this is okay,' he told her hollowly.

'No. It's not,' she said softly, putting a hand to his jawline. His eyes fluttered shut as he breathed in the scent of her and allowed her nearness to soothe the raw, open grief. Maybe he was being a selfish bastard, but he wished that he could forget about everything else going on at the moment and stand here, alone, with Hadley forever.

Six

Hadley could hear Ollie's heart under her ear, beating strong and steady, and she squeezed her eyes shut tight. Luke's death had shaken her more than she cared to admit. Maybe it was because he represented part of her childhood—her carefree teenage years. When she thought about Luke, she saw his big cheeky smile and heard his slow, larrikin drawl that had entertained everyone over the years. It seemed impossible that he was gone.

She'd witnessed death and destruction more times than she could count, and while she wasn't immune to it, she'd had to find a way to compartmentalise her emotions so she could do her job. This was different. Try as she might, there was no way she could compartmentalise Luke.

She knew Ollie would feel particularly strongly as they'd been such close mates. She'd taken one look at him leaving the pub and known he needed someone. Griff had Liv to comfort him, but Ollie, as far as she knew, had no one to give him a shoulder to cry on. Not that men around here would be caught dead admitting that's what they needed, and Ollie, left to his own devices, would have been the same. But after her brother's breakdown last year, she'd vowed never again to let someone suffer in silence if she could help it.

If only Luke had had someone there to do that for him. Would it have made a difference? She wasn't so sure. The culture out here was to always be strong. Men were supposed to be dependable. Tough. They got stuff done. If things were getting you down, you didn't sit around discussing it, you got back to work and ignored it.

Her heart ached for Ollie. Strong dependable Ollie. He had such a kind heart and she hated seeing him take the burden of guilt over Luke's suicide. It wasn't fair. It wasn't his fault. And yet now, in the aftermath, not just Luke but everyone was left with the sickening feeling that they should have done something, said something . . . anything, to give Luke a reason *not* to go ahead and do what he did.

She breathed in the clean smell of his shirt beneath her cheek and felt his hands tighten around her a little. In his arms she felt safe and sheltered. Since her marriage had fallen apart she'd felt alone and defenceless, but right now she felt protected.

She wasn't sure exactly when her initial instinct to offer comfort began to turn into something else, but one minute she was feeling an overwhelming urge to protect and comfort one of her best friends, and the next . . . she could feel where they connected, all the way from chest to waist, the warmth of his larger body dwarfing hers.

It felt so . . . right.

Like a bucket of cold water being thrown over her, common sense came flooding back. She was supposed to be comforting a friend in need, not turning it into some, well, she wouldn't allow her mind to find an appropriate word for whatever had just happened, that would only make it real. It was better to forget about it and concentrate on what was important. Which was Ollie.

Hadley eased out of his arms and ran her hands down the front of her T-shirt, wishing she didn't miss the warmth of him against her.

'Hads?' he said, making her look up. 'Thanks. For being here.' He shrugged. 'For bringing me up here.'

She managed a smile and felt it wobble slightly when he gave a small one in return.

The drive back into town was as quiet as on the way out, only this time there was more of a lightness—a sense of relief, maybe. On the way out there'd been pent-up grief and she suspected Ollie had still been in shock. Now, having been able to release some of his torment, he seemed almost back to his old self, only he wasn't and probably never would be after today. Something had changed in all of them.

Ollie pulled his ute up alongside her car and she glanced over at him. 'Are you coming back in?'

'Nah, I think I'm just gonna head home.'

'Are you sure?'

'Yeah. I'm good. I just don't feel like going back into the pub and listening to the same old shit. No one has any answers and, until they do, I really can't handle sitting there listening to it anymore today.'

She understood what he meant, she wasn't particularly looking forward to it either, but she wanted to at least make an appearance. 'If you want, I can come home with you?'

'That's okay. I'm just going to finish some work. But thanks again for, you know, earlier.'

'You're welcome. Call me if you need anything,' she said, opening her door and sliding out.

She watched him drive away and tried to ignore the tiny flutter of abandonment that followed. *Stop it,* she told herself irritably. She put it down to concern for a friend but a little niggle of doubt played on the edge of her mind. What else could it be? Nothing she felt like overanalysing right now, that's for sure.

Her phone let out a burst of music and she looked down to see Linc's name on the screen.

'Hey, Hads. I just heard the news about Luke Patterson.'

'Yeah. It's been a bit of a shock.'

'Not wrong. How's everyone doin'?'

'Mum's all over it—she's with the Pattersons now. Griff's pretty cut up and poor Ollie—he's taking it really hard.'

'I can imagine. They've all been playin' footy and cricket together since they were kids.'

'Everyone's down at the pub at the moment, but maybe it'd be good if you gave Griff a call a bit later tonight.'

'Yeah. I will. I'm at work but I just wanted to call and see how everyone was. Speaking of which, how are you?'

'I take it you heard from Mum and Dad.'

'Yeah, they called last night. I'm glad you finally told them.' She heard muffled voices on the other end of the line before Linc came back. 'I gotta go, but it'll be good to get back home. I'll see you soon.'

'Give Mia and Cash a kiss for me,' she said before saying goodbye and turning to walk inside.

It was sombre inside the old pub. Groups of people sat at tables, half-drunk beers in front of them. Hadley greeted a few people she hadn't seen since her wedding and hoped she wouldn't be going to hell for the little white lies she mumbled when asked how Mitch was going. Surely she'd be forgiven for that today.

She saw Griff and Olivia at a table towards the back of the room and made her way across to them.

'I haven't been able to get hold of Ollie,' Olivia told her a few minutes later.

'I was with him for a bit earlier. He wanted to get back home.'

'I knew he'd be taking it hard. Mum said he was pretty cut up.'

'He feels responsible,' Hadley said with a long sigh. 'Ollie thinks he let Luke down.'

'Well, that's ridiculous.'

'I think he's in shock . . . like the rest of us.'

'You're not wrong. I just can't get my head around it. I mean, *suicide*?' Olivia almost breathed the word, horrified. 'There've been so many over the last few years around the place, but they've never been people we went to school with . . . people we really *know*, you know?' Olivia said, searching her friend's face.

Hadley shook her head slowly. Olivia was right, it was one thing to hear about it and only vaguely know who these people were, it was another thing altogether when it was someone you shared memories with.

There was a low hum in the room as people spoke quietly—so different to the usual roar—and Hadley felt a heaviness blanketing the room. She understood why Ollie had wanted to leave—it was suffocating. There was nothing to accomplish sitting here, and she knew that after a few more rounds shock and disbelief would lead to anger and frustration—not a great combination to mix with alcohol. Hopefully the fact that most people in the room were in the middle of harvest would cut things short, but some wouldn't let that deter them from drowning their sorrows and finding an outlet for their grief. Hadley wasn't going to hang around for that.

The sombre mood of the pub seemed to follow her home to Stringybark. There was so much going on inside her right now, she felt dizzy trying to separate it all. Maybe the Ollie incident was just a spin-off from shock—or grief—or both. That had to be it. It was so far out of the realm of anything she'd ever considered before that it had to be some kind of *reaction*. She slowly nodded as things began to fall into place and relief seeped through her, restoring calm. *It was just a reaction. Completely normal*, she told herself firmly in the mirror. Her respite lasted only as long as it took to walk to the house from her car, when a little voice whispered, *But what if it wasn't?*

❦

At the Pattersons' place it could have been Christmas Day or a party of some kind going by the number of cars parked in front of the house and the people coming and going. Only it wasn't. Ollie gritted his teeth against the sick feeling that rose at the thought of going inside. He didn't want to face Luke's parents like this. He didn't want to see first-hand the devastation that would be on their faces. And part of him was terrified that he'd see something else . . . blame. Deep down he knew it was crazy and yet he couldn't help but feel there had to be something he could have done to stop this from happening. Why wouldn't Luke's family blame him? He'd been one of the last ones to see their son alive.

His boots felt as though they were made of concrete, the weight of his steps slow and reluctant as he made his way up the path towards the house. He knocked and barely had time to drop his fist before Luke's dad was there, pushing open the squeaky screen door with its peeling green paint. For a moment the two men simply stared at each other. The leathery skinned farmer looked tired, his eyes red-rimmed. Ollie tried to speak but nothing came out. He didn't know what to say. Usually he'd just walk inside, calling out to Luke to hurry the hell up or they'd be late getting to the footy game. For the briefest of moments he expected Luke to appear behind his dad, but then he remembered, and was swallowed up again by the sorrow and despair brewing inside him.

'Come in, son,' Terry Patterson said gruffly. 'Good to see you.' He stood aside to allow Ollie to enter.

Alice Patterson moved around her kitchen, dodging the family and friends who stood by helplessly watching. He knew this reaction all too well. It was how his own mother dealt with stress. She couldn't sit, she had to be doing something—anything but sitting and thinking. He saw the concerned looks the women swapped and wished he could turn around and escape. Alice looked up at his arrival and summoned a shaky smile.

'Hello, Ollie.'

'Mrs Patterson,' Ollie said, hoping his voice sounded stronger than he felt.

'Would you stop calling me that. You're a grown man now. Call me Alice,' she said with a weary shake of her head. 'Thank you for coming over.' She looked older, as though she'd aged overnight. Her eyes, usually full of reluctant amusement, were dull, as though someone forgot to turn on the light inside on a grey, dreary day.

Ollie stepped closer and carefully hugged her. She felt smaller somehow, like a fragile bird, and he was scared of breaking her. Her grip, though, as she hugged him around the waist, was strong. For the briefest of moments he thought he felt her shoulders shake, but she pulled away quickly and turned back towards the counter, taking a mug from the cupboard. 'You'll have a cuppa?' she said without turning.

'Yeah. Sure,' he said, looking over at the sympathetic faces of the women in the kitchen.

'Here, let me,' Alice's sister said, taking the cup from her hand. 'Why don't you go and have a lie-down?'

'No, no, I'm fine,' she insisted doggedly.

'I might just go out and see Terry for a bit,' Ollie said, feeling as helpless as the others, unable to offer anything other than his presence.

The men were gathered in the lounge room, talking quietly. There was discussion about the weather and the recent footy scores, although it lacked its usual passion. It was just token conversation in lieu of discussing the massive elephant in the room. No one wanted to go there. What was the point? There were no answers, but the questions still hovered just under the surface. *Why?* There was an oppressive sadness—Ollie could feel its weight. His own grief and guilt pressed down on him. He risked a glance at Terry and saw the gritty-eye sorrow etched on his usually jovial face. He felt his own eyes sting. There was a reason no one was making eye contact with anyone here. It was all just too painful.

∽

Ollie went through the motions for the next few days. He got up and went to work like he always did. He concentrated on the harvest and buried himself in the day-to-day running of it, knowing that he couldn't afford to drop the ball. He'd worked too hard to get them where they were to pack it in now. His dad had finally started to ease up on the pressure, allowing him more freedom to run things. They were on track for a bumper year and he couldn't risk making any stupid mistakes that might jeopardise that.

The relationship between his dad and himself had been a prickly one over the past few years. It had been all right when he'd been a kid and had just done what he was told, but once he'd got older, and had more of his own ideas, things had changed.

It wasn't anything new. Plenty of his mates had the same story to tell. Hell, Griff and his old man fought like cats and dogs over how to do things too. It was only natural. His situation, though, was a little different in that he'd been forced to take over the property when his dad had had a serious accident the year before. For Bill, it had been difficult to let go of the reins when it hadn't been of his own making. Ollie had taken over running of the place because he'd had to. He got how difficult it must have been for his dad—stuck in hospital and then rehab for most of the past year. He'd had a huge life change, and losing the ability to run the place as he wanted to was probably the biggest of those adjustments.

Ollie had tried to keep his old man in the loop as much as possible. His dad needed to feel part of everything still and Ollie had learned not to take what he said as some kind of challenge. He'd begun to listen and take notice of his dad's suggestions. He'd lost the defensiveness he'd been carrying after the accident when his dad had come home expecting to pick up where he'd left off. They'd both had to learn a few things—not easy for two headstrong farmers living under the one roof. They still had their moments, but on the whole things ran smoothly.

Which was why he didn't want to lose his focus now and risk some kind of stupid mishap ruining everything. It only took one dumb mistake, like forgetting to clean out under a harvester so it caught on fire, which had happened last year. It could have taken out the entire crop—and, worse, everyone else's crops as well. He still felt sick to the stomach when he thought about it. He would *never* make that mistake again.

It was good that the crazy harvest season had gotten underway. It meant long days and nights in the harvester, which made him fall in bed and drift into an exhausted sleep. It gave him less time to be around people, and right now that was good. The only downside was that in a harvester there was way too much time to think.

He parked the machine and climbed down from the cabin, ready to head to bed, only he couldn't yet. He still had to clean the harvester.

Diesel wandered over to him and he bent down to rub the dog's head. 'Hey boy.' He missed his mate during harvest. He'd taken his dog in the harvester with him once and he'd had to keep stopping to open the cab door every few minutes because Diesel kept letting off the most toxic farts. Turned out his dog got car sick in a harvester.

He checked the various points under guards, where dust and chaff build-up could go unnoticed, making sure exhaust pipes and mufflers were free of chaff and then using the large air compressor to blow down the machine. He was just finishing when he saw his father ambling over. He was surprised to see his old man up this late.

'Machine going all right? How's it yielding?' his dad asked, resting an arm on the front of the harvester.

'Auger drive belt was slipping a bit but I tightened her up and she's all good now.'

'Good to hear. Yeah, so . . . your mother . . .' Bill started, stopping to clear his throat. 'She, ah, thought maybe . . .' He trailed off.

Ollie frowned. He was beginning to get alarmed; maybe his old man was having some kind of stroke.

'Well, the thing is, your mother's worried about you.'

'About me? Why?'

'Over this Luke Patterson thing.'

'What's she worried about?'

'Well, it's not so much that she . . . *we're* worried,' he corrected gruffly. 'I just want you to know that nothin's ever bad enough to warrant doing what young Patterson did.' Bill's voice shook a little and there was a glisten in his eyes.

Ollie swallowed hard, his throat feeling as though it had seized up at his father's unexpected emotion.

'If something ever does go that wrong, you come to us. Got it?' he said in a tone more brutal than the concerned expression on his sun-weathered face.

Ollie managed a quick nod, unable to trust his voice right at that moment.

'Righto. Well, get back to it and then grab some sleep. It's gonna be a bastard of a day tomorrow for everyone.'

He couldn't have put it better himself. He'd been dreading it all week, and now it was finally here. Tomorrow they buried his mate.

Seven

Hadley climbed out of her parents' car and spotted Griffin and Olivia nearby. It was rare to see her brother, or any of the men in town for that matter, dressed in suit jackets and pants and she wished it was for any occasion other than a funeral.

Both Griff and Ollie were to be pallbearers, and while dark sunglasses could hide red-rimmed eyes, they did little to disguise the torment and devastation in their body language.

Ollie was already at the front of the church, standing to one side quietly as they approached. While her parents were busy greeting neighbours and friends, Hadley moved over to him. He looked so alone, even in this crowd of people.

It was always so hard to say anything worthwhile at these things. *How are you? How are you holding up?* It was plain to see he wasn't doing great, and he was barely holding up, so both greetings sounded ridiculous. She opted instead for no words, simply slipping her arm in his and hugging him tightly. He needed support now, more than words or empty-sounding platitudes. They all did.

Beside him, she could feel the effort it was taking for Ollie to hold it together. He shouldn't have to—none of them should—and, yet, that's what he and pretty much every other generation of men here had been brought up to do. It wasn't just the men—she'd also learned in her own line of work that to show weakness, particularly as a woman, whether it be in combat or during some horrific natural disaster, made her somehow less of a reporter. If she cried when she reported on the innocent victims of war—the wounded children in hospital, the little ones killed in bombings and wars around the world—then she was being an 'emotional woman'.

At the same time, if she managed to speak to the camera dry-eyed and steadfast, she was a cold-hearted bitch. She really couldn't win. But in order to get the jobs—to be chosen alongside male journalists—she'd had to learn how to mask her grief and do the job. Over time, that hardness had seemed to eat away at her. Her mother often looked at her with a sad kind of wonder as she'd told some awful story around the dinner table. She knew what her mother was thinking: *Where did my passionate, kind-hearted daughter go?* The one who'd been offended and outraged on behalf of some underdog, even as a child. She was still in there, but she'd learned not to let her emotions get in the way of the story she had to tell, because people in her line of business didn't know how to react to displays of emotion. They knew how to exploit it well enough, they just didn't know what to do with a TV journalist who cried each time she reported a horrific story. So she'd learned how to bury that part of herself.

It was harder today, when she personally knew the man . . . the boy she'd gone to school with. When she knew the family who stood here grieving for their son, and the friends who were left shocked and shaken by his sudden death. But she'd hold it together for everyone else's sake—be the strong one who was able to talk when others couldn't finish a sentence or find any words to say. It would be her job to be strong today, so others didn't have to be.

People began to move into the church, so Hadley and Ollie followed them. They found a row of seats and before long the rest of the Dawsons and Callahans were sitting down beside them.

The minister's words were heartfelt and kind. The eulogy was read by Luke's cousin and his sister, and although they did their best to colour it with humorous anecdotes, the laughter from the gathered mourners was somewhat forced and bittersweet. It felt good to remember him in funnier times, until the brutal reality of his final moments robbed any joy from the memories.

When the service was finally over, Hadley gave Ollie's hand a final reassuring squeeze as he stood and made his way to the front of the church along with the other pallbearers. She heard the gentle sobs from Luke's mother and sister in the front row. Terry Patterson stood by the casket that held his only son, ready to carry him out of the church. The heartbreak on his weathered face spoke volumes. A father should not be carrying his son's coffin. It just wasn't the natural order of things.

Hadley had been to her fair share of funerals over the years—none of them were nice. It didn't matter if it was someone who had lived a long and full life, they were all a goodbye. But this one was even harder to process because it felt so wrong. Luke shouldn't be in a casket. He shouldn't be having a funeral at all. He had the rest of his life ahead of him. He hadn't had some horrific terminal disease that had unfairly robbed him of his life. He hadn't been in some terrible accident . . . he'd planned his death. Waited till his parents weren't home, took a gun from the house, walked down to a back shed and pulled the trigger. At any point he could have changed his mind, but he hadn't. That was the part Hadley knew haunted everyone the most. If things were that bad, why hadn't he tried to get help? Why hadn't any of the people closest to him suspected he could do such a thing?

Logically, she knew that depression was like a disease in its own way, but it didn't *have* to be terminal. It didn't *have* to reach this point. There was help available . . . if he'd only asked.

Why hadn't he asked?

❧

Ollie had never been so glad to see the back end of a day. He'd been dreading the funeral, and thank Christ now it was over.

He'd thought that maybe once it was done, he'd feel different—relieved, maybe—but he didn't. He just felt gutted. He couldn't look at Luke's parents. He couldn't talk to either of them. The anguish he'd seen on their faces when they'd walked into the church had been enough to shake any resolve he'd built up. His eyes felt gritty and sore. His throat ached from holding back his grief. He couldn't lose it in front of everyone. There were people who were depending on him to be strong. He was no use to anyone if he gave into the urge to pour out his grief and frustration like he wanted to do. What would that achieve? It wouldn't bring Luke back. It wouldn't give him the answers he needed. And it sure as hell wouldn't wash away the guilt that continued to hang over him like a big black rain cloud. He should have done something.

Ollie looked up as Hadley sat down beside him on the tailgate of his ute. He didn't know how she'd found him out here in the dark.

'You okay?' she asked gently.

'Not really.'

He heard her sad sigh next to him and closed his eyes. He felt so damn tired and old.

'I needed to get out of there for a bit,' she admitted, and he knew exactly how she felt. The wake was being held at the pub and was still in full swing, but after a while everything had started to get on his nerves and he'd needed to find some quiet.

'I can't handle listening to the endless cycle of "I can't believe it" or "I had no idea" anymore today,' Hadley said.

'Me neither.' It was bad enough that those same things were swirling around in his own head constantly.

He could feel the warmth where her arm brushed against his, and her touch felt as though it were slowly melting the cold, empty sadness that had wrapped around him ever since hearing about Luke's death.

Where the evening night air had filled his senses before, now suddenly it was all Hadley. Her scent, a delicate floral smell, and the warmth of her nearness shut out everything else. He looked down when her hand covered his, braced beside his thigh on the tray back. When he looked at her the gentle expression on her face soothed his saddened heart.

Right now he couldn't think of anyone else in the entire world he'd rather be with. All around them were the sounds of early evening—birds settling in the trees for the night, crickets chirping—he was aware of all of it and yet somehow he felt as though he and Hadley were in a vacuum. There was nothing between them; she was so close he could see the movement of her chest as her breathing quickened. Surely he was hallucinating. This couldn't be happening, and yet her eyes seemed to soften, and her lips parted slightly, beckoning him closer.

At the first touch his head began to spin. Her lips moved beneath his, gently at first and then with more insistence. He was certain she'd pull away and shriek in horror, but to his surprise the kiss continued. He felt her move closer, and adjusted his position so she could slip between his thighs. His hands moved to cup her head, his fingers sliding into her thick hair as they deepened the kiss. He was lost in her. He would have scoffed if he'd ever spoken the words aloud, but right here, right now, that's exactly how it felt.

∞

This was crazy. She'd only meant to comfort Ollie. He'd seemed so alone and she couldn't turn her back on an old friend who was hurting. Only, somehow, comfort had turned into . . . this.

Hadley eased back. Her hands trembled slightly against his chest and she struggled to regain her composure. 'I, ah, don't really know where that came from,' she said with a wince at how unsteady her voice sounded. When Ollie didn't reply she risked a glance up at his face and saw him watching her intently. A flutter began in the pit of her stomach. *He's not sorry.* The thought made her reel. Why wasn't he as surprised by this as she was?

'It's all right,' he said in the gentle voice someone might use on a startled animal. Which was probably what she looked like right at this moment—a kangaroo caught in headlights.

'This is not all right,' she said when she found her voice again. 'You're my friend and you're grieving and I shouldn't have . . . done that.'

'It's the best thing that's happened to me in a long time, if you wanna know the truth,' he said, his gaze still locked on hers.

Hadley shook her head sadly. 'My life is a mess right now and the last thing I want to do is drag you into it.'

'Nobody's dragging me.'

Why wasn't he more freaked out about this? They'd been friends since childhood and now suddenly here they were, making out . . . and he was sitting there all calm and rational? What the hell?

'I'd better get back inside,' she said, her words trailing off feebly as he lifted an eyebrow slightly but made no move to stop her. Hadley swallowed hard. When had he gotten so . . . good-looking . . . so mature? She would have thought she was the one who had it together, but right now she felt like a blubbering idiot while he was being this stoic tower of strength. 'See you,' she said, backing away quickly before she said or did anything else she might regret.

Her lips still felt warm from his and she pressed them together firmly to stop the annoying sensation the memory of it caused. Like she didn't have enough to deal with. She did *not* need to add a complication like falling for her best friend's brother on top of everything else.

'Pull yourself together, Callahan,' she muttered, heading inside and resisting the urge to look back at Ollie.

∽

'Are you going to tell me what's going on with you?'

Hadley looked up at Olivia and frowned. 'What?'

'You've been sitting there staring into your coffee for the last ten minutes. You haven't heard a word I've said. What's wrong?'

Hadley picked up the mug and took a sip of the luke-warm coffee and sighed. 'Something happened yesterday.'

'What happened?'

'I don't want you to freak out, and you have to swear to me that this stays between the two of us. You can't tell Griff . . . or anyone,' she said, holding her friend's eyes sternly.

'Okay,' Olivia said, folding her arms and leaning on the table.

'Yesterday, after the funeral, I wanted to make sure Ollie was doing okay so I went out to sit with him for a bit,' she said, biting the inside of her lip as she stared down into the caramel-coloured coffee. 'I don't know how it happened, but . . .'—she closed her eyes tightly—'we kissed.'

When Olivia didn't immediate gasp or laugh out aloud, Hadley opened her eyes and looked at her friend, to see a slow smile spreading across her face. 'Well, it's about time.'

'Excuse me?' Of all the things she'd anticipated Olivia saying, this had *not* been on the list.

Olivia rolled her eyes and shook her head mournfully. 'Hadley, I love you, but for a savvy woman of the world, you are so dumb sometimes.'

The shock must have shown on her face, because Olivia gave a small chuckle. 'How can someone who makes a living investigating stories not see what's been staring her in the face for most of her life?'

'What are you talking about?'

'Ollie, you twit. He's been in love with you for as long as I can remember.'

'Don't be ridiculous.'

'Maybe if you actually looked around you instead of only ever thinking about where your next story's coming from, you'd have noticed.'

The barb stung, but it was dulled slightly by the shock of the revelation that apparently other people knew Ollie had feelings for her. How had she missed it? 'Why didn't you say anything?'

'Because Ollie asked me not to.' She shrugged.

'You're my best friend,' Hadley said, feeling a little betrayed that Liv had kept such a huge secret from her for all these years.

'Yes,' she agreed simply, 'but he's my twin, and we both knew there was no point saying anything.'

'Why not?'

Olivia sent her a look that made Hadley feel as though she was a child and Liv the adult was considering how much information she could deal with. 'You were on your way to start a career. You never held back telling anyone who'd listen how you were going to travel the world and have these amazing adventures.' She smiled sadly. 'Ollie knew he couldn't compete with that, and he didn't want to. He wanted you to go out and live your dream.'

It was as though she was hearing a completely different version of her life. The Ollie she remembered had been the strong, silent type. Dependable, brotherly. Now she was being told that he hadn't felt that way about her at all and somehow she'd missed all the signs. Or had he just been really good at hiding them? An empty kind of regret filled her chest at the thought. He hadn't needed to hide it too deep; she'd been oblivious to everyone else back then, especially through her high school days. She'd known exactly where she was going—as far from Stringybark as she could get.

She blinked away a sting in her eye. For so long she hadn't really considered anyone else's feelings, she'd been so obsessed with her career, so busy immersing herself in the world's problems that she hadn't spared a thought for friends and family back here. She tried to get home for special occasions, but work always seemed to take over. Mother Nature often didn't consult Hadley's schedule before unleashing a natural disaster. She was inconsiderate like that.

It hadn't been until after all this mess with Mitch and Harmony unfolded that she'd realised she'd been burying her head in her work to escape some pretty uncomfortable and painful truths. Now to find out this . . . How self-absorbed did a person have to be not to pick up on something this big?

She didn't want to be that person anymore. She wanted to be involved with her family and friends. She wanted family dinners and morning cups of tea with her mum and her gran.

'I feel really stupid,' she admitted quietly as Olivia watched her silently from across the table.

'You shouldn't. We all had to grow up and move away to find out what it was we wanted to do with our lives,' she shrugged.

'It's like I've been living with blinkers on.'

'That's sometimes how it has to be. You have to focus on things, but eventually there comes a time when you take them off and you realise there's a whole lot of other stuff to look at.'

'I don't know how I'm going to face him after yesterday.'

'The same way you have every other day. He's still Ollie.' She paused before asking, almost hesitantly, 'Did you like it?'

'The kiss?' she asked, and felt her heart flutter briefly as she remembered it. 'I guess. It's just . . . weird.'

'No kidding,' Olivia said drolly. 'You're my best friend and he's my brother . . . I'm torn between wanting to know every last detail and being completely grossed out.'

'It just happened.'

'And yet I'm assuming you didn't run away screaming. So does that mean you've discovered some feelings for him?'

'I don't know.' Hadley shook her head helplessly. 'I was too surprised to say much . . . Nothing can come of it,' she finished decisively.

'Why not?'

'Well, I've still got my career . . . and Ollie belongs here. It's just not workable.'

'Trust me, from one career-obsessed city dweller to another, anything's possible if you want it bad enough.'

But did she want it? That was the big question. Did she even want to figure out what this thing was in the first place? At the moment she could just put it down as an accident . . . a mistake, a grief-induced moment of madness. It didn't have to go any further. It didn't have to get messy. And yet ... Last night she'd replayed that kiss over and over in her mind and couldn't shake the fact that there'd definitely been something there. A spark. Chemistry. Whatever they called it, it was not brotherly in any way, shape or form, that much she knew for certain.

Eight

Hadley's phone rang on her bedside table and she groaned when she saw Mitch's name on the screen. It was far too early in the morning to be dealing with him. She hadn't even had coffee, for goodness sake. However, when he tried calling for a third time, Hadley finally answered, not bothering to hide her annoyance in her clipped greeting.

'I wanted you to know they're running a story in the papers about the split,' Mitch said without a greeting.

'I'm surprised it took them this long,' she commented after the initial surprise wore off.

'I've managed to hold them off as long as possible, but my agent and the network seem to think it's best that we come out with a statement and head off any tabloid sensationalism.'

'*We*, as in they want *us* to give a statement?'

'Well, no. *We* as in the network and I. It's important to protect the image of the show as much as possible.'

Of course, he was only really concerned about his image and TV ratings.

'I just wanted to prepare you. It'll be in the papers tomorrow morning.'

'Thank you for the opportunity to contribute to the decision,' she said archly.

'There was really no need for you to get involved. In fact, after our last conversation you made it pretty clear you wanted nothing to do with it.'

'Considering you really didn't give me any say in anything before having an affair with my sister,' she added. 'So how are you spinning that one?' That should be great for his ratings.

'We're just focusing on the separation and pending divorce at this stage. It's been an amicable decision and hopefully it'll all blow over and there'll be no need to involve anyone else in all this. I'm sure you wouldn't want your sister and family dragged through the media,' he added pointedly.

'So basically, if I get asked, we're not mentioning the fact that we're getting a divorce because you were cheating on me,' she said dryly.

'Hadley, we've been through this. I'm sorry Harmony and I have hurt you, but I think we both know that you and I weren't working out. Can you really hold a grudge against us for finding love? Surely you want your sister to be happy?'

Hadley gave a disbelieving snort. These last few weeks had been a real eye-opener for her. She knew where his career was concerned, Mitch had always been ambitious, but she hadn't realised just how self-centred he'd become and how single-minded he was about keeping his job. He knew any scandal connected to him would not put him in good stead with his employers, especially when he made his living as the face of a program that prided itself on family values and speaking up for the underdog. Having their wholesome poster boy linked to a marriage break-up, one in which he cheated on his wife *with her sister,* would not be a good look for the network.

She couldn't think of anything worse than having everyone know the truth behind the story either—it made her look like an idiot. Of course she didn't want the story plastered all over the newspapers and gossip magazines any more than he did, but it rubbed her the wrong way when he felt it necessary to add the threat about her family getting caught up in it all. That bit really annoyed her.

'Yes, my sister's happiness is the most important issue in this whole fiasco,' she said sarcastically. 'Don't think for a moment that I believe this call has anything to do with Harmony. Or my family,' she added bitterly. 'This is about you, Mitch, and your precious image. I just hope the job you seem to have sold your soul for is worth it, because you're not the man you used to be.'

He hadn't been like this when they'd first met. Yes, he'd always had his dream job firmly in mind even back then, but he'd been decent and kind, and despite the vanity and the overconfidence she knew drove other people insane, he had been a good man. She just hadn't been around him often enough after his promotion to really understand the changes he'd undergone. Not until it was too late.

'Goodbye, Hadley,' he said briskly and the phone call disconnected in her ear.

Good riddance. She let out a long sigh as she tipped her head back on her pillow. Maybe it was a positive thing this was about to break. For the last few weeks it'd been like waiting for the other shoe to drop. The sooner it was out there the sooner everyone would lose interest in it and move on to the next unfolding drama.

Hadley bit the inside of her lip as she sat at breakfast later that morning with her parents and grandmother. *Just bring it up and get it over with.* 'I had a phone call from Mitch this morning,' she said, reaching for a piece of toast she didn't feel like eating.

'What'd *he* want?' her father asked, looking up from the rural report.

'Apparently he's decided to break the story about our divorce before someone else does. He gave a statement to the paper, so I guess we can expect the phone to start ringing any time now.'

'Bloody reporters,' her dad muttered, before glancing up at his daughter. 'Not you, love,' he added reluctantly.

Hadley gave a wince. 'Thanks, Dad.'

'Did he say what was in the statement?' Lavinia asked.

'Not really, other than he's explained that we decided that it wasn't working out.'

'It's a bit bloody hard to work on a marriage when the bastard's cheatin' on you, isn't it!' Bob snarled.

'Robert,' Lavinia cautioned gently.

'He's not even man enough to stand up and take responsibility for his actions,' Bob said, his brow creased in a way that reminded Hadley of his reaction when Griffin had taken his brand-new four-wheel drive for a joy ride with mates when they were fourteen. 'I say we tell whoever calls the real reason behind it.'

'No,' Hadley said quickly. 'There's no point in doing that. All it'll do is create an even bigger story. They'll never let it go then. Please, Dad, if they call, just agree with Mitch's version. Work commitments drove us apart or something, or, better yet, no comment,' she said, trying to keep her tone casual. The last thing she needed now was her dad to get all protective and offended on her behalf and give the reporters ammunition to go digging around to uncover the truth.

'I don't understand why you're happy to let the bastard off scot-free, after what he's done.'

'Because I don't want the whole world knowing my business, Dad,' she said and didn't have to try for a hurt tone. It was the truth. She was hurt and she didn't want to be exposed to public scrutiny when she felt so vulnerable.

'Your father and I won't say anything about it to anyone, darling. It'll be okay,' her mum said, patting her hand. 'Right, Robert?'

She saw her parents exchange a look that eventually changed her dad's belligerent expression to one of resigned agreement. 'Right.'

'I just want to move on from all of this with as little fuss as possible.'

'We understand,' her mother said. 'We're just worried about you. We don't want to see you get bulldozed into something because Mitch thinks it's right. You've been hurt by all this and he's trying to cover up his part in it. I just hope this other woman is worth it.'

Hadley swallowed past the sick feeling that began to rise. Maybe at first she'd felt a small stab of vengeful satisfaction at her parents' wrath against the unknown woman, but now it was starting to make her feel uncomfortable. It wasn't fair on her parents to let them vent their anger against some nameless woman when, if they knew it was Harmony, they'd be reluctant to speak out against her so vehemently.

It would be hard for her parents to be torn between two of their children. Unfortunately, it had gone on too long. How did she tell them it was Harmony now? Especially after hearing their opinions on the kind of woman who would do something like this. They were going to be utterly devastated. No. It was better not to say anything. She was fairly sure Harmony and Mitch had a plan in place. A way to spin the situation in their favour. She figured they'd say they met afterwards and realised they shared common interests, *mainly themselves*, and fell for each other.

If they lasted that long. Hadley supposed there was always the possibility that the relationship wouldn't survive once it became less of a novelty and more of a reality. Then again, Harmony was into all the lifestyle extras that went along with Mitch's job: the parties and the functions, fundraising events and balls. Hadley hated that part of his career. In fact, she'd really only gone to a handful of events while they'd been married. She was usually away on assignment, for which she was grateful. Evening gowns and social chit-chat had never been her forte; it was, however, Harmony's. So maybe they would survive. Mitch needed a partner who could handle that side of things and Harmony had always dreamed of being in the limelight.

She managed half of her toast before taking the scraps to the kitchen and putting her plate in the dishwasher. She might be willing to go along with whatever fabrication Mitch wanted to spin for the media, but she knew that at some point she and Harmony needed to talk about it. Her parents were beginning to get worried about the fact that Harmony hadn't been out in a while and seemed to be spending a lot of weekends away. It wouldn't be long until they began to suspect she had a new man in her life, and once that happened her mother wouldn't let up until she had all the details. There was no way Harmony was going to be able to keep this quiet once their mother started to suspect a secret boyfriend.

∽

Hadley parked out the front of her sister's house and drummed her fingers on the steering wheel. The house itself was fairly old and had been rather outdated when Harmony bought it several years earlier, but it had an impressive front entrance and the gardens were beautiful. Hadley had to admit her sister had impeccable taste; the woman could seriously make a career out of interior decorating if she ever set her mind to it. She'd overseen the renovation of the house and it was nothing short of breathtaking.

Hadley walked to the front door, taking a deep breath before knocking, and waited as she heard the click-clack of heels on the polished timber flooring inside.

The large, somewhat overcompensating door opened to reveal her sister looking just as surprised as Hadley had imagined she'd look, since she hadn't phoned ahead to tell her she would be dropping by. Part of her had hoped Harmony would be out. That way she could at least feel as though she'd made the effort, without enduring any of the confrontation. No such luck.

'Hadley. I expected you to show up sooner or later,' Harmony said quietly.

'As opposed to you making the effort to come and see me,' she said lightly, holding her sister's wavering glance.

'It was a little difficult, seeing as Mum and everyone would be there.'

'I thought it was time we talked.'

'I don't have very long. There's a luncheon I need to attend.'

'It won't take long,' Hadley said, stepping into the open foyer. The polished timber floors and large leafy foliage of scattered pot plants gave the house a cool, summery feel. They bypassed the kitchen, which was done in white timber and elegant antique fixtures, in favour of a windowed sitting room, which opened up with expensive folding glass doors onto the back yard overlooking the swimming pool and gazebo.

'Would you like coffee?' Harmony asked politely.

The thought of drinking or eating anything right now made her feel a little ill. 'No, thanks.'

Harmony surprised her by launching into the subject without preamble. 'I want to thank you for not saying anything to Mum and Dad.'

'I did it for them, not for you and Mitch,' Hadley said stiffly, then sighed. She hated this—hated so much that she had a sister who clearly thought nothing about betraying her and was little more than a stranger to her. How had that happened? How had they managed to grow so distant?

'I guess you heard that Mitch has spoken to the press,' Harmony said, looking down at her fingernails.

Hadley glanced down at her own short nails and realised she hadn't been to a beautician since before her wedding. 'Yes, he called this morning.'

'I know you have every right to be upset, but I really hope you can see past everything that's happened and realise that anything you say will only hurt Mum and Dad.'

Hadley closed her eyes briefly, praying for the strength not to jump across the table and strangle her older sister. 'Do not,' she articulated clearly, 'use Mum and Dad as leverage in all this. If either one of you cared about Mum and Dad's feelings, neither of you would have gone and done what you did, in the way you did it, so please spare me the lecture. What you really mean is don't let Mum and Dad find out what *you* did, because you know damn well it's going to break their hearts.' She felt a moment of regret when she saw the flash of pain cross her sister's face but she steeled herself against it. 'I just hope you realise that while you might be genuinely worried about our parents, Mitch's reasons for keeping me quiet are solely based on what it'll do for his reputation and career.'

'Well, of course he's worried about that, Hadley. Look at everything he has to lose.'

'Harmony, are you listening to yourself?'

'What?'

'It doesn't concern you that his only regret about all this is that his career might take a hit? Really?'

'He does have other concerns. He's not the monster you're making him out to be, but he is a man with ambition and drive. He's worked hard to get where he is. Of course that would be a huge concern for him.'

'And you're okay with the fact he's willing to lie about your relationship in order to protect his career?'

'He's not lying. It's none of anyone else's business.'

'Of course not. Neither of you should feel the least bit guilty for anything you've done to anyone else.'

'Hadley, I *am* sorry that we didn't tell you before this got serious. I *do* feel bad about that, but you can't tell me that you are devastated about this marriage being over. You did nothing to try to save it. All that working away from home—how often were you two even together? Neither of you was seriously committed to the relationship, so please don't play the victim in this.'

'Don't play the victim?' Hadley repeated, stunned by her sister's words. 'Play the victim?' She demanded louder as her outrage gathered momentum. 'You're my *sister*, Harmony. What's wrong with you?'

Harmony's gaze hardened at that. 'I saw a chance to be happy. I found a man I could admire, someone I knew I would be happy with. You're always so vocal about taking chances, following your dreams. Well, maybe I was taking your advice for once.'

'Oh, please. You talk about me acting like a victim? *Seriously?*'

'I don't think we're going to get anywhere here, do you?'

'No, sadly, I don't think we are,' Hadley said after a moment of silence.

Hadley hadn't been sure what this visit would achieve; maybe she'd been stupid to think it would change things. She stood to turn away, but stopped, looking back at her sister. 'Why are we like this?'

At least Harmony didn't bother pretending that she didn't know what Hadley was asking. 'We grew up and went in two very different directions. We're different people.'

'We're still family. A man shouldn't be what comes between us.'

'I can't help who I fell in love with. It just happened. It wasn't planned. Mitch and I belong together. He's who I'm meant to be with. You weren't happy with him, so why

87

should I throw away a chance at an amazing future with the man I love because you chose him first and got it wrong?'

'You may not have deliberately gone after him, but you sure as hell knew at some point that what you were doing was wrong.'

'I'm sorry for hurting you,' she said again softly. 'If I could go back and change how it all happened I would. The truth is, I was in a really bad place at the time. Mitch . . .' She paused, giving a small smile. 'He was the only person who seemed to see me. The real me, Hadley. The woman. He listened to me, *really* listened,' she said, searching her sister's eyes for some kind of understanding. 'I thought with Don I'd have the life I'd been dreaming of, but he turned out to be . . . well, less of a man than I'd expected,' she said darkly. 'Mitch is everything Don isn't. He is charming, and for the first time in years I feel as though I'm beautiful and that the things I have to say are important. I can't even remember the last time I was asked my opinion or taken seriously about something. I'd never believed in soulmates before Mitch.'

Hadley wanted to feel outraged, but the truth was, all she felt was deflated and empty. There was no way her sister could know that she wished for exactly the same thing. She wanted that magical soul connection with someone, and for a long time she'd lied to herself that it would happen with Mitch. It never had. Part of her was hurt far more by the death of that fantasy than by the fact her sister had had an affair with her husband. She was jealous. Harmony had found her soulmate in the man who Hadley had hoped would be hers.

'I have to go,' she said, stepping away from the table. Her heart felt heavy and sad. She'd come here so angry and wanting to unleash her righteous fury as the woman wronged, only deep down she knew that even though her sister and husband had hurt her, her cries of injustice weren't coming from a broken heart. She felt like a fraud holding on to her anger. Yes, she had a right to be angry and feel betrayed, but knowing that she wasn't really in love with Mitch and probably never had been, it felt wrong to accept her parents' outrage and pity on her behalf.

'One day I hope we can put this behind us, Hadley,' Harmony said softly behind her.

Hadley's footsteps faltered slightly at the slight quiver in her sister's tone, but she didn't reply. She was hurting. Not over the loss of her marriage. Over the loss of her sister. Maybe one day they would find a way to start over, but it wouldn't be today. Today it still hurt too much.

Nine

Ollie wiped his hands on a rag and fought the rush of
nerves exploding inside him as he spotted Hadley walking
towards the machinery shed. They hadn't spoken since the
wake. He'd wanted to call her but had had no idea what
he would say.

Diesel ran up to her, jumping on the spot to get her to
pat him. He watched his dog look across at him with a
big dopey grin on his face as she rubbed behind his ears
and crooned at him lovingly. *Yep, I know just how you
feel, mate.*

'Hey,' he said, tossing the rag on the workbench as she
came to a stop in front of him. As he was wondering how
to bring up the matter of the kiss, he caught the look on

her face. 'Are you okay?' She looked tired and her eyes were red, like maybe she'd been crying.

She shook her head and he saw tears begin to brim on her lower lashes. He didn't think about it, he just pulled her close and held her tightly, feeling her shoulders shake. He was pretty sure this wasn't about the kiss.

For a long while they just stood there in the middle of the shed. Her tears subsided and he felt her take a few deep, calming breaths before she stepped out of his arms, wiping her fingers across her face and collecting herself.

'I'm sorry about that. I don't know why I came here, actually.'

'Is everything okay?' Clearly it wasn't, but he had no idea what else to ask.

'I just had a long-overdue heart-to-heart with Harmony. I'm sorry, I just . . . I don't know, seeing you was all I felt like doing.'

Inside, her words were making his ego do crazy high fives, until he realised what the conversation with Harmony must have been about, and the thought instantly doused his joy with anger. 'I'm sorry. That must have been rough,' he said gently.

'It was, but not in the way I expected,' she said, crossing to the bench and picking things up and putting them down again distractedly.

'How do you mean?'

'I just realised the thing that hurts the most isn't losing Mitch. It's that I miss my sister. Isn't that weird?'

'Not really,' he said slowly.

She turned to look at him and he swallowed over a painful lump in his throat as she gazed at him with big, solemn eyes. 'I just wish it had been anyone else but her,' she said and the pain in her voice broke his heart.

He wanted to take all that pain away and make it better, but he knew he couldn't.

'There's going to be an article in the paper tomorrow.'

'About Mitch and Harmony?'

'No. Just about the divorce. The official story will be work and long-distance commutes broke up our marriage.'

'Official story,' Ollie scoffed. 'Yeah, right. You're not going to let them get off that easy, are you?'

Hadley shrugged listlessly. 'It's partly the truth. Things weren't going great.'

'Before or after he started bangin' your sister?' At her sharp glance, he let out a frustrated sigh. 'Sorry.'

'Truthfully? I don't know. Maybe it took him meeting her for at least one of us to come to our senses and do something about it.'

'He's still a coward and a jerk in my book. The only reason you found out was because they got caught. He should have been man enough to tell you before things got that far.'

'We can't do anything about it now. I just want it over and done with, and to make sure Mum and Dad don't have to hear about it.'

'They're going to hear about it anyway. At some point Harmony will have to tell them about him.'

'Yeah, eventually. And I'm sure they'll work it to their advantage somehow.'

'I can't imagine your parents accepting Harmony and Mitch even if they take another year to come clean.'

'It won't be pretty,' Hadley agreed. 'But at least it's not as horrible as them finding out she was cheating with him while we were still married. That would crush them.' She took a seat on a nearby box.

Either way, he figured it would be pretty uncomfortable. It didn't look like family gatherings were going to get any less awkward any time soon.

'I guess we should talk about the other day,' she said when silence fell between them.

He wasn't sure where this was heading. Did she regret it? Was she about to tell him to stay the hell away from her from now on? He hoped not, but who knew?

'I had no idea, Ollie,' she said, looking up at him.

'About what?'

'How you felt,' she said, and his gut dropped. 'About me.'

The ability to open his mouth and speak was beyond him.

'Liv told me.'

'Told you what?' he asked slowly.

'That you've . . . had feelings for me . . . for a long time. I swear I didn't know, Ollie. I would never have . . .'

Never what? He screamed inside but couldn't speak.

'Well, I mean, I would have said something . . . I wouldn't have just ignored it.'

'I can't believe she told you,' he managed to get out, feeling mortified that she must think he was some pathetic loser after all this time.

'No, it's not her fault. I went there after we ... you know. Anyway, I told her what happened and that it took me by surprise ...'

'You told her that we kissed?'

She looked up at him uncertainly. 'She's my best friend. We always tell each other stuff like that.'

Just great. If his sister knew, then Griff would know by now too. He'd never hear the end of it. 'Look, I don't know what Liv told you ...' he started.

'That you've had a thing for me ... forever,' Hadley supplied, holding his gaze even as he swallowed in discomfort.

It was worse than he'd thought. 'Well, you know, the thing, is ...' he began again.

'Actually, her exact words were that you've been in love with me for as long as she could remember.' She cut him off and the look she levelled at him dared him to deny it.

'Right,' he said, shoving his hands into his pockets. 'I guess I used to have a crush on you when we were kids.'

'So when did it stop?'

'When did what stop?'

'The crush.'

'Oh. Ah, I don't know ... I guess at some point. I don't remember. You know, we all grew up ... and you got married,' he said, hoping his voice still sounded off-hand and not as uncertain as he feared it did. He saw her lower her eyes but not before he caught the slight flinch. 'It doesn't matter,' he said, reaching out a hand instinctively to touch her arm.

'It does matter, Ollie,' she said, lifting her gaze to his, and making him catch his breath at the pain he saw there. 'What kind of person is so wrapped up in her own self-importance that she doesn't even pick up on something like that?'

'You're the last person anyone would think was wrapped up in self-importance and you didn't know because I never said anything.'

'Why didn't you?'

'Because . . .' he shifted his weight awkwardly and rubbed his chest. 'I don't know, you were always destined for big things. There was nothing I could offer you here.'

'How could you have known that back then?'

'It didn't take a genius,' he said with a small grin. 'There was always something special about you, Hads. You were too big for this little place. That and the fact you pretty much only ever talked about the day you'd leave . . . that was kinda a big clue.'

'I guess I was a little obsessed with that.'

Ollie shrugged, 'You knew what you wanted to do in life. I always liked that about you. You had drive.'

'I'm still sorry that I was so busy looking ahead that I didn't take time to see what was around me.'

∽

How could she have been so blind? Now that she knew, she thought back to all the times over the years she'd come home and Ollie had been there. She knew he'd never be the kind of man to hold a grudge and grow bitter with unrequited love, but how hard would that have been, to have feelings for someone and never get more than a friendly hug or smile in return? All those Christmases and family celebrations over the years. *Her wedding.* She almost gasped aloud as the realisation of that struck home. He'd had to stand there and watch her marry someone else.

Logically she knew she had nothing to feel guilty about, she hadn't even known how Ollie had felt about her, and yet she *did* feel bad. It wasn't difficult to imagine how painful that must have been.

He kicked the dirt at his feet and she knew he was embarrassed that she'd found out.

'Forget it,' he said.

'It's a bit hard to forget when I haven't been able to stop thinking about the other day.'

He looked up at that, eyeing her apprehensively.

Hadley wiped suddenly sweaty hands on her jeans, fidgeting nervously. 'The thing is, it kinda caught me off guard. I wasn't expecting . . . that.'

He watched her intently, waiting for her to make some kind of sense, she supposed. If only she *were* making sense. What was she doing? She knew they had to talk about the kiss, but she hadn't been planning on doing it today. Today she'd driven here after seeing Harmony because . . . She paused, a strange sensation passing through her body, because . . . there was no one else she wanted to be around right now.

'Hads?' he asked, concern filling his face.

Hadley blinked. 'Ah, sorry. I . . .'

'It's okay,' he said gently. 'We can just forget it ever happened if it's freaking you out that much.'

'It's not,' she jumped in quickly. 'I'm not freaked out.'

Ollie gave her a crooked grin, the kind she'd seen a thousand times before but until today hadn't ever made her stomach flip-flop like this. 'I can see that.'

'I'm not. I'm just . . . surprised.'

'About what part?' he asked. 'The kiss or that I'd been wanting to do that since we were in high school?'

'Pretty much all of it,' she said, feeling side-swiped once again.

He leaned back against the side of the tractor and folded his arms across his chest. 'If it makes you feel any better, I haven't stopped thinking about it either.'

She was momentarily distracted by the tight pull of the fabric of his shirt and the soft denim that covered his thighs. This was Ollie. Only it wasn't. It was Ollie as she'd never seen him before.

'I just don't know where we go from here,' she said, forcing her focus back on track. 'My life is a mess at the moment. I don't know if this,' she waved a finger between them, 'is something that I need to add to my life right now. I mean, I'm not even sure how long I'm home for.'

'I know it doesn't change anything,' he shrugged. 'To tell you the truth, I've never really thought past what would happen if I did ever get to kiss you. Reality always gets in the way of a good fantasy,' he added dryly.

'I don't want you to think it didn't mean anything,' she said softly. 'It did. I just think the timing's really bad right now.'

'Story of my life,' he smiled sadly. 'It's all good, Hads. Don't worry about it. It was a stressful day and we were just in the right place . . . at the wrong time.'

'Maybe if things weren't so crazy,' she said, feeling somehow disappointed that he wasn't arguing a case for why she was wrong, then getting annoyed at herself for being the kind of woman who wanted drama in her life. Here she was, knowing that any kind of involvement with Ollie would only add more stress to her already tumultuous life, and she was still tempted to throw caution to the wind and ignore all the logical reasons why it was a bad idea.

He opened his mouth to speak, but her phone interrupted them as it rang loudly from her back pocket. 'It's Mum. I better answer it or she'll send out a search party. I've been gone for most of the day.'

'Yeah, sure. I've got to get back to work anyway.'

'I'll see you later,' she said.

She sent him an apologetic smile before backing out of the shed as she answered the call, feeling a mixture of relief and dread at the timely interruption.

Harvest was always crazy. Long days and long nights were spent out in the paddocks, and Hadley was happy to be thrown back into the thick of it, keeping busy with urgent runs into town to pick up parts or taking out meals to her father and brother to give her mum a break.

The newspaper story came out as expected and, with the exception of only a handful of calls asking for a response from her, there'd been very little hounding from the press so far.

She should have known not to be too relieved.

She parked the car in the main street out the front of the small general store and takeaway, needing to grab a few things for her mother, as well as to pick up the mail. So far the locals had been sympathetic about her marriage breakdown, and much to her relief she hadn't had to answer too many awkward questions.

'Hadley.'

She turned at the unfamiliar voice and her smile abruptly slipped as she caught sight of the journalist walking briskly towards her.

'Hadley, can you give us a minute of your time?' called the young man in a suit, zeroing in on her. 'How are you holding up?'

Hadley forced a polite expression onto her face, having no alternative as the reporter gestured to his cameraman to zoom in on her.

'I'm doing okay.'

'Your marriage breakdown has come as a surprise to the Australian public as you and Mitch Samuals were dubbed the golden couple of Australian prime-time viewing. Is there anything you'd like to say?'

Hadley bit back what she really wanted to say, but instead flashed a tight smile at the mock sincerity behind the question. 'It's a private matter and Mitch and I would both appreciate the time and space we need in order to deal with the situation.'

'You can appreciate the interest from the public though? I mean, Mitch is a media celebrity.'

'I appreciate all the good wishes the public has been sending but, again, this is a private matter between Mitch and myself.'

'Is there any truth to the rumours about another woman being involved?'

It took all Hadley's strength not to flinch at the question.

'Hey, mate. Get out of the lady's way.'

Hadley's gaze shifted abruptly to Ollie, who seemed to have appeared from nowhere and was now towering over the reporter with a threatening scowl.

'And who would you be, Mr . . . ?'

'None of your bloody business. Get that camera out of my face.'

'It's all right, thanks,' Hadley interjected quickly, sending Ollie a pleading look she hoped said, *Just shut up!*

'Are you a relative, sir?' the reporter went on, unperturbed.

'I'm a family friend. Now get out of her way.' Ollie pushed past the reporter and the cameraman and hustled Hadley into the driver's seat, closing the door behind her securely.

She threw one last desperate look towards Ollie and the reporter before deciding to make good her escape while she could. When she glanced in the rear-view mirror, she saw Ollie, tight lipped and unimpressed but thankfully walking away. She let out a shaky breath as her attention returned to the road ahead. Although grateful for Ollie's intervention, she really wished he'd left things alone. They were sure to use today's footage in some form to add to the breaking story. She just hoped they didn't try and make a big deal out of it.

Ten

'*Wife of Mitch Samuals, Hadley Callahan, was reluctant to comment on her marriage breakdown. Having headed back to the small community of Rankins Springs, Ms Callahan was not in the mood to speak with journalists today, and our reporter, Cameron Sheffield, had a close encounter with a mystery man who objected to our presence. It leaves us wondering, what was the reason behind this sudden unexpected split of TV's golden couple? Could it be that Ms Callahan has found romance back in her home town? And who is this mystery man?*'

Griffin turned the TV off and swore, tossing the remote on the coffee table with a disgusted snort. 'You have got to be kidding me. How do these bastards get away with this kind of crap?'

Hadley's fears had turned out to be founded. She'd come home and told Griffin and Olivia about the fiasco in town, and for the rest of the day she hadn't been able to shake the niggling sensation that things were about to get ugly.

Ollie had dropped by to apologise, but she hadn't been able to get angry with him. He'd only stepped in to help. It was just unfortunate that it had been caught on film. She glanced over at him now, half hitched on the armrest of the lounge, arms crossed, still glaring at the television.

'I can't believe these people tracked you down out here and had the hide to ask you about your divorce,' Olivia said, furious. 'Would they like someone asking them about their personal business?'

'No, they wouldn't,' Hadley agreed. 'But Mitch is big news. I guess I knew that was part of the package when I signed on.'

'No one deserves that kind of invasion of privacy. I don't care how famous they are, or who they're married to.'

'I'm really sorry that I made it worse,' Ollie said.

'It's not your fault, Ollie.'

'Bloody oath it isn't, mate,' Griffin cut in. 'They're just lucky it was you instead of me. I would have knocked the bloke's head off his shoulders if I'd been there.'

'I'm *really* sorry *that* didn't happen,' Hadley said sarcastically.

'Well, what a knob,' Griffin said, disgusted. 'What gives them the right to harass people on the street like that?'

'They're just doing their job. They have to get a story for their network.'

'It's messed up, that's what it is,' Griff said with a shake of his head.

'It'll be okay,' Hadley said, forcing a confident smile she didn't particularly feel. 'It'll all blow over eventually.'

'Why do they think anyone has the right to invade someone's privacy like this?' Olivia said, frowning.

'They know viewers like a juicy story.'

'Well, that's stupid. I'm not interested in chasing down people to ask them about their marriage breakdown.'

Hadley shrugged. 'The ratings say differently. If it's on the TV, people will watch it. The more it's talked about, the more invested people become in the story.'

'Society is going to hell in a handbasket,' Griffin said miserably.

'Another story will come along soon and everyone will forget all about this one. Until then I'll just keep my head down and wait it out.'

It wasn't fair, and Hadley was as indignant about losing her privacy as the others were, but she also knew how the system worked. One day no one would even remember she'd been married to Mitch Samuals and she could go back to living her life again.

∽

A few days later Hadley was walking back to her car after dropping over some containers to Sue when Ollie's ute pulled up beside her.

A funny fluttering stirred as she watched him get out of the vehicle. His faded jeans and big work boots were so incredibly ... manly. 'Oh dear lord,' she muttered under her breath. Manly? Seriously? She better than anyone knew all about manly kind of men—she'd worked in enough military zones during her career to know the alpha male type. Sure, they may be easy on the eye—all that muscle and brawn and cockiness—but in reality they were rarely compatible with a strong-headed independent woman. From her experience, they liked their women agreeable and pretty and willing to swoon. Hadley didn't do the swooning thing too well. Till now.

She was *not* swooning.

'Hey, Hads.'

His deep voice made her swallow awkwardly then wince. 'Hey. I was just running an errand for Mum.'

'Thought I saw you heading this way earlier.' He rested his backside against the bonnet of her car and braced his arms either side of his hips. Dragging her eyes to a respectable level, she noticed how tired he looked.

'You look like you need a week of sleep.'

'At least,' he said with a weary smile, 'but who doesn't. Nah, it was pool night last night.'

'Maybe you should have got some sleep instead of playing pool,' she said, wondering how on earth these men found the energy to socialise between the hours they were doing.

'Probably would have been the smarter move,' he agreed. 'Actually, I didn't feel like playing but I went because, I don't know, I felt like I owed it to Luke or something. We hadn't played since the last time he was there. I don't know what I was expecting, I didn't want everyone to be moping about or anything, but not one bloke mentioned him. It was the weirdest thing. I was sitting there waiting for someone to say something, anything, but no one did. It's like they've all forgotten about him. It's only been a bit over a week since his funeral,' Ollie said, staring hopelessly at her.

'People don't know how to deal with the fallout,' Hadley said, gently.

'It's bullshit. This whole situation is bullshit,' Ollie snapped, rubbing a hand through his hair, before standing up and staring out across the paddock. 'It's like he never existed. Like everyone's ignoring the fact he killed himself. He *killed himself*, Hadley,' he said, turning to face her, his voice full of pain.

'I know,' she said softly, approaching him slowly, 'but everyone's still hurting.'

'So, what, we're all going to sweep it under the carpet and pretend everything's normal?'

'Maybe it's time to bring it out into the open,' she said, stopping before him. 'Nothing's going to change until we start talking about it.'

'That's the problem. No one *wants* to talk about it. It's all they could bloody talk about after it happened,' he said, bitterness edging his tone. 'No one could get enough of the hows and whys then, but now the funeral's over, it's off limits again. Like we've all gotta move on and forget.'

Hadley heard the torment in Ollie's voice and felt her heart go out to him, even as a simmering rebellion began to bubble inside her. She hated injustice in any form and although these people were her community and didn't mean any malice by their actions, this culture of 'Don't talk about it. Don't bring up all the pain and sadness. Let it go' was actually doing more harm than good. It alienated people who *felt* a need to talk about it.

'Maybe we need to think of a way to change things.'

'How?' Ollie asked and his gaze was fixed on her with a solemnity she'd never seen before.

She wished she had an answer for him, but she didn't. Not yet. But she was determined to find one. He was right, things couldn't continue to go this way. They couldn't afford to lose anyone else.

∽

It was good to be busy, she enjoyed lending a hand when things were hectic—more so now than when she'd been a teenager. She gave a soft snort as she recalled how grudgingly she had helped out back then. She'd done it because that was what you did—everyone got in and pulled their weight. Looking back, she knew that it had made their family stronger, having to work around the clock harvesting, racing to finish before rain or strong winds approached, or worse, crops over-ripened and lost value.

She didn't mind being dusty and sweaty—she'd spent more than her fair share of days that way. Life as a foreign correspondent was not glamorous in any shape or form. She understood the romance of farming, the thing that separated those who worked the land and those who didn't. It was that need to be outdoors, not stuck inside an office; the simple joy of feeling the sun on your face, and the soul-filling satisfaction of watching something you planted or raised, something you toiled and sweated and worried about, grow into a healthy crop or animal. She had the soul of a farmer, and even in the worst of situations she had encountered in her work she could find something to hold on to. A child's reunion with its mother after an earthquake. A birth after a death. A tiny green shoot pushing from the ashen earth after a fire. There was always light even in darkness.

Today she was over at Moorbrook with Griff and her father, lending a hand to the Dawsons to finish off the last of their harvest. It was a hard slog but they were determined to finish it today.

Ollie, her father and Griff were all out in the big harvesters, gliding across the paddocks, perfectly aligned. It was Hadley's and Olivia's job to drive the chaser bins, lining up with the harvesters as they filled the bins with the freshly harvested seed, then headed off once more. It was a job that took quite a bit of concentration and skill, but Hadley had been doing it since she was old enough to reach the pedals of the truck.

The farm was a hive of activity. Huge semitrailers crawled along the dirt roads leading to the silos Olivia and Hadley were filling with the seeds they'd collected from the harvesters. Utes were scattered the field that had only a few weeks earlier been full of crops waiting to be harvested. Radios constantly burst to life with chatter from drivers and harvesters and chaser bin drivers. It was all part of a well-rehearsed routine. Today had a celebratory feel about it—subdued but still noticeable. You didn't get too excited about the last day of harvest until the last of the bins had been loaded. You never knew when something might go wrong—and it usually did. It was all part of the game. Farmers learned early how to live with frustration. It didn't make it easier to cope with when the crap hit the fan, but it wasn't unexpected. But so far today at least, everything seemed to be working like a well-oiled machine.

Hadley hadn't seen Ollie for a few days but she'd heard his voice over the radio and was relieved that he still sounded like the Ollie she knew—maybe a little quieter than usual, but he was still there.

At the end of the day, when the last bin was emptied, they gathered around the stationary machinery and quenched their thirst with cold beers. Silence echoed beyond the chatter and celebration—for the first time in weeks there were no harvesters, no tractors, no machinery at all rumbling in the distance. As a small child Hadley had loved driving out with her mother to take a picnic basket of food and an esky of cold drinks to feed the workers. Even when it wasn't the end of harvest, it felt like a party. Today the atmosphere was even more festive with the Callahans, Dawsons and workers all happily lounging on the ground or perched on the backs of vehicles, feasting on delicious food baked and delivered by two of the best cooks in the district.

As the afternoon faded, people slowly began drifting off, leaving only Hadley, Griff, Olivia, Ollie and a handful of others to continue unwinding. She wasn't sure if it was the beers or the release of long hours of work and the stress of Luke's funeral, but a few of the men started to act the larrikin, led by Griff, as per usual, and closely followed by his best mate, Ollie. Hadley couldn't recall who brought it up but suddenly a dare was made. And everyone knew that combining beer, country boys and a dare was going to end in either something hilarious or illegal, or maybe both.

Either way, she was glad she'd brought her camera along.

'Let me get this straight—you dare me to jump in the back of the chaser bin?' Ollie was saying to Griff when she came back from retrieving her camera from the ute.

'Yep,' Griff drawled. 'Naked,' he added smugly.

Hadley froze in the process of taking off her lens cap. *Naked?* Her stomach gave a weird lurch. He wouldn't do it.

'You're on.'

Hadley felt her mouth drop open and quickly shut it. A warm flush began creeping up her neck and she turned away quickly. Oh. My. God. *Pull yourself together, Callahan.*

The cheers and egging-on started and Hadley knew without turning that Ollie had started disrobing. Swallowing hard, she turned her head. She was going to look pretty damn stupid if she didn't snap out of whatever this thing was.

'Are you getting this, Hads?' Griff called, spying her holding the camera.

Automatically she lifted the camera. At least behind here she could hide her stupid reaction. Surely Ollie wouldn't really get naked? It had been funny when they were kids— seeing someone streaking about naked was a regular occurrence then—but they weren't teenagers anymore. Lord, she was sounding like a grandmother.

Ollie tugged his T-shirt up over his head and dropped it on the ground.

No. Ollie was *definitely not* a teenager anymore. Hadley swallowed painfully as her gaze swept across his chest, resting on the two quite prominent pectoral muscles he'd just revealed.

'Sorry?' Olivia said, beside her.

'What?' Hadley dragged her gaze away from Ollie to his sister.

'I thought you said something.'

'No,' Hadley said quickly, turning her head back in time to see Ollie unzipping his jeans.

'All right,' Olivia said, holding her hands up. 'Hello? Your sister is standing right here. I do *not* need to see your hairy butt in all its splendour, thank you very much.'

Relief filled Hadley at her friend's intervention, and she firmly squashed the little pouting voice that protested at the interruption.

'Fine. I didn't want to climb into the bin bare-arsed naked anyway,' Ollie said, strutting over to pull himself up the ladder on the side of the bin and gracefully swing over the top. Shortly afterwards a pair of denim jeans flew over the side, followed by some boxers.

A chorus of hoots sounded through the air and Olivia shook her head. 'How old are you guys?'

'Get up there, Hads. We need photographic evidence,' Griff announced.

'Unless he magically has a spare pair of jeans and boxers up there, I'm pretty sure we can take his word for it that he's naked,' she said drolly.

'Then give me your camera,' Griff said, walking towards her.

No one touched her camera. Ever. 'Okay, I'll take a stupid photo,' she agreed reluctantly, moving towards the ladder. She hauled herself up and closed her eyes for a moment. This had started out as a joke, but the way her hands were sweating suggested this was no longer funny. Seeing his hat hanging off the top of the ladder only added to her dread. Dread. Yes. Not excitement. *What the hell?*

'It's okay, Hads. I'm respectable,' Ollie called out teasingly.

'Yeah right,' she scoffed, gingerly pulling herself the rest of the way to the top and looking over. She gave a nervous chuckle. There was Ollie reclining on his side, one arm casually bracing his weight, stretched out looking for all the world as though he were casually sunbaking on the beach. Except for the pile of lentils he'd scooped up over his hips.

'I don't think I'll be eating any lentil-based products for a while,' she said dryly, raising her camera and clicking off a few shots.

'I'm pretty sure I'm more at risk of catching something from this stuff,' he reasoned.

'This is so wrong,' she said. 'Here,' she tossed him his hat, 'sit up and place that strategically.'

'It's only supposed to be proof I'm actually in the nuddy, not a photo shoot,' he complained, but followed her instructions.

Hadley moved her camera up and down a few times, getting her focus right before snapping a few more shots. 'Move your arm a bit to the left.'

'Seriously?'

'Just do it,' she said, forgetting for a minute her earlier discomfort. She was loving the colour of the grain against the strong lines of the man half buried in it. The texture and feel of the image excited the photographer in her. When was the last time she'd enjoyed the actual artistic appeal of a photo session?

'Put your hands behind your head,' she said, cocking her head slightly as she studied him.

Her gaze followed the slow movement of his arms as he linked his fingers and placed them behind his head, the movement making his biceps bulge. Hadley licked her suddenly dry lips as her eyes moved lower across the trail of hair that dipped below the strategically placed lentils.

'Ah, Hads?'

Hadley gave a start, causing her to momentarily lose her balance. Ollie was halfway to his knees before she righted herself and called out an alarmed, 'I'm okay! Stay where you are.'

'Everything okay up there? What are you doin'? Is he naked or not, Hads?' Griff called.

'Ah. Yeah.' She cleared her throat quickly. 'You owe him fifty bucks.' She saw Ollie relax slightly now that he knew she wasn't in danger but found him watching her with an expression she found hard to read.

She shifted her gaze from Ollie's as she felt her brother climbing up behind her, his loud chortle breaking the strange moment. 'That's gold.'

'Yeah, okay, show's over. Throw up my gear,' Ollie said wryly.

'You sister's gone home, so I think you can get down and grab 'em yourself.'

'What? Hey, Griff, don't be a dick,' Ollie said, sitting up straighter, digging himself out of the heaped grain.

'Whoah. Okay. I'm done with the official photos. Get out of the way, Griff,' Hadley said, elbowing her brother so she could climb back down.

'Comin' down, Ollie?' Griff called from the ground once he'd reached the bottom.

'Toss up my stuff, Griff,' Ollie yelled from inside the bin.

'Griff, throw him his clothes,' Hadley said, trying to keep a straight face. It wasn't funny, and yet . . . well, maybe it served him right for agreeing to such a stupid dare in the first place.

'Nah, let him come down and get 'em himself. You don't have to look,' he said, sending her a narrowed-eye stare, 'unless you want to,' he added, wiggling his eyebrows suggestively.

'Whatever,' Hadley scoffed, stepping around her brother. 'Like I've never seen a naked man before.'

'Don't let Dad hear you say that,' Griff warned to her back, before his loud hoot of laughter made her turn and gape at the sight before her.

Tired of waiting for Griff to send up his clothing, Ollie had decided to get them himself, ignoring the catcalls from below. The stark white of his backside and ankles stood out in almost comical relief against the rest of his tanned skin and she clicked off one more photo.

Hadley bit her lip to hide the grin that had formed as she'd watched his defiant descent down the ladder. When he reached the bottom, Ollie took his hat off his head and shielded his groin with it, storming past to pick up his clothes.

She chuckled the rest of the way to her car and was still wearing a smile when she eventually pulled up back at Stringybark.

You'd think once the craziness of harvest was over that things would settle down, but there was no such luck. If it wasn't time to harvest something, then it was time to prepare the next paddock to sow something, and then there were the cattle that always needed drenching, marking, feeding, weaning and selling. The list of jobs never ran out.

Ollie found himself thinking back to yesterday and the whole naked dare thing. It hadn't been the smartest idea, and he'd only done it to show off. Sure, as a seventeen year old, getting naked to impress the girl you liked was understandable—seventeen year olds were not renowned for making the best choices—but you'd have hoped he'd have grown out of it by now. He wanted to blame the beer, and the hot weather, and sheer bloody relief that harvest was done and dusted . . . but, really, he was just showing off.

He glanced at his wrist and felt a twinge of irritation at the cracked screen that greeted him. Another reason he should have behaved more sensibly—he had broken another watch. That was the second one in the last year. Why didn't they make anything that actually lasted anymore?

He forced away his frustration and went back to thinking about Hadley. Over the last few weeks they'd gotten closer. She'd helped him through a pretty rough time and he knew without her he would be in a lot worse shape now than he was. Maybe it was in his head, that strange feeling that something was happening between them. Up until the other day, he'd almost convinced himself he was imagining it, but then they'd had that moment. They'd looked at each other and something had happened. He didn't know what; maybe it was the first time she'd seen him as someone more than her brother's best friend or her best friend's brother. Maybe it was the first time she'd allowed herself to see him as someone different. A ripple of excitement ran through him, just as it had when she'd looked at him that way.

Was it possible he and Hadley might finally have a shot at something? It seemed hard to believe after wanting it for so long. Yet if these past few weeks had taught him anything, it was that you never really knew what life was going to throw at you. Where he'd been content to sit back and wait before, now he felt an urgency to act. At night he found himself lying awake thinking about where this thing with Hadley might go—was there any point starting something that had no hope of becoming long-term? He knew how much Hadley's career meant to her and he wouldn't want her to give it up. He gave a mental snort: if he were being truthful, he knew he wouldn't stand a chance in a contest against Hadley's career. Very little in this world could. And yet there was a burning inside his chest that he couldn't ignore. How many more years was he going to sit back and wait? An image of himself old and alone floated before his eyes. He pulled himself up abruptly. When the hell had he become so melodramatic?

Eleven

Hadley was busy writing an article for one of her freelance projects when she heard the ping of her phone alerting her to a new message. She glanced across and felt a smile spread across her face as the name flashed across the screen. Ollie.

Hadley's gaze fell on her camera sitting on the table nearby and she reached to pick it up. She'd been out earlier that morning taking photos. Her spontaneous photo shoot in the chaser bin had sparked a renewed interest in photography. The morning air had felt cool on her face, summer mornings were her favourite time of the year. Everything smelled fresh and sweet. She'd walked down to the stock yards and caught the first hint of the sun peeking up from the horizon, the solid old timber posts silhouetted in stark contrast against the soft colours of the morning sky as dawn gave way to daybreak. Hadley scrolled through the images, particularly loving the one of a single dew-drop hanging like a diamond from a silver-threaded cobweb.

As she scrolled through she came to the photos of Ollie and gave a strangled kind of chuckle. While the image itself was hilarious, of a handsome young farmer laying naked, in a bin full of lentils, his groin covered with a hat, there was also an undeniable prickle of something that felt very much like attraction. He was a good-looking, virile male and she was finding it difficult to remind herself that this particular guy had been like another brother to her growing up. She should not be having these kinds of thoughts about him. She'd known Ollie all her life—why was she suddenly seeing him like this? Maybe it was some kind of reaction to Mitch's betrayal. Maybe this was a rebound response because Ollie was safe—maybe that made him appealing all of a sudden. Whatever it was, it seriously baffled her. How did you go from having platonic feelings for someone to, well, very *unplatonic* feelings?

'Morning tea, darling,' her mother called through the kitchen screen door.

Hadley jumped, turning the camera off quickly, before placing it on the table carefully. *You're acting like a twit. Knock it off.* Was it creepy to be having these feelings about Ollie? She felt like a teenager again. In fact, the last time she'd been this stupid over a boy had been when she *was* a teenager.

'Everything all right?' her mother asked as Hadley came inside.

'Yep. Right as rain.'

'Morning, Gran,' Hadley said, leaning over to kiss her grandmother's soft cheek.

'Good morning, dear. Let's see who we've managed to offend today, shall we?' Gran said, dragging the newspaper across the table towards her.

Hadley bit back a chuckle. She loved this woman so much, but political correctness was not part of Gran's vocabulary. 'It's nice to see the headlines not dominated by that scoundrel of yours for a change. Thank goodness the politicians have created another scandal. They're always good for that.'

'I think we've seen the last of Mitch for now.'

'Good riddance. His eyes were too close together.'

'Ida,' Lavinia sighed, and Hadley gave a snort.

'You were right, Gran,' she admitted.

'Of course I was. But what's the point of being young if you can't go and make a few mistakes now and again? If you don't make mistakes, how will you ever know when something's right?'

Hadley smiled sadly at her gran. 'I'm not sure I want to make any more mistakes of those proportions.'

Gran patted her hand gently. 'It wasn't the worst one ever made.'

'I feel like a failure, Gran,' she admitted. 'You and Grandad, Mum and Dad ... you guys all managed to stay married.'

'We came from a different era, sweetheart,' Gran said gently. She placed a hand on top of her granddaughter's and it felt cool and soft against Hadley's. 'I don't think you can really compare the two. In my day you married young, had your children, worked from dawn to dusk. We were too tired to think about finding someone else and getting a divorce. Besides, the stigma attached to a young woman who left her husband was huge,' she went on, her eyes narrowing slightly. 'It happened, don't you worry. There were women who left husbands, but they had a wretched life. My cousin Eunice left her husband. He was a brute of a man, but her family couldn't take her back in, they still had five children at home. She ended up moving in with another aunty for a while.' Gran shook her head slightly. 'She was such a beautiful girl when she was young, happy and carefree, but after her marriage and divorce she was never the same. I never saw her smile. Most men her age were already married and those that weren't, well, their mothers didn't want them marrying a divorced woman. Poor Eunice.'

'What happened to her?' Hadley asked when Gran stopped talking.

'Oh, she ended up marrying some older man from church. He was *much* older than her. Years later when I saw her again, she still had the saddest eyes,' Gran sighed.

'But what about you, Mum? You were well and truly in the free love, women's lib era, but you managed to stay married to Dad all these years.'

'Well, it might have been all well and good if you lived in the city back then, but out here growing up there was no such thing as free love, I can tell you. My parents would have skinned me alive,' she said with a wry grin. 'I know it seems like it must have been all smooth sailing for your father and I, but it hasn't been,' she said, a small frown crinkling between her eyebrows. 'There have been times I've felt like packing up and moving out, but I guess I was raised to believe that divorce wasn't an option. Maybe I was just lucky, finding a man like your father,' she shrugged. 'Yes, we had rough patches, when things were bad with the farm and we were tired and stressed and we fought a lot. We could have let that drive us apart, but the reality is that we love each other. We love the family we created, and in the end the tough times brought us closer. I don't know what the answer is, darling, but I think it depends on who it is you're marrying and whether they're the right person for you. I think two people can survive anything together if they're right for each other.'

The truth of her mother's words struck home. Had she married Mitch for the right reasons? She'd known her family had their reservations about him, but their relationship had been so easy. They liked the same things; they knew the same people. They worked in the same industry. They were friends. Inwardly, Hadley sighed. There'd been a small part of her that had kept on with the wedding out of pride. She'd been determined to have the perfect wedding. She'd wanted to prove to her family that the man she'd chosen was the right one, even if now, with the clarity of hindsight, maybe they had just fallen into a comfortable friendship with benefits. But were fireworks and giddy feelings really what made a successful marriage? She knew plenty of couples who'd been absolutely smitten with one another only to have their marriage fail too ... so what was the answer?

'You know what I think the secret is to a long and happy marriage?' Gran piped up, as if reading her mind.

'What, Gran?' Hadley smiled, before taking a sip of her coffee.

'Sex,' she said simply. 'Your grandfather was a magician in the bed,' she sighed.

Hadley coughed, then choked on her sip of coffee, managing to snort some of it out of her nose. She took the tissues her mother handed over and dabbed at her nose and eyes.

'Well, it's true,' Gran said with an indignant sniff. 'He was very talented.'

'Ida,' her mother tsked, with a hopeless shake of her head.

'I bet that was the problem with that Mitch fella, wasn't it?' Gran nodded sagely. 'He was a dud between the sheets.'

'Oh, for the love of Pete,' Lavinia muttered.

'Well, he was ...' Hadley wasn't exactly sure how to answer. She hadn't ever imagined having a conversation like this with her grandmother. 'He was fine,' she ended uncomfortably.

'Fine!' Gran chortled. 'My darling, when you're with the right man you won't use the word *fine*,' she promised. 'Didn't I tell you that boy's eyes were too close together.' She turned to look at Lavinia. 'I told you so,' she announced smugly.

Hadley swapped glances with her exasperated mother. Life was never dull around Gran.

A car pulled up outside and Lavinia craned her neck to look out the window. 'Oh, it's Ollie. I wonder what he wants.'

Hadley set her cup aside and forced her expression to remain as nonchalant as she could. 'He mentioned he might be dropping by. I'll go see.'

She ignored the slight raise of her mother's eyebrow and the less than subtle curiosity on her grandmother's face and left the room before any questions could be asked.

∞

Ollie took a breath before opening his door and getting out of his ute. Just do it. Don't think about it. Just say it and get it over with. His step faltered slightly. Say what exactly? What was he supposed to say?

'Hi.'

Hadley's greeting cut through his momentary panic and he cleared his throat. 'Hey.'

'I got your message you were coming over. Everything okay?'

'Yeah,' he said, rubbing the back of his neck awkwardly. 'Everything's fine. I just . . . I was driving and I . . .' He paused. 'The thing is, Hadley,' he said starting again, 'I've been doing a lot of thinking lately.' He risked a glance at her. 'Life's short,' he said simply. He saw her eyes widen a little as he took a step towards her. 'I guess what I'm trying to say is, I'm not imagining there's something different between us lately, am I?' It wasn't really a question. 'The kiss the other night and then the other day . . .'

Hadley opened her mouth to speak but he didn't give her time. He didn't want to be wrong and, if he was, this would probably be his last chance to kiss her, so he did.

The first time had caught him off guard with the unexpected spark it created, and even though he was expecting it this time, their first contact still went through him like a bolt of electricity. Her lips beneath his were warm and soft, and they moved with a growing curiosity that soon turned to hunger. His hands slipped up to cup her head and he felt her push closer into his body as the kiss deepened. He'd only meant to kiss her like the other night—a gentle, tentative kiss—but something had definitely changed over the last few days. Maybe she'd been thinking about the kiss just as often as he'd been.

He felt her ease back slightly and fought the disappointment that swiftly followed. He closed his eyes briefly. This was it. If she told him she didn't want things to go any further, it'd be the last time he held her like this.

He slowly let his hands slip to his sides and braced himself to hear the 'We're just friends' speech.

'You're not imagining it,' she said softly.

For a long moment he could only stare at her. 'Okay,' he said uncertainly.

He saw her lips tug into a soft smile. 'So what happens now?'

'I don't know really. To be honest, I was just wingin' it.' He grinned at her chuckle and gingerly slid his hands down to loop around her waist. 'We could try again just to make sure?'

'I think we've more than established we've got that part down pat,' she said dryly. 'Actually, I'm more worried about what everyone else is going to say.'

'It'll be a bit of a surprise, but I don't think it's going to be an issue.'

'I just think we need to take this slow. I haven't got *my* head around this thing yet.'

'Yeah. Me either. I mean, you're all I've been able to think about for the last few weeks, but now that we're here, it kind of feels like I'm dreaming.'

'If you are, then we're both having the same dream.'

'Oh, yeah? Well, in that case, in my dream I need to kiss you again,' he said simply. When she didn't argue he took it as a yes and lowered his head. The effect was the same. Kissing Hadley had just become his favourite thing in the world.

A sound edging closer alerted him to the fact they weren't going to be alone for much longer and he reluctantly lifted his head. He couldn't help the small grin that tugged at his mouth when he saw the sleepy-eyed look on Hadley's face. It gave him a cocky kinda kick to realise she was just as affected by the kiss as he was.

'My brother has *the* worst timing ever,' she muttered when she glanced over her shoulder at the tractor returning to the shed.

'You're not wrong.' Bloody Griff. 'Can you come over tonight? To my place? I'll cook you dinner.'

Hadley shot him a doubtful eyebrow lift. 'You know how to cook?'

'Oh, ye of little faith,' he scoffed.

'Faith has nothing to do with it. I've never seen you cook. Ever.'

'Doesn't mean I can't. I'll have you know I plan on having a feast set out for you tonight.'

'You know, I'm going to say yes, purely because I'm calling your bluff,' she said, folding her arms across her chest, which only managed to stretch her T-shirt tighter across her breasts and distract him from their banter.

'I'll see you tonight then,' he said, holding her amused gaze as he backed away. It wasn't until he got into the ute that he was capable of thinking clearly again and realised he was going to have to come up with something pretty impressive if he was going to live up to the big-mouth claims he'd just made. Bugger.

❧

'What did Ollie want?' Griff asked later as he strolled across to Hadley.

'Nothing. He was just sayin' hi.'

'Since when does he have time to stop and say hi?'

'I don't know,' Hadley snapped irritably. The last thing she needed was her nosy brother making too big of a deal out of whatever this was. 'I didn't ask him what he was over here for. He just stopped on his way out.'

Griff sent her a side-eyed glance. 'Everything okay?'

'Everything's great. I've got things to do. See ya later.'

Hadley didn't have to look at her brother to know he would be wearing a somewhat suspicious look on his face. He must have noticed how close they'd been standing, or maybe he'd just picked up on the chemistry between them. Either way, she wasn't going to stick around and fan any flames. She wasn't ready to admit to herself what was happening, let alone to her brother. It was way too soon for that.

Twelve

Hadley pulled up in front of Ollie's small cottage. It felt strange driving past the main house. *It's just Ollie,* she reminded herself firmly as the nerves began fluttering once more. Only it wasn't *just* Ollie. It wasn't the old Ollie. This was something new. Something very different. This was Ollie as she'd never known him before. This was *hot* Ollie. An image of him lying back in the lentils flashed through her mind once again and she pushed it away. She couldn't think about that right now. She was distracted enough as it was.

The old wooden boards groaned as she stepped up onto the tiny front verandah and knocked on the door. From inside the cottage she heard something drop and a sharp explative, followed by hurried footsteps up the hallway.

A somewhat flustered Ollie appeared in the doorway and Hadley bit back a smile. 'Am I too early?'

'No. No, come on in. I'm just . . .' He waved his hand vaguely towards the direction of the kitchen at the rear of the house. 'Diesel. Get out, go on,' he said, letting the dog out the front door. 'Don't look at me like that,' he warned when the animal tilted his head slightly at his owner.

'Don't kick him out on my account,' Hadley said, crouching down to rub the dog's head.

'He's getting under my feet in there. He usually stays outside anyway.'

'Is something burning?' Hadley asked.

'Shit. Bugger it.' Ollie turned and jogged down the hallway. 'Come on in,' he threw over his shoulder as he disappeared into the kitchen, leaving Hadley to follow cautiously.

The kitchen was remarkably tidy. She'd been expecting a sink full of saucepans and bowls; food spilled all over the benchtops. A small table was set up with a white tablecloth and a candle, two crystal wineglasses and fine bone china plates.

Ollie was at the oven juggling an oven mitt and blackened tray of what appeared to have once been garlic bread.

'Do you need a hand?'

'Nope. I got it all under control,' he said, dumping the tray on the sink with a clang. 'Sorry. Burned the bread.'

'We didn't need the carbs anyway,' Hadley shrugged. 'So what else is on the menu?'

'Ah, well, we've got,' he paused, lifting the corner of the foil-covered tray still in the oven, 'peas, potatoes and roast . . . lamb,' he said hesitantly.

'You're not sure what you cooked?' Hadley asked innocently.

'Of course I am, I just . . . Look, you go sit down and I'll serve up.' He ushered her away from the oven.

Hadley settled herself at the table and gently ran her fingers over the silver cutlery that she knew for a fact belonged to Ollie's mum. How many times over the years had they eaten in the good room for some special occasion and used this cutlery?

Ollie brought over the two plates and carefully placed hers on the table before her. 'Here you go.'

She looked down at the plate filled with roast vegetables and thinly sliced lamb, with a hefty drizzle of gravy, and felt her mouth water. She was starving.

'I'll take that apology any time now,' Ollie said smugly, taking his own seat across from her at the small table. Beneath the table she felt his knee rest against her own.

'Oh, please. As if you managed this on your own. Come on, spill. You got your mother to cook this for you.'

'I said I'd have a feast for you and here it is.' He filled their glasses from the bottle of wine sitting in the centre of the table.

'Fine. I'm too hungry to care. It looks amazing.' There was no way he'd cooked this himself but she was touched that he'd gone to so much trouble for dinner.

The clinking of cutlery on plates sounded loud in the small kitchen. Hadley felt as though she were on a first date with someone she'd just met. Which was ridiculous. She'd known Ollie forever. They'd eaten meals hundreds of times together, only it had never been a meal like this and they'd never really eaten alone before. There had always been someone around. This was all new territory. But it was still Ollie, for crying out loud.

She risked a glance up at him and licked her bottom lip. She swallowed hard when he looked up at the same moment, his eyes fixed on her mouth. He had an uncanny ability to make her knees wobble without even trying. The look she read in his eyes set the earlier butterflies launching into the sky like a flock of startled galahs.

Hadley reached out and picked up her glass, taking a hasty sip of her wine. The alcohol warmed a path down her throat. She forced herself to concentrate on finishing her meal.

'How did your parents take it when you said you were coming over here for dinner?' Ollie asked.

Hadley focused on pushing the vegetables onto her fork. 'I didn't really mention it. Just said I was going out . . . to visit friends.' She risked a quick glance and saw him frown a little. 'Is that a problem?'

'No,' he said, returning to his own meal. 'I just wondered if you said anything to anyone.'

'I don't think we should,' she said, before hurrying on. 'I mean, why get everyone all hyped up about something that . . .'

132

He raised an eyebrow, waiting for her to finish the sentence.

'I mean . . . we don't even know . . . we haven't . . .'

'It's okay, Hads.'

Damn it. It wasn't okay. But what did he want her to do? Go and announce to everyone that she had feelings for him? The last thing she wanted was for her family to start asking questions and, God help her, start planning a wedding date before she was even free of her current husband. 'You know what they're like,' she told him. 'They'll all get carried away.'

'Yeah. They would. No, you're right,' he said, shaking his head. 'I just wasn't sure how you wanted to play it. But Griffin's gonna figure out something's going on sooner or later. You've already told Liv about the kiss . . . I know my sister, she's gonna let something slip.'

'Do *you* know what this thing is?' she asked, feeling a little helpless.

She watched as he put his cutlery down and looked at her. His gaze held hers with a steadiness that felt like a touch. 'I know what this is . . . to me,' he said slowly. 'But if you need more time to work out what it is for you, I'll wait as long as you need me to.'

'What is it . . . to you?' she found herself asking, watching as his gentle smile crinkled the corners of his eyes.

'I don't want it to be something casual, but if that's the only way I can have you, I'll take it,' he said, surprising her with his honesty. 'I'm hoping it'll be a lot more, but if it's not, the time we've had together is more than I ever figured I'd get, so I'm not going to complain.'

She mulled over his words and found that thinking about starting a relationship with Ollie didn't freak her out as much as she'd imagined. It should, shouldn't it? She'd already failed at marriage and was feeling more than a little disheartened about relationships. The last thing she thought she'd be doing was considering diving headfirst into a new romance. And yet here she was.

Ollie collected her plate and she stood to help clear the table.

'No, sit. I've got it,' he said.

'After all this cooking you've done today?' she said, eyeing him with a dry look. 'You must be exhausted.'

'Well, you know how it is. A man's work is never done,' he grinned.

Hadley rested her chin on her hand as she watched him place the plates into the sink. Her gaze followed the long length of his back down to where it tapered into a narrower waist and a denim-covered butt. *Country boys in jeans should really come with a warning label*, she thought weakly. She'd been around men in denim all her life, but she'd never really *truly* appreciated it until right this very moment.

There was a restlessness inside her that had been fighting to get out for a while now and this afternoon's kiss had only increased the desperation. Before she could talk herself out of it, she stood up and crossed to the sink where Ollie stood.

'Seriously, Hads, I got this. Just sit down,' he said, turning around.

'I don't want to sit down,' she said, his body tantalisingly close to her own.

For a long moment they stood looking at each other. She felt his eyes searching her face, and she was unsure what he was looking for, but in case it was for some kind of sign not to kiss her, she decided to make the first move and put his mind at ease. Pushing onto her tip-toes, she touched her lips to his, sliding her hands up around his tanned neck. The kiss wasn't the gentle exploration of the last few times. This time it was a statement. She knew what she wanted.

His arms circled her waist and he pulled her tightly against him, leaning back against the sink. Nothing else mattered. Her earlier nerves seemed to have vanished and all that remained was simple desire. She couldn't remember the last time she'd been so consumed with need like this. She knew it was probably in the early days with Mitch, but she was sure it had never been this potent. She was struggling to retain any coherent thought in her head as Ollie's kisses continued to send her plummeting over the edge of reason.

∞

Ollie had never been one to question good fortune when it happened to fall into his lap, and he was not about to start now. All through the meal he'd been trying his hardest not to think about Hadley and her mouth, which had been pretty damn difficult when her tongue kept darting out to wipe gravy from her lips. He hoped she couldn't read minds—she'd think he was some kind of pervert if she knew the things he was thinking about that tongue of hers and what he wanted her to do with it.

She felt so good in his arms, pressed up against him like this. Her soft curves moulded against him as though the two of them were designed to fit together.

He moved his lips away from her tempting mouth, needing a moment to control the burning desire he felt building way too quickly inside him. He traced a path down the soft skin of her neck, smiling when he felt her tremor and moan softly. His smile soon faded when he realised how those small whimpering moans managed to harden certain parts of his body at an alarming rate. Goddamn it, how old was he again? Fourteen?

Hadley tilted her head back, allowing him greater access, and his tongue darted out, tasting the slight saltiness of her skin. He breathed in the warm, heady smell of her that filled his senses almost to point of overdrive. She was everywhere, and still he needed more.

His hands moved to the hem of her shirt and he heard her gasp as his fingers touched her bare skin and skimmed their way up the sides of her ribs and across the lace of her bra.

He paused momentarily when she pulled back, fearing he'd misread her signals, until he caught her sultry smile as her hands moved up his torso, pulling the fabric of his T-shirt higher and working it over his head.

'You're overdressed for the occasion,' she told him simply.

'I could say the same for you,' he said and held his breath as she wordlessly pulled her own shirt over her head, tossing it on the floor without breaking eye contact and sliding her hands up his chest as she leaned in and kissed him.

The friction of the lace against his chest sent an involuntary shiver down his back and he pulled her closer as their kiss deepened. He could feel the heat of her against his thigh as it pushed in between her own and he held back the greedy lust that just wanted to take her right here.

'Come with me,' he said, taking her hand and tugging her along behind him towards his bedroom.

'Ouch,' she said, laughing and hopping on one foot. 'My toe.'

'Sorry!' He stopped abruptly to check her foot, and she ran into his back, her hands going to her face automatically as she gave a muffled curse. 'My nose.'

'Damn it, Hadley, I'm sorry.' This was great: in the middle of his big seduction scene, he'd so far managed to break her toe and her nose and they hadn't even got naked yet. Well, broken may have been going a tad far, but still . . . this had not been part of any fantasy he'd ever had. 'Here, let me.' He bent down to lift her into his arms, just as she was straightening from checking her toe, and he felt a blinding pain that sent stars dancing before his eyes as the top of her head smashed up under his jaw. They both cried out in pain at the same time and staggered away from each other.

'Son of a b—'

'Mother . . . trucker,' Hadley bit out tightly over Ollie's sharp retort, rubbing the top of her head.

'Let me,' Ollie started to speak, moving towards her, but stopped abruptly as Hadley put out a hand in alarm.

'Stay there. Do *not* move,' she said firmly. 'I'm going to walk over to you. Stay absolutely still,' she warned.

This was so stupid. Ollie did as he was told and remained perfectly still. Stupid or not, she had a point: another incident and one of them would wind up in emergency at this rate.

Her hands went to his chest, slowly moving in a gentle touch. His breath caught as he felt the barest brush across one taut nipple, and a shiver ran through him that he couldn't quite conceal. When he made to move, she lifted an eyebrow sharply, making him stop.

He watched as her gaze slowly travelled up across his pecs and along his shoulders and arms, then shivered again as her hands followed the same path, moving from his wrist to the waist of his jeans. He drew in a sharp breath as the coolness of her fingers came in contact with the warm, sensitive skin just under the waistband of his jeans.

She gave a small smirk at the sound before lifting her face, her eyes heavy with sultry desire. Never had he been so turned on in his whole life.

'Move back towards the bed,' she instructed him, her voice as smooth as aged bourbon.

He found himself doing as he was told almost without thought. She followed him, her hands against his chest, lightly guiding him until the back of his legs touched the foot of the bed.

'Sit down,' she ordered, and Ollie did as he was told. Who knew he was into being dominated? He frowned a little at that and hoped she wasn't about to pull out a pair of leather chaps for him to wear or, worse, dress him up like a My Little Pony, something he'd recently read about on Facebook as the new freaky sex craze. He definitely wouldn't be into that.

There were no signs of whips or chains as he sat down on the end of the bed. Hadley moved forwards between his knees. Instinctively his hands came up to rest on her hips and he leaned forwards to nuzzle the soft skin exposed above the black lacy bra she wore.

He watched as her hand moved to the front of her jeans and slowly unfastened the button then began shimmying out of them. Ollie's eyes followed the denim sliding down her thighs. Hadley stepped out of them and straightened, placing her hands over his on her waist and prodding them away lightly. 'Lie back.'

He did so without protest, his eyes never leaving hers. They widened slightly as she followed him, crawling with feline grace to straddle his lap, setting off a million nerve endings and sending his libido into overdrive. With steady hands she reached behind her and unfastened her bra. With another of those sultry smiles that did dangerously erotic things to pretty much every part of his body, she peeled it away, making him groan slowly at the picture she made before him. Never in any of his wildest fantasies of her—and there had been a lot over the years—had he ever pictured her looking like she did at this very moment. She was beautiful.

'Is there something wrong?' Hadley said, and he saw her arms hover in front of her chest, realising he'd simply been staring at her.

'No,' he said quickly. 'God, no. I'm sorry, I . . . you're perfect,' he gave up trying to untie his tongue and just let it spill out.

She looked surprised by his words, and a little embarrassed, but had lost the uncertainty of a few moments before. 'You're the perfect one,' she murmured, leaning forwards to whisper against his lips. 'How have I been missing out on this for so long?'

'Good things come to those who wait,' he told her, nipping at her bottom lip gently, her nearness surrounding him and clouding his mind.

'Then be prepared to have some very, very good things happening tonight,' she whispered in between hot, deep kisses.

Thirteen

Christmas was looming. It didn't mean the work eased around Stringybark, but it did mean that the community festive season was at its peak.

Hadley shook her head as she watched her mother move around the kitchen, preparing for the upcoming week of Christmas parties and end-of-year functions. On the calendar there was a mind-blowing number of commitments written neatly in red pen and just looking at them made Hadley feel exhausted.

'Can I do anything, Mum?'

'I think everything's under control, darling, but you could come along if you like. We're having the CWA Christmas lunch.'

'Thanks, but I have a few things I need to get sent off today.' She was enjoying the break from the relentless travel her job usually entailed, but her workload hadn't diminished that much. She had a number of projects she'd been needing to finish, and she'd managed to write a number of new articles that she'd been itching to do but hadn't had the time to pursue until now. She went back inside after waving off her mother.

It was nice to have some downtime. Even if it had been in order to keep out of the public eye until the whole divorce thing blew over. This wouldn't be such a horrible way to work. She pulled herself up short. What was she thinking? This was not her plan. *Neither was a divorce,* a small voice echoed. True, but when had she begun to think this could be part of her future? She wasn't, was she? She groaned and dropped her head into her hands.

It was all very well to give into her feelings for Ollie, but at some point the two of them had to address the issue of the future. *What future?* Would it be the occasional hook-up whenever she came home or he managed a weekend to fly to the city? What more could it be?

The sound of tyres crunching on the gravel outside put a stop to Hadley's endless circle of questions. The white four-wheel drive could have belonged to anyone around here, but the rental car company logo on the back window gave it away.

Her smile widened as she reached the bottom of the stairs, throwing her arms wide to hug her eldest brother as he took his sunglasses from his face and hooked them onto the front of his shirt.

'You two are risking actual bodily harm from Mum by not telling her you were coming today.'

'Don't look at me, I told him to call,' said Cash, Hadley's sister-in-law, turning from the back passenger side of the car with a dark-haired bundle of baby in her arms. 'But I figured Mia would be a good distraction,' she added dryly.

Hadley's heart almost exploded with a powerful surge of love as Cash handed across her daughter. 'Mia,' Hadley breathed softly. 'Look how much you've grown.'

'It's hard to believe she's already eight months old.'

'She's so gorgeous. Look at those big brown eyes,' Hadley crooned down at the small face blinking up at her and looking surprisingly settled.

'Just like her mum's,' Linc said, slipping his arms around Cash's waist and smiling adoringly down into his wife's shining eyes.

They were disgustingly in love . . . still . . . even with a newborn in the house. A small twinge of envy snaked its way through Hadley, but she squashed it immediately. She was not going to feel sorry for herself. Just because she was soon to be divorced didn't mean she had a right to feel cheated about not having a baby of her own. For a moment she thought about her miscarriage, remembering that children hadn't been part of her and Mitch's plan, not for a long while—if ever. They hadn't discussed starting a family. Kids did not fit into their work schedule. Hadn't fit, she corrected before stopping. *Still didn't.* Good grief!

Having a baby was even less likely to suit her lifestyle now that she was single. It must be that warm, snuggly baby-powder smell messing with her mind. Gingerly she handed back her niece to Cash and waved the trio towards the house. 'Mum's at the CWA Christmas lunch, but she should be home soon. She's going to freak when she sees you all.'

'Linc, can you bring up Mia's bag so I can change her?' Cash asked over her shoulder.

Hadley bit back a smile as she watched her tough, ex-commando brother hoist a delicate floral nappy bag over his broad shoulder as he retrieved their luggage from the rear of the vehicle.

'So how's things, sis?' Linc asked as they trailed slightly behind Cash, who'd already reached the top of the stairs.

'Not too bad.'

'I heard there was some trouble with a reporter. Is that still a problem?'

Hadley looked up at her brother and shook her head. 'It wasn't as bad as you probably heard. Things have settled down.'

'Mitch is just lucky he isn't here. I can't believe that jerk would dump you in it like that and leave you to face the press alone.'

Hadley gave a shrug as they climbed the front steps. 'We both knew it was going to cause a stir. It's old news already.'

'If you want to talk about it . . .' Linc said, stopping at the top of the stairs.

'I don't,' she said quickly, then softened her words with a smile. 'Thank you, but I'm fine. Really. As soon as Christmas is over I'll be able to return to my old life. Until then I have my family and the cutest niece ever to keep me occupied.'

'She is pretty cute. Gets that part from her dad,' he added without modesty.

'Really?' A loud, insistent crying came from inside the house. 'Now *that's* more like her father.' Hadley flashed a smug smile at her brother as he reached the screen door and sent her a dark look.

It was actually insane how one small baby could make so much mess.

'No wonder you're so cranky,' Cash was crooning above the red-faced, angry baby kicking her legs wildly on the bed. 'Let's get you cleaned up.'

The nappy that Cash was changing was so potent that Hadley had to back out of the spare room. 'I'll put the jug on,' she called over her shoulder.

By the time the two parents came out of the room, she had their coffee and a plate of her mother's biscuits on the kitchen table.

'Dear God, was that smell normal?' Hadley asked Cash as they sat down.

'That was a rather large one, even for us,' Cash said, eyeing her daughter sternly, which melted into a look of pure adoration within seconds. Clearly mothering involved the ability to instantly forget all unpleasant memories of their child, including pooey nappies. She supposed it had to be that way or no one would ever have a second baby.

'So where's Dad?' Linc asked as he reached for a biscuit.

'He went to a sale.'

'I guess this was that one time that surprising the olds backfired on me, huh?'

'Mum warned you,' Hadley said, sipping her coffee. 'She's going to freak when she gets home.'

'Nah, she loves it. She'd be disappointed if we ever turned up when we said we would.'

'Only in this family would that remark sound logical,' Cash drawled.

The three of them caught up over a cuppa and chatted, before Cash decided to go and put Mia to bed before the grandparents came home and all hope of any kind of routine went flying out the window.

❧

It amazed Hadley that her mother could turn a simple Tuesday night meal for three into a family feast without so much as a blink of an eye. After an afternoon of cooing over her grandchild, Lavinia headed out to the kitchen and within minutes had enough food cooking to feed a small army.

Griff and Olivia arrived, further lengthening the queue to play with the baby, and Hadley excused herself to take a phone call from Ollie.

'Hey,' she answered, her voice quiet as she made her way across the room to head outside.

'Hey. Why are you whispering?'

'I'm just going outside.'

'Sounds like you have a crowd there.'

'Yeah. Linc and Cash arrived out of the blue earlier. I meant to text you but I haven't been able to get away. There's no way I'll be able to get out of dinner here tonight.'

'Nah, that's all good. I understand.'

'But I was thinking maybe I could come by afterwards?'

'Sure,' his voice seemed to brighten, and she was relieved to realise he'd been as disappointed about them not seeing each other as she'd been.

'Last night was—' he paused and then breathed '—freakin' awesome?' She felt her stomach flip as memories of the night before flashed though her head. God, the things they'd done ... the things *she'd done*. She felt a flush creeping up her neck.

'Yeah. It was,' she said, her voice a little unsteady. The screen door opened and Hadley turned away. 'I've gotta go. I'll see you later,' she said, hanging up just as her father and brothers came out onto the verandah with all the subtlety of a herd of elephants, abruptly putting an end to any further lustful thoughts.

She didn't like sneaking about, but the alternative was being interrogated by her family and dealing with what everyone may or may not be thinking about her relationship with Ollie. It was too soon for all that; besides, she already had more than enough on her plate that *hadn't* been dealt with yet.

∽

Ollie looked down at the phone thoughtfully. When Hadley had said she was going to have to cancel coming over tonight, he'd had a moment of panic. Had she decided it wasn't going to work out between them? It only lasted a few seconds, until she'd added that she'd come over later, but the speed with which the devastation had struck surprised him. So much for playing it cool and seeing where this thing took them.

He knew he was already too attached but, then again, he hadn't expected anything less. Sure, he'd said he'd be happy to take whatever came out of this, but in truth he wasn't sure how he was going to cope when Hadley left. He could deal with a long-distance romance if he had to, but he wasn't sure how he'd go if things simply ended between them as though nothing had even happened. They were going to need to talk but right now he was too scared to bring it up in case she told him something he didn't want to hear.

He didn't like the sneaking around though. Hadley was right, it would complicate things if their families all got involved, and he'd already had to lie to Griff about meeting up last night, which sadly, thanks to his unexciting social life, had immediately sparked his mate's curiosity.

He wasn't sure how Griff would take the news if they told him. The Callahans were funny like that—Griff and Linc had always been fiercely protective of their sisters growing up. Ollie knew that a number of potential boyfriends had, without Hadley's knowledge, been given a detailed description of what would happen to them if they did anything to hurt her. Hadley hadn't had very many long-term relationships in high school. He was probably overreacting. Griffin was engaged to Ollie's sister for goodness sake. It'd be a bit pot calling the kettle if he did, and yet Ollie had a funny feeling Griff wasn't going to be overjoyed by the news. He hoped he wasn't going to lose his best mate over it.

Yeah, there was a lot riding on a relationship that had no real name yet. A hell of a lot.

∽

'Is it just me or is it kind of boring not to end up with a broken nose and black eye?' Hadley said, turning her head on the pillow to look over at Ollie.

'Boring?' He lifted an eyebrow at her.

'Okay, poor choice of words. Anticlimactic?'

'Woman, if you're trying to castrate me, you're going about it in the right way.'

Hadley chuckled and slid her hand into his. 'I wouldn't want to do that. It's just a relief there were no trips to Emergency and awkward explanations. I was worried after the first attempt that it could become a thing.'

Ollie looked down at her hand inside his. It looked incredibly small and delicate. It was such a small hand to be holding his whole heart. Whoa. Part of him wanted to pull on the brakes. He wasn't even putting up a fight? A saner part of him just shook its head—what was the point? Seriously? He'd been in love with the woman forever.

'I wasn't sure if this would happen again,' he admitted quietly, hoping he wasn't pushing his luck opening this conversation.

'You had second thoughts about your physical safety?'

He grinned but shook his head, 'No. I was half-expecting you to realise you'd made a terrible mistake.'

'Why? Have you? Realised you've made a terrible mistake, that is?' she asked slowly.

'God no,' he answered quickly and felt her relax slightly. 'Just when you called earlier, it crossed my mind.'

'I don't regret this,' she told him earnestly. 'It's taken me by surprise,' she admitted. 'I mean, the last thing I expected when I came home was to discover I had all these weird feelings for someone who I've always thought of as a—'

'Do not say brother,' he warned her darkly.

'Cousin?' she said helpfully.

'That's still pretty much frowned upon in most places too.'

She chuckled and rolled over on her side to look at him and he instantly felt a stab of attraction all over again. She was so damn beautiful. Messy hair, no makeup and all.

'This is all so new and unexpected, Ollie. It's really taken me by surprise.'

'But not in a bad way, right?'

'Definitely not in a bad way,' she agreed, sliding a leg along his thigh under the sheet that covered them.

Okay, so she might be using sex to distract him from continuing along the path of serious conversation, but who was he to complain? He could wait to talk about all this . . . as long as she wanted.

∞

'Morning.'

Hadley jumped, letting out a muffled curse as the whispered words seemed to echo in the quiet room. 'Jesus, Cash. You scared the hell out of me.'

'Sorry,' she said, smiling serenely as she fed Mia in the dark room.

Hadley moved across to her and eased down into the chair opposite, trying not to make any noise and disturb her niece from feeding. 'Bit early for breakfast, isn't it?'

'This is the pre-breakfast breakfast,' Cash said, looking down at her child's face tolerantly. 'And where have you just come home from, missy?' she asked, glancing up.

'Ah, nowhere. I was just out . . . for a walk.'

'Really . . . and wearing the same clothes you were in yesterday? Come on, Hads, my entire life right now revolves around feeding and changing a baby. I've got cracked nipples and stretch marks. I *need* to hear something adult and juicy right now before I lose my mind.'

Hadley studied her sister-in-law silently for a few moments before letting out a long sigh. 'Fine, but you can't tell Linc.'

'Okay. Now spill. And don't leave out any details.'

'There are no details. I've just recently developed feelings for someone I've known for a long time. It's still new and I don't really know where it's going.'

'Who?'

'I'd rather not say. I mean there's no point if it doesn't go anywhere. I'd rather not have everyone know.'

'It's Ollie, isn't it,' Cash said.

'What?' Hadley hurried to adjust the level of horror in her tone. 'Why would you think that?' *What the hell?*

'Just a hunch,' Cash shrugged, before switching the baby to her other breast and settling back once more. 'I remember seeing him at your wedding. I thought then that maybe there was something going on with you two. He just seemed . . . different that night. I'd never seen him quite that drunk before. Actually, it was only a guess until I saw the look on your face just now.'

She must be getting out of practice if she was giving away her thoughts so easily. She'd interviewed more than her fair share of difficult people over the years, and she had been pretty sure she had the ability to hide what she was really thinking.

'You can't breathe a word of this to Linc,' she said finally.

'I won't, but I doubt he'll figure it out,' Cash dismissed. 'Men rarely pick up on the obvious.'

'It's not *that* obvious,' Hadley protested.

'So?' Cash drawled. 'Details?'

'There's not that much to tell. I was there for Ollie at Luke's funeral and things just kinda progressed.'

'How long have you been together?'

'Not long . . . and we're not really *together*,' Hadley clarified. 'It's complicated.'

'Of course it is. All the best relationships are.'

'I don't do complicated. In fact, I've always had very *uncomplicated* relationships.'

'And how's that been working out for you?' Cash asked, lifting an eyebrow. The early morning sun was beginning to peek over the horizon and a faint glow was creeping into the room.

Hadley gave a small surprised snort. From anyone other than Cash, she'd probably have taken offence, but it was hard to be offended by the woman who'd won her brother's heart and with whom her whole family had fallen in love. 'I don't know how it can go anywhere.'

'You said it's only new? Maybe just don't think about all the complications right now and just enjoy being together and getting to know each other.'

'We've known each other all our lives.'

'You've known each other as friends,' Cash said with a shake of her head. 'This is different. You have to start all over again.'

'I don't know, Cash. If there's no point in it, why put ourselves through all this?'

'You don't know that there's no point. Trust me, once you find the right person you can open up to, it's life-changing.'

'That's the bit I'm worried about. I'm not sure I want my life to change.'

'Oh, come on, Hads. Change doesn't have to be scary. It can be a good thing.'

'I'm a foreign correspondent, Cash. I've had to work hard to get where I am. It's not a job that you just turn your back on.'

'Do you have to? I mean, is there some kind of rule that says if you have a relationship you have to give up your job?'

'You know how crazy my work schedule is. I'm away for months at a time. That's no way to live in a relationship.'

'You won't know until you try. I think you're putting all this pressure on yourself, and thinking of all the negatives, when you haven't even given the relationship a chance. Don't write it off too soon. I'm telling you, the hardest opportunities are the ones that ends up being the most worthwhile.' She stood up slowly, a now sleeping baby cradled in her arms. 'Just do yourself a favour and open your mind to the possibilities before you shut the idea down completely.'

Hadley found herself staring down the hall after her sister-in-law. Maybe Cash was right. There was nothing really stopping them from continuing their lives as they were and still working on a relationship. Only, what if they found themselves falling further into something serious and not being able to make it work because of her job? Wouldn't that be worse than ending it before it got that far in the first place?

With a frustrated groan, she tipped her head back against the headrest of her chair and closed her eyes. This wasn't getting her anywhere.

Fourteen

Ollie glanced up as a ute pulled over in the paddock. He turned off the tractor and climbed down out of the cab. 'You got the day off or something?' he called as he crossed towards Griff.

'Just brought back the generator.'

'Righto. Thanks.' Ollie's eyes narrowed a little as he watched his mate. He couldn't put his finger on it, but there was something not quite right. 'You okay?'

'Huh? Yeah. Nah. All good,' he said, shuffling slightly with his hands shoved in his pockets. 'I s'pose I should get back and do something before the old man starts jumpin' up and down.'

'Okay. Catch ya later then.' Something was definitely up.

He turned away as Griff waved, but turned back when he started speaking again.

'Actually. While I've got ya here,' Griff started. 'Look, it's probably none of my business, but . . .' He paused and then blurted, 'Is there anything going on with you and my sister?'

Ollie bit back the denial that instantly sprung to his lips—this was his best mate. He wasn't going to lie to him. He knew Hadley wanted to keep things quiet till they figured things out, but he'd seen how keeping secrets had caused problems for other people around here lately. They always managed to snowball into bigger lies and before you knew it you were stuck in the middle of a huge shit storm. 'Maybe you should ask Hadley about that, mate.'

Griffin straightened at that and his gaze locked onto Ollie's. 'I think I'd rather hear it from you.'

'Griff, your sister doesn't want to make a big deal out it. She asked me not to say anything.'

'So it's true? You've got to be shittin' me,' he said, staring at Ollie with a dumbfounded look. 'And you're happy to have a fling with her on the quiet?'

Ollie knew Griff and Hadley were close—hell, he had a twin sister, he knew how protective a bloke got over his sister but Griff was treading a very thin line at the moment. 'You were right, this is probably none of your business.'

'This is my sister you're talkin' about,' Griff said through clenched teeth.

'Exactly. It's Hadley. You should know better than to ask something like that. You know damn well I'd never treat her like a fling.'

'Then what the hell? Where did this thing even come from? She's practically your family.'

'And you're marrying my sister,' Ollie pointed out.

'It's not about that,' Griff snapped. 'This is to do with timing.'

'I'm not talkin' about this with you. If you want to know any more, go speak to your sister.'

'I can't believe you'd sneak around behind everyone's back like this. Christ, Ollie, she's still married.'

'As if you give a toss about Mitch. You're really reachin' for straws now.'

'I'm trying to get my head around the fact my best friend has decided to pounce on my sister when she's at her lowest.'

'Pounce? Griff, I think you better shut your mouth right now before you say something that's gonna be really hard to ignore.'

'Pretty disappointed, mate.' Griff turned away abruptly and stormed back to his ute, leaving Ollie to stare after him, clenching his jaw.

Ollie climbed back into the tractor and slammed the cabin door before starting the engine. How had everything blown up in his face like that? Trust Griff to get the wrong end of the bloody stick. Who the hell was he to come storming over here and get up in his face like that? It was none of his bloody business. He eyed his phone and fought the urge to call Hadley. It wasn't a good idea while he was still seething, but she had a right to know that her brother was on the warpath. No doubt she'd be hearing from Griff soon enough. Although he was willing to bet

Griff wouldn't get away with calling her out on it the way he had just now. He almost wished he could be there when that particular conversation took place. If he were a betting man, he'd have his money on Hadley. She may be tiny, but growing up with two older brothers, she'd learned pretty fast how to stand up for herself. Nope, he wouldn't be underestimating Hadley.

∽

'So when were you going to fill the rest of us in on your latest news?'

Hadley glanced up from the wedding magazine she'd been flicking through as she and Olivia decided on bridesmaid styles.

'What latest news?' She eyed Griffin curiously. Oh, great, what had happened now?

'You and Ollie. Want to tell me what the hell's going on there?'

Hadley's stomach dropped a little, before her brother's slightly aggressive stance registered. Her eyes narrowed dangerously. 'Want to tell me why you think you can stand there and demand anything from me in that tone?'

'I've just been over to see Ollie. He didn't deny it.'

'You did what? Why would you think you had the right to do that?'

'Because you're my sister and he's my best friend. I've had the feeling something's been goin' on for a while now. I wanted to hear it from him.'

'It's got nothing to do with you, Griffin.'

'So it's true? You and Ollie?'

'It's none of your business.'

'Okay. How about we all calm down,' Olivia said, getting to her feet to stand between the siblings.

'Calm down? Where does he get off attacking me like this?'

'Haven't we had enough secrets in this family?' Griff shot back.

'It wasn't a secret—God, is it too much to ask for anything to stay private in this place?' Hadley snapped, before turning to Olivia. 'I knew once he found out he'd carry on like this.'

'Coffee anyone?' Olivia tried again.

Griffin stared at his fiancée. 'You knew about it?'

'I told her in confidence,' Hadley said, eyeing her friend sternly.

'So I'm the last one to know anything around here?'

'Stop being such a drama queen,' Hadley said, rolling her eyes. 'Look. Ollie and I . . . I don't know where it's headed. It just happened. I don't want to make a big deal about it.'

A loud rap at the front door of the cottage made all three turn around as the screen door opened and Ollie came inside.

Hadley had that weird stomach flip thing happening as Ollie strode across to her side. Her eyes trailed across his pale blue work shirt and she was momentarily distracted by the tanned forearms revealed by the rolled-up sleeves.

'I figured Griff was on his way here and I wasn't going to let you take it all alone,' he said before Hadley could ask what he was doing here. 'Griff, despite what you think, you don't have to know everything that's going on in your sister's life . . . or mine for that matter. You're my best mate and I don't want anything to change that, but if Hadley wants you to back off about this, then I'm gonna make sure you do.'

'Whoa. Hold up,' Olivia said, stepping in between her brother and soon-to-be husband like a human shield. 'That's enough. No one is going to make anyone do anything,' she said, glaring at the men sternly. 'This is getting ridiculous.'

'Ollie,' Hadley said gently, putting her hand on his arm and feeling the solid strength beneath her fingers. 'Thank you, but it's okay.'

'It's not okay that you have to deal with everyone asking about us. We're in this together.'

The way his voice dropped would have made her knees tremble if she'd been that kind of girl. Wait a minute. Turned out she was that kind of girl. Where had this strong, stoic Ollie come from?

The tender way he was looking down into her face made her swallow over a surprised lump in her throat. She couldn't recall the last time she'd had someone this protective hovering over her. Mitch certainly had never had this streak. It wasn't altogether unpleasant, despite the fact it was her brother whose arse Ollie was getting ready to kick, and she was more than capable of kicking his arse herself.

This was a man you could depend on. The thought came like a blinding flash of light. He didn't deserve to be kept hidden like some dirty secret. Ollie had never wanted to keep this a secret, and the fact he was willing to do whatever it took to keep it quiet *for her,* proved just how selfless he was. Hadley didn't think about what she was doing as she leaned up and kissed him.

She felt the split second of surprise the action caused, before he recovered and kissed her back. She didn't care that they had an audience; in fact, she was glad. She didn't want to keep this thing quiet anymore. She had feelings for Ollie—real feelings—and she didn't want to hide them.

'Oh, for God's sake, get a room,' she heard Griff mutter in disgust.

She pulled away from Ollie, taking a breath as she risked a glance up at him. 'Griff, consider yourself informed about our current relationship,' she said, without taking her eyes from Ollie's heavy-lidded gaze.

'Was that so hard to do? A little consideration wouldn't have gone astray is all I'm sayin',' Griff said grudgingly, and Hadley knew that Olivia would be sending him a withering glare.

'Great. So you two boys all good now?' Olivia asked, sounding like a schoolteacher talking to two kindergarten kids.

'I'm okay,' Ollie said, sliding his arm across Hadley's shoulder and pulling her close against his side.

'Yeah. All good,' Griff said grudgingly. 'I may have been a bit out of line . . .'

'May have been?' Hadley said, narrowing her eyes.

'It's all good,' Ollie said, giving her a squeeze. 'You were just lookin' out for your sister. I get that,' he said pointedly, nodding towards his own sister.

'Yeah, well, I may be okay with it, but you've still gotta tell Linc and Dad yet,' Griff said with a touch too much glee in his voice to be considered comradely. It was her turn to give Ollie a comforting squeeze. She wasn't sure, but she thought maybe he'd lost a little of his colour.

'It'll be fine,' she said. At least she hoped it would be. She still didn't have any answers as to what their future would look like. *Oh, well, it's too late to back out now,* she thought, and was glad.

'Come over for dinner tonight,' she said, turning in Ollie's arms. 'We'll make it public. We'd better invite your parents too. May as well kill two birds with one stone.'

She walked Ollie to the door and kissed him goodbye, lingering in the doorway as they rested foreheads together quietly. 'Are you sure you want to do this?' he asked.

'Not really,' she smiled weakly. 'Yeah, I'm sure. I don't want to hide things from our family anymore. I'm tired of always keeping secrets.'

'Whatever you want to do, you've got my support.'

'Thank you. For everything.'

'I haven't done anything.'

'Yes, you have. You came over here to take on my brother. You've got my back. That means a lot.' It was something she hadn't really experienced before. It also highlighted how one-sided her marriage with Mitch had been. He'd never really had an opinion about her career—or anything else in her life for that matter. They'd led two separate lives under the same roof. This was nice. Different, but nice.

∽

Hadley had organised the dinner. Dodging her mother's questions had proven challenging, but it was easier to distract her with Mia in the house, and the suggestion of a night off from cooking so she could enjoy her grandbaby prevented the grilling Hadley would normally have gotten.

The atmosphere was festive, not unusual this close to Christmas and the two families always enjoyed any excuse for a gathering.

Her gaze settled upon Sue and Bill and she found herself briefly considering how this new relationship might affect them. With a wry smile she realised Olivia and Griff had already eased the path for her and Ollie in that regard. The families used to joke about marrying all the kids off to each other and joining forces like some medieval clan, although she was fairly sure none of them ever actually thought it might come true. Not that she and Ollie were anywhere near that serious yet, she reminded herself quickly. She pushed the thought of marriage and going through all that again—ever—from her mind, choosing instead to focus on her unexpected happiness right now.

She loved being home. She had missed it when she spent so long away. Over the last few years she'd found herself making excuses for not coming home because Mitch was uncomfortable around her family. He wasn't used to their open affection and good-natured ribbing. She should have pushed him more, but she hadn't. Maybe on some level she'd known that if she'd tried to force Mitch to be part of her family he'd eventually decide not to get married after all. It made her equal parts angry and ashamed of herself. Why had her ego—her need to prove herself to everyone—let her ignore the red flags that had waved for so long over her relationship with Mitch?

Her thoughts drifted back to her sister, and her mother's announcement earlier that Harmony was out of town and wouldn't be coming along tonight. Hadley felt a twinge of guilt over her relief when she heard the disappointment in her mother's voice. The reality of how things were going to change—had already begun to change—was not lost on her. Hadley assumed that from now on one of them would always try to find an excuse not to attend family functions to avoid the awkward situation. She felt sad that her parents, who always looked forward to having all their children home together whenever possible, would be the biggest losers in this whole, horrible mess.

She glanced up when Ollie walked into the room and felt a warm sensation spreading from her stomach to her toes. The man seemed to get better looking every time she saw him. She'd never taken any notice of how his jeans fitted oh so perfectly, not skinny jeans designed for city chic, but real jeans made to fit a real man. He didn't wear what was on trend, he wore what was comfortable, and yet somehow he managed to make what the models wore look like kids' wear. How had she been able to look past those arms? Everything about the way he moved, the way he held himself, seemed to ignite primal urges in her. She inwardly scoffed at herself, but she couldn't stop herself responding to him. Her gran would say she was smitten, but that sounded far too innocent for the things her imagination was coming up with right now.

'Hey,' Ollie said softly as he stopped before her, having greeted everyone on the way across the room. 'How's this thing going to go down?'

'I have no idea. Should we do it before we sit down or at the table?'

Ollie looked around as though trying to gauge the audience. 'Well, they seem to be pretty loosened up,' he said, eyeing the various glasses of beer and wine. 'Maybe we should get it out of the way now?'

'I don't think I've had enough to drink yet, but okay.' She felt ill. This wasn't the worst thing she'd had to announce, she told herself . . . For someone who detested drama, she was certainly having her fair share of it lately.

Ollie took her hand and looked down into her eyes intently. 'We're in this together, okay?'

His words cocooned around her and made her smile. 'Okay.'

Still holding her hand, Ollie gave a whistle and conversation instantly stilled in the room. 'If I can interrupt for a minute,' he started, and Hadley saw a few curious gazes dart from their joined hands and back to their faces. 'There was a reason behind tonight's get-together. Some of you might have suspected something's been going on. Well, it has. Hadley and I have some news.'

'What did he say?' Gran piped up from her position on the lounge. 'Is there another baby on the way?'

'No!' Hadley said, jumping in and swallowing hard at the sudden frown that had appeared on her father's face. 'No, Gran. I'm not having a baby. Ollie was about to say, we're . . .'

'Getting married?' Gran supplied hopefully.

'Ah, no,' Hadley said, feeling the rest of the room getting restless as the situation began to get out hand.

'Ollie and I have been . . . seeing each other,' Hadley said quickly. 'We just wanted to let everyone know. So it would be less . . . weird.'

'Oh,' Lavinia said, her eyes wide and her smile fighting to stay in place.

'You're . . . together? As in a couple?' Sue said, as though to clarify.

'And there's no baby?' her father said, his eyes narrowing.

'Nope. No baby,' Hadley said, forcing a bright smile.

'Yet,' Gran added cheerfully.

'Well, that's lovely,' Lavinia finally said, getting to her feet and handing the baby to Cash before coming over to hug them both. It opened the gate to more good wishes and Hadley could finally breathe a sigh of relief. Thank goodness that was over and done with. She knew they'd now be facing a million and one questions about the how, why and what this meant for the future, but at least Ollie was there to help field them.

'So, Dawson,' Linc said, coming over to slap Ollie on the back. She heard Ollie bite back a grunt at the slightly overenthusiastic greeting. 'As the older brother, I guess it's up to me to point out that if you ever hurt my sister, you'll have me to deal with,' he said with a friendly smile, which on closer inspection had a slight tightness to it. 'Family friend or not,' he added, and Hadley glared at her older brother.

'Okay, thank you, Linc,' she said, intervening quickly.

'It's okay,' Ollie said calmly. 'I've said the same thing to Griff. It's a brother thing,' he said without his gaze leaving the other man's. Clearly there was some unspoken brotherhood exchange going on between the two, so Hadley left them to it.

She hugged Olivia and her mother and accepted Cash's smug embrace. 'I knew it,' she said, nodding sagely. 'You two were meant to be.'

'Yeah, well, we're not sure how it's all going to work . . . but I guess we'll see.'

'This is the best news,' Sue said, smiling warmly. 'Something that Bill and I have been secretly hoping might happen for years.'

So it was official: apparently she was the only one completely blinded to what pretty much everyone else had somehow suspected over the years. So much for investigative journalism skills. In the kitchen, having waved Lavinia away, Cash, Olivia and Hadley began serving up the meal.

'So how does it feel to come clean?' Olivia asked.

'I don't know. No one really seems overly surprised.'

'Told ya,' Olivia shrugged as she served the peas.

'I thought your dad was going to bust a gasket there for a minute when he thought Ollie had knocked you up,' Cash chuckled.

'As though *that* would have been the biggest scandal I'd put the family through,' Hadley scoffed.

'It'd have given Mitch something to think about,' Cash said harshly, unable to hide her contempt for the man.

'Mitch wouldn't bat an eyelid,' Hadley said, dishing the potatoes out onto the many plates spread out before them.

'He should. The jerk,' Olivia added.

'He never really wanted kids.' Her thoughts briefly touched on the still tender memory of the baby she'd lost a little over a year ago. The sadness had dulled, but it was always there. She often wondered how things would have turned out had she not lost the baby. She doubted Mitch would have changed; if anything, he probably would have only grown resentful. He'd never liked it when something intruded on his pre-ordained plans.

She looked up and saw her friend's expression soften to one of understanding. It wasn't often you had a friend who'd shared the very best and worst of times with you. Olivia had always been her rock and she blinked quickly as her eyes stung and threatened to well up. 'We better get these out before the natives get restless.'

Hadley smiled as Olivia moved past her and bumped her with a hip on the way out. Maybe things hadn't been going great lately, but she still had to be one of the luckiest people in the world to have her family and good friends to support her. Her gaze searched the table until she found

Ollie. And she had this amazing man in her life now. For better or worse, it was now public knowledge. Maybe it would put more pressure on them to make this thing work, but then again, everyone knew the obstacles they were up against, so surely they'd cut them some slack. One thing was certain though—at least now everyone wouldn't be sending her any more of those 'Poor Hadley' looks that she'd been trying to ignore since she'd been home. If only one good thing came from all this, then that would be a pretty good one.

Fifteen

'Do you realise,' Olivia said, looking at Griff after the meal was finished and they were recovering from a food coma, 'that this is the last Christmas we'll be single?'

Hadley watched her best friend and brother exchange a smile and swallowed back a little ping of regret mixed with a touch of nostalgia. Two Christmases ago she had been in the final stages of planning her dream wedding.

She looked around at the small group gathered and realised just how much had changed for all of them since that Christmas. Linc and Griff had almost split the family in two when they'd fought over Cash. Who could have known then that Griff would go on to find the woman he was really supposed to be with had been right under his nose all these years? Linc had fought his demons and won—won his girl and now had a baby—and she was an almost divorced, disillusioned journo hiding out at her parents place to avoid becoming fodder for the gossip magazines. Her gaze shifted to Ollie and she saw a sad, faraway look on his handsome face as he stared down into the beer he held in his hand.

'What are you thinking about?' she asked him quietly.

His eyes shot to hers as though startled from deep thought. 'Nothing much.'

'You looked like you had the weight of the world on your shoulders.'

'I was just thinking about Luke's family,' he said, sitting up a little in his seat. He'd been to visit the Pattersons a few times since the funeral and had dropped by the day before to have a quiet beer with Terry. He couldn't help but think while he was there that it should have been Luke sitting with his old man out the back having a drink to see in the Christmas season. Alice had joined them later and he'd listened to her reliving some of the more amusing antics from Luke's childhood. Ollie had listened and grinned at some of them—he'd been part of one or two and had forgotten about them—but the stories, as funny as they were, were full of sadness. That's all they'd have of him now—stories.

'Christmas is going to be hard for them,' Hadley acknowledged.

'I feel like we've let him down somehow,' Ollie said, picking at the label on the side of his beer bottle. 'That something needs to be done. We need to *do* something.'

'How do you stop people taking their own life, Ollie?' Olivia said sadly. 'It's a choice they make. That's why it's so hard to understand.'

'Then maybe the answer's about finding a way to stop it before it gets to that point,' Ollie said.

'There're a few programs about that deal with suicide. Maybe you need to get in touch with them and see what they suggest,' Linc said thoughtfully.

'I feel as though we need something aimed at farmers. How many local families do we know that this's happened to over the last few years? We need to aim something at blokes like us. I think it needs to come from someone who isn't a doctor or a psychologist, from someone like us, you know? It needs to be relatable.'

'I think you might be on to something there,' Cash said after a few moments.

'But that's all I got. I don't have any idea how to go about making it happen.'

Hadley put a hand on Ollie's leg. 'You'd be surprised how many ideas can spring to life with enough heads put together.'

'Dessert time,' Sue called out, clapping to get everyone's attention and breaking the sombre mood that had fallen over their small group. Clearly, the mothers had taken over the party.

'Hey,' Hadley said, pulling Ollie back into his seat when everyone else got up and moved inside. 'Don't give up. We'll think of a way to make something work. I'll help you.'

Ollie leaned over and kissed her gently, resting his forehead against hers. 'In case you haven't noticed, I don't give up too easy.'

'Lucky for me,' she said softly.

∽

'Hadley, good news,' her mother called as she walked into the kitchen the next day.

Hadley had been reading through her emails and looked up as Lavinia put her handbag down on the bench.

'I spoke with Ollie the other night about young Luke. He's still terribly upset, isn't he?' she said sadly.

'Yeah. It's hit him pretty hard,' Hadley agreed. She hadn't known that he'd spoken with her mum about it.

'Well, anyway, today at the meeting I raised the idea of doing something as a fundraiser towards mental illness on behalf of Luke's family. Ollie's right, everyone feels helpless and we need to do something positive. So I put forward the idea of a high tea, to raise money for an organisation that can do something useful with it.'

'That's great, Mum,' Hadley smiled.

'Normally we wouldn't be looking at any kind of event until well after the Christmas season, but seeing as so many people are home during the holiday period, I think this would be a wonderful opportunity to do something.'

Her mum was right. Christmas was one of the very few times of the year that everyone came home to the area. There would be a lot of old schoolfriends of Luke's who would probably like to attend an event in his memory, many of whom hadn't been able to return for his funeral.

'I'm very excited about it actually. I'm going to invite as many influential people as I can so we can spread the word. We need councillors and our local member . . . health professionals,' she said, listing them off and growing more enthusiastic with each new thought. 'I spoke to Martha Williams, you remember she had a daughter—I think she's a bit older than Harmony—anyway, her daughter is a psychologist and she's very interested in getting on board, and I've asked if she'll give us a bit of a talk about mental health on the day. I think we need to make this as much about raising awareness as raising money. What do you think?' she asked, looking at Hadley expectantly.

'I think that's a fantastic idea, Mum.' They did need to target the people in power, people who could make a difference, but it was kind of throwing her off balance the speed at which it was taking off. Still, leave it to her mother and things always ran at full speed until they were done.

The rest of the day passed in a blur of emails, phone calls and arrangements, and by the end of the day Hadley had a renewed appreciation for her mother and her remarkable ability to pull together an event in such a short space of time.

Later that afternoon, when Hadley had arrived at Ollie's with the news, she looked up at him from where she reclined against his chest on the lounge and frowned a little. 'You don't seem as excited about this idea as I imagined you would be.'

Ollie gave a half-shrug and stared down at their entwined fingers. 'I am. I think it's a great idea. Your mum's fantastic at raising money for things like this,' he said.

'But?'

'I don't know . . . it's not enough,' he said, then looked down at Hadley quickly. 'I know it sounds like I'm being a jerk. I'm grateful that your mum and the other parents are stepping up, but I just don't see how it's getting the message across the way it needs to. We have to target the groups that this is happening to. Do you know what I mean?'

'Yeah, I do actually. What you're saying makes sense. We just haven't been able to think of a way to make that happen yet.'

'I know. I've been thinking, but I don't know, it has to be something special. Something different. Something that makes people sit up and take notice.'

'Maybe we can get a group together and brainstorm some ideas around a bonfire one weekend?'

'Yeah. I'd like that,' Ollie said, looking at Hadley before a gentle smile touched his face. 'It's really great that you and your mum got this thing up and going though.'

'I think Mum and the other women at the CWA know they have to stick to what they do best. I'm always gobsmacked when I see how much influence these women and their groups have. The CWA has been campaigning for rural health and regional investment for years now. I'm in awe of how passionate and motivated they are. In fact, I've just finished doing a story on them. Now I have a bit of free time, I've been able to explore a lot of the stories I've wanted to write but haven't had the opportunity.'

'That's great. I'm glad. You seem less stressed lately.'

'And I suppose you're fishing for a compliment in there somewhere, are you?' she asked, lifting an eyebrow.

'Well, I do happen to know for a fact that I've been responsible for some of that release of tension,' he said smugly.

Hadley had been worried about how things would be between them once they announced they were a couple. But so far everything was going along as normal. Of course, it was partly due to the fact that everyone else was still buried under the last of their harvest, and farming never really stopped, so her time alone with Ollie had been rather limited since their announcement.

She'd walked into the room a few times when her parents had been deep in conversation and they had stopped talking abruptly, making her suspect she and Ollie had been the topic of discussion. However, it can't have been anything too concerning or she would have been sat down for a deep and meaningful by now. It was probably genius on her part to time the announcement just as her mother was in full Christmas preparation mode and had very little time for anything else.

Hadley's writing had become an exciting outlet for her; she was sending more and more freelance work out and loved the change of pace these stories provided. She was missing her assignments, but strangely not to the point where she was becoming restless. Maybe when she began running out of story ideas she'd feel a need to get back out in the thick of it all, but at the moment she was enjoying having less deadline pressure and not having to write about the worst in human and Mother Nature.

It was hard to believe it was almost Christmas. Her time here had been flying past, mostly because of Ollie. They were caught up in the new relationship where everything was exciting and fresh and fun. But would it last? She wasn't sure. After all, she knew the pressures that a long-distance relationship could put on a couple. She'd seen many of her colleagues go through rough patches with partners who weren't in the business, and she wasn't overly confident that Ollie understood what he was getting himself into. How could he?

She'd tried to bring it up a few times over the last few days, but each time Ollie stopped her. 'Can we just focus on here and now for a while before we worry about the future?' he'd asked last time.

'Not talking about it isn't going to make it go away, you know,' she'd said gently.

'And it's not going to change anything either, so let's just deal with it when we have to.'

Unfortunately that time was rapidly approaching and Hadley knew the conversation couldn't be put off forever.

∽

Hadley was answering emails while her parents sat and watched the news later that evening. She smiled to herself as she glanced up at the familiar scene. Other than at meals, it was the only time of the day that her parents sat down together. It had been that way ever since she'd done her first on-air story. They never missed it. They'd always been there for her, supporting her from the sidelines.

'*We now cross live to our foreign correspondent, Amber Latoy.*' The newsreader's smooth voice cut into her memories and drew her attention to the television. The tall, attractive woman on the screen talking earnestly into the camera wasn't unfamiliar to Hadley. They'd bumped into one another now and again during assignments, but this was the first time Hadley had seen her doing *her* job. She'd known they'd be replacing her during the somewhat forced leave the network had persuaded her to take, but she hadn't known it would be by Amber.

'I don't know this one,' Lavinia said, turning a curious face to her daughter. 'Is she new?'

'She's been around for a little while,' Hadley said, trying to keep the surprise from her tone. Not long enough to be landing the foreign correspondent role, though, she added silently. She'd been told Marcus, her long-time colleague, would be handling things until her return. Something big must have come up to take him away. Already her mind was sifting through the possibilities. Crap. What was she missing out on?

'She's very pretty,' Lavinia said.

Hadley narrowed her eyes slightly as her mother's comment registered. She *was* very attractive, and quite young. And ambitious. She gave a silent, self-deprecating chuckle at that. They were all ambitious—it came with the territory. You had to fight for your stories and always be ready to jump on the slightest lead. But she'd never really warmed to Amber. Admittedly, she hadn't spent a great deal of time with the woman as Amber hadn't been working in the field very long. Maybe she just needed a bit more time to get to know her once things went back to normal.

The throw ended and returned to the studio, but Hadley was left uneasy. Too many changes had been happening and she wasn't sure all of them were temporary. If she wasn't careful, things may never go back to normal again.

∽

Ollie walked into the shed and frowned as he saw his father bent over, changing a tyre.

'Jeez, Dad. Here, let me do that,' Ollie said, as he reached his father's side.

'The day I need someone to change a bloody tyre for me will be the day I roll over and die.'

'Would you stop. You don't need to be doin' this stuff. Just ask for help.'

'I don't need help.'

'Why do you always have to be so damn stubborn?' Ollie snapped, as he stood watching his father struggle.

''Cause I'm sick of everyone fussin' over me. I've been home for months and anyone would think I'd got out of hospital yesterday.'

'The doctor said not to push yourself,' Ollie reminded him.

'He also said layin' around wasn't good for me, but if your mother had her way I'd be tucked up in bed reading flamin' *New Idea* all day.'

'We're all worried that you're taking on too much, with the farm tours and stuff. It's a lot of pressure to put on your body. You're lucky to be walking again.' It wasn't the first time he'd had this conversation with his dad.

'That's right. I'm lucky,' he said, straightening with a grimace. 'Layin' in that hospital bed gave me a glimpse of what my life could have been like,' he said, holding Ollie's gaze. 'I'm not takin' anything for granted anymore. I'm not completely useless, despite what your mother and sister think.'

'Come on, Dad. They don't think that. They just don't want you pushing yourself too hard.'

'I know what you kids were thinking when you came up with this little venture. It was so I had something to keep me busy and out of the way.'

Ollie opened his mouth to protest, but closed it when his father held up a hand.

'I get it,' Bill nodded. 'I can't do as much around the place as I used to, but I can still do some things,' he said, spreading his arms to indicate the flat tyre before them. 'You don't understand what it feels like to suddenly go from being a capable, able-bodied man to one who has to relearn how to walk, to climb steps and to dress himself. I hope you never have to go through that, son,' he said stiffly. 'That's why I need to do things around here—normal, everyday things.'

'I do understand, Dad,' Ollie said, his earlier frustration draining away. He knew that if he was in his dad's situation he'd struggle with the sudden loss of independence and he'd hate giving up the job he loved. But it was hard to stand by and watch him struggle.

'Okay,' Ollie said with a defeated sigh, stepping back from the ute. 'You change the tyre. Under one condition,' he added firmly. 'In future, if there *is* something you need help with, you ask. No one thinks any less of you for needing some help now and again, Dad. Everyone's proud of how far you've come. I know I am.' He cleared his throat roughly and studied the cement floor under his feet. 'I've got some stuff to do. Yell if you need anything.' Ollie turned away to head across to the workbench where he'd left the battery from the Toyota that had been flat that morning.

For the next few minutes he listened to his father's slow movements, determined not to look over and watch his progress.

'So you and young Hadley, huh?' his dad said, grunting as he tightened the wheel nut on the ute.

The question, and it was a question rather than an observation, surprised him. 'Yeah. Kind of snuck up on us both.'

'Did seem to come out of the blue,' Bill agreed. 'You sure you've thought this one through?'

'What do you mean?'

'Don't get me wrong—I love those Callahan girls like one of my own—but Hadley's always been different ... bit of a parrot among the pigeons. I'm not sure I can see her settling in back here after all this time. How're you planning on making that work?'

'We're not sure yet,' Ollie eventually admitted. 'I don't know where it's headed.'

'I reckon you better start figuring it out soon. One way or the other. Way I see it, you only have two options. Make it work or end it.'

His father's words stayed with him long after his old man had gone back inside. That gnawing sensation had started back in his gut again. What were they going to do?

They would most likely end up with some kind of long-distance arrangement and, as much as the thought of that sucked, the reality was that it was the best outcome he could hope for. Did he like the thought of only seeing Hadley whenever they could arrange a weekend for him to fly to the city? Hell no. But what was the alternative?

Sixteen

'You're quiet tonight,' Hadley said as she and Ollie sat on his lounge the next evening, holding hands as they watched TV.

He flashed a quick smile and rubbed his thumb along the inside of her wrist distractedly. 'Just been a long day.'

'You sure that's all it is?'

The conversation he'd had with his father had been playing on his mind. Things were pretty much black and white. They either had a future or they didn't. Hadley's leave wouldn't last for much longer and she'd be returning to her life of travel and excitement, leaving Rankins Springs behind her without a backwards glance. That's not how she'd put it, of course. He knew if he asked her right now, she'd sweeten it, tell him that everything would work out, but they both knew deep down that there was no simple solution to their dilemma.

'I knew it,' she said, leaning forwards on the lounge, her eyes glued to the TV screen.

Ollie switched his confused gaze from her face to the news presenter talking solemnly into the camera and tried to work out what had caught her intense focus. They were crossing to something live and the camera switched to a man in his early forties holding a microphone and standing in front of a large motel. The newsreader finished, '*Marcus Beercroft is in Lagos with more on the events unfolding.*'

'*Early this morning, militants invaded the prestigious hotel, a popular place for businessmen and travellers to stay in Lagos, taking eighty-six people hostage,*' the journalist said gravely. '*It's understood that French Special Forces were deployed and, upon storming the hotel, encountered heavy gunfire. Currently the death toll stands at sixteen and there is no sign of the insurgents surrendering. So far the nationalities of the deceased are not known. I'll be standing by with further updates as they come to hand.*'

'I knew there was something big going on. That's why Amber was replacing Marcus.' Ollie sent her a confused frown and she shook her head abruptly. 'Sorry, just something that happened last night.'

'Would that have been you, if you weren't here? Covering that story?' Ollie asked.

'Maybe,' she shrugged.

'You wish you were there,' Ollie said and tried not to sound as deflated as he was feeling.

'It's a pretty big story. It would have been a good one to be on.'

'Reporting on a terrorist situation, with hostages, in . . . wherever the hell that place is? You're *disappointed* because you're not there right now?'

'It's in West Africa and, yeah, of course I'm disappointed. It's a big deal.'

'It's dangerous,' Ollie pointed out firmly. Christ, there were pictures of armed soldiers running around the place and the sound of guns firing. People were being killed.

'Of course it's dangerous. That's why they're over there . . . to report on it.'

'Even if it means putting yourself in harm's way?'

'We don't put ourselves in harm's way. We're just there to tell the story to people back home. Document what's going on. We're kept back from the actual action.'

'Except when you're on tour with some military unit in Afghanistan or Iraq, or doing a story on training camps in Al Qaeda territory,' he pointed out dryly.

'Ollie, it's my job.'

'I guess I try not to think about it too much. At least that's what I used to do. It was none of my business before.'

The look she gave him made him pause. He could have sworn it said, *It still isn't*, and mentally he took a step back. *Was* it his business now? They weren't married or anything—he gave a small grimace at that—even when she *had* been married it hadn't stopped her. *Did* he want to stop her? His immediate reaction was no, of course not. He didn't want to become some overbearing dick, but seeing the violence on the TV unfolding behind the reporter at this very moment, knowing that would be her again one day soon, chilled him to the bone.

He wanted to ask whether it was his business. But he was too scared of what her answer might be. They sat together on the lounge without talking much after that, both caught up in their own thoughts, and Ollie had a sick feeling inside that refused to go away. One day soon he wouldn't be able to avoid the question—and he had no idea how he was going to cope with the fallout of that.

Ollie greeted Bob Callahan and Linc as he bounded up the stairs. Christmas spirit hung in the air and everyone seemed to be in the mood to celebrate. Well, almost everyone. It wasn't that he wasn't looking forward to Christmas—they'd had a great season, harvesting had finished earlier than expected and was even better than last year, and this year he had Hadley. That still took some pinching. He had a lot to be happy about, and yet he found himself thinking about Luke and all the joy got sucked out of him like a vacuum. The Pattersons wouldn't be celebrating this year. Christmas would never be the same for them with an empty place at the table. This year in particular would be hell on earth—the pain still so raw. He wished there was something he could do. The need to take some kind of action—to try and ... that was just the problem. Try and do *what*? He didn't know what to do, all he knew was this could not be allowed to happen again. But how to stop it? He didn't have any answers, all he had was an empty, sick feeling inside.

He looked over Linc's shoulder and that sick, empty feeling eased a little as Hadley saw him and a smile lit up her face. 'Sorry, mate, I'll be back in a sec,' he said, stepping around him and heading towards her.

He didn't care that they were surrounded by both their families, he needed to feel her against him, and the moment she was in his arms he felt the sadness he'd been carrying inside him all day ease a little.

'Hey, you,' she said softly, leaning back a little after sharing a deep but all too brief kiss and looking up at him with a puzzled face. 'What's wrong?'

'Nothing now. I just missed you all day.'

'You saw me this morning,' she said, giving him a look that instantly made him wish they were alone. 'You do remember this morning, don't you?'

How could he forget? It was the reason he'd been late starting work—he had been lucky he hadn't bumped into his father and needed to try to explain.

'I remember,' he said sending her a slow grin. 'It's been playin' on my mind most of the day.'

'Ollie, there you are,' Lavinia brushed past and kissed his cheek. 'I was worried you weren't going to make it.'

'Wouldn't dream of missing Mr and Mrs Claus making an appearance.'

Lavinia's laugh, much like Hadley's, had a melodious ring to it and she gave a wave of her fingers as she continued on her way.

'Can you believe my parents still do this every year?' Hadley said with a chuckle and a shake of her head.

'It's tradition,' Ollie shrugged. 'They've been doing it for as long as I can remember.'

'I know. But I'm a bit worried: I heard Dad suggesting it might be time to pass the Santa suit down to the next generation. I don't think I'm ready for that kind of responsibility.'

'Surely Linc or Griff will get it before you?'

'Do you honestly see either of my brothers dressing up as Santa? Seriously?' she added dryly, and Ollie gave a grunt. She had a point.

'I don't think your mum will be willing to give it up anytime soon.' Lavinia Callahan was Christmas personified. The house was decorated to within an inch of its life, and as much as Bob Callahan grumbled about it, Ollie was pretty sure he got just as big a kick out of the whole thing as his wife did.

He noticed Harmony inside and looked back down at Hadley. 'How're things with your sister?'

Hadley shrugged. 'We've been civil. She's been pretty quiet. Mum and Dad are worried about her. They had a bit of a chat when she first got here.'

'No sign of mentioning Mitch?'

'No,' she said bluntly. 'Doesn't seem she's planning on telling them too soon.'

'Buggered if I know how she can live with something like that. Secrets always backfire on you.' The fact that this particular secret stood to hurt so many people once it was out of the bag only made the waiting worse. Maybe

Harmony and Mitch had a plan; maybe they would contrive some cock-and-bull story about getting together after Mitch's divorce was official in a few more months—who knew—but it didn't sit well with him. He couldn't stand dishonesty in a person.

'I'm staying out of it. This is their problem to deal with. All I know is I'm the happiest I've been in a long time and I'm not going to let the two of them ruin it for me.'

Ollie smiled into her blue eyes and felt his heart clench tightly. Right here, in this very moment, surrounded by friends and family and holding this woman he'd loved for most of his life in his arms, he had everything he could ever want. The realisation shook him.

He was about to tell Hadley and opened his mouth to do so but there was a call for everyone to take a seat at the table and the moment was lost in good-natured barging and hustling. He wasn't sure what he was going to have to do to make this thing work, but he knew, whatever it took, he'd do it.

∞

Hadley walked into the kitchen carrying dirty plates and saw her mother and two brothers deep in conversation. She paused, getting ready to walk back outside, but her mother stopped her. 'Hadley. Maybe you can shed some light on this.'

Her mother's tone instantly set her on high alert.

'Linc was just bringing up the fact he's noticed Harmony's not herself. See, it's not just me. Do you have any idea what's going on?'

'She doesn't tell me anything,' Hadley hedged.

'Well, maybe it's time I brought her in here and we got to the bottom of this,' Lavinia said firmly.

'No,' Hadley said quickly, drawing strange glances from her mother and eldest brother. She instantly sent Griff a pleading glance and saw his wary expression. He'd wanted to come clean about all of this earlier. She wouldn't be getting any help from him. 'I mean, clearly she doesn't feel like talking about whatever it is.'

'Well, she needs to. I know better than anyone what can happen if you don't get shit off your chest,' Linc said.

'Can't we just be happy that for one year we're having a nice, peaceful, drama-free Christmas?'

'Hadley. This is your sister we're talking about,' Lavinia said with a disapproving frown.

'Exactly. You know Harmony. There's always some kind of crisis going on.' As far as dramas went, this was in fact a big one and, yes, she wanted nothing more than to finally get it all out in the open, but the timing sucked. This would devastate her parents and that just wasn't fair when there was still Christmas to get through. 'Let's just hold off on the intervention until after Christmas, okay?'

Hadley noted the look exchanged between her brother and mother and plastered on a smile before making a quick exit. She wished she could just say, *Trust me,* but then they'd know for sure something was up. Maybe she was wrong, maybe it wouldn't matter when the news broke, it was going to be terrible regardless, but surely ruining Christmas was only adding insult to injury?

∽

'I'm not sure Harmony will be able to hold Mum off for much longer,' Hadley said to Ollie later.

'Maybe that's a good thing. Get it over and done with.'

'We just need to get through one more day.'

'You know, the fact your Mum's suss about something means she's probably worried, so it's not like everything's fine and dandy just because it's Christmas.'

'Yeah, well, it's in Harmony's court now. I'm willing to bet she won't be able to keep up the front for much longer.'

Olivia's laughter drew their attention. She and Griffin were making cooing noises at baby Mia.

'Get ready to be an aunty again soon,' Ollie said, watching his sister's besotted face.

'She's so clucky. And don't let Griff's tough guy exterior fool you. I caught him playing with Mia the other day and that kid had him wrapped around her little finger.'

They shared a chuckle as they watched the scene quietly for a few moments.

'Do you want kids?' Ollie asked.

Hadley didn't answer straightaway. That weird empty feeling was still there whenever she thought about a baby of her own.

'I don't know,' she said slowly. She glanced across at him and saw he was watching her thoughtfully. 'I mean, well . . . you know about the . . . when I lost the . . .' She couldn't say it. She didn't want to say baby. It hurt too much when she thought of it that way. 'The miscarriage,' she said instead.

She assumed Liv had told him about everything that had happened during that horrible time. It had been the reason Olivia hadn't wanted to tell Hadley that she'd accidentally discovered Mitch and Harmony together.

'Yeah. I knew about it. I'm sorry you went through that all by yourself.'

'Miscarriages happen a lot more often than people realise,' she said, trying to keep the tone matter-of-fact. 'I actually remember doing a story about it once.'

'Yeah, but this wasn't a story. It happened to you,' Ollie pointed out, and she knew from the serious look on his face that he wasn't going to let her shrug it off.

'In hindsight it was probably a blessing. I'd be connected to Mitch forever if I hadn't . . . you know . . . lost it,' she said, faltering again.

'If he and your sister work out, you'll be connected to him anyway.'

'Maybe. But sharing a child?' She shook her head. 'I can't even imagine having to be that civil for the rest of my life.' God, the thought of her ex and her sister having joint custody of her child was a complete nightmare.

Usually when she passed women with babies, there was a moment of wistfulness, of wondering what her baby would have looked like, but it was fleeting. The timing had been all wrong. She couldn't even imagine herself as a mother, and yet she *had* mourned the loss of the baby she hadn't gotten to meet.

Her attention switched back to the man beside her. Ollie. So strong and dependable. Her heart flooded with a fullness that still surprised her. She could see him with one child in his arms and another on his shoulders, looking as comfortable as he was when he was driving a tractor. 'Yes,' she said softly, 'I do want kids.' *With you.* The words floated through the air between them and for a moment she wondered if she'd said them out loud.

Ollie's eyes softened and crinkled in a familiar smile and for one brief moment she forgot about the world around them. There was no family crisis, no work commitments, just her and Ollie and the rest of their life together. If only reality were that simple, she thought as Christmas carols belted out of the stereo and Mr and Mrs Claus arrived.

Seventeen

Hadley had always loved Christmas mornings. That moment after you opened your eyes and suddenly remembered what day it was. The burst of excitement that followed and the eager anticipation of running into the lounge room to see if Santa had been.

Today she still awoke with that bubble of excitement inside her, but she was a little less eager to get out of bed this early.

She lay in bed and listened to the stillness of the old house she'd grown up in, and a swell of contentment surrounded her. There really was no place like home. The familiar creaks and the odd groan sounded from the roof and she smiled at the sounds. A new sound came to her and she pushed aside the blanket and climbed from her bed. She made her way down the hall to Linc's bedroom and eased the door open quietly. Cash was sitting on the edge of the bed gently rocking her daughter in her arms. Mia looked like she had no intention of going back to sleep.

'I'll take her so you can go back to sleep for a bit,' Hadley said, reaching out to take the soft bundle into her arms.

'You're an angel,' Cash said gratefully.

'That's me,' Hadley agreed. 'Isn't that right, Miss Mia?' She closed the door softly behind her and carried the baby out to the lounge room. It didn't matter how old she got, a Christmas tree lit up with twinkling lights and tinsel always made her happy. She turned on the stereo, making sure the volume was low, and sat cross-legged on the floor with Mia, enjoying the time with this precious little person while the rest of the house slept.

Slowly, one by one, the family emerged from their beds and gradually the room began to fill with the soft murmur of voices.

'I hope you're all enjoying the last civilised Christmas morning we'll have for a while,' Hadley said, handing Mia over to her parents as she got up to help her mother make coffee before they opened the presents. By the next year Mia would be mobile and it would be an early morning start for everyone. It would also bring back that special magic to Christmas that only small children could bring. She couldn't wait.

Christmas carols were in full swing by the time everyone was seated back in the lounge room with coffee. Hadley unwrapped her gift from Linc and Cash, feeling a little nervous at the way her brother was watching her so closely. She half expected something to blow up in her face as she opened the box inside, only to discover three smaller boxes. She pulled one out and opened the top, revealing a delicate bone china cup inside. The pretty pink, aqua and brown flowers made a garland around an elegantly swirled message. 'Aww, guys, this is . . .' she paused, her mouth dropping as she read, *Oh, for fuck's sake,* scrawled beautifully across the front.

Linc laughed at her reaction, and Cash watched her cautiously. 'I told him it wasn't a good idea.'

'And I told you, as soon as I saw it on the shelf of that gag shop, it was perfect for Hadley,' Linc shot back. 'You gotta read the others,' he said, reaching out to help her before she slapped his hand away. Making sure no one who may be offended was nearby, she carefully put the first mug down and stole a glance at the others. The second one said simply, *Fuckity, fuck, fuck,* in exquisite writing, making Hadley giggle. The third one had her shoulders shaking with sheer mirth. It was so wrong—*Off you fuck,* it said in writing that should be on wedding invitations, not inappropriate Christmas gifts.

'What did you get, darling?' Lavinia said, coming across to them before Hadley could close the lid of the box. 'Oh, how pretty,' her mother said, reaching to inspect one of the cups, before hearing her name called from the kitchen. 'Honestly, I don't know what your father does all day out there without me. Once he's home he can never find a blasted thing on his own.'

Hadley sent her older brother a look and shook her head. 'You better hope Mum doesn't see these or she'll wash your mouth out with soap.'

'I'll tell her it was Cash's idea.'

'Hey!' Cash said indignantly.

The morning was full of lazy teasing and Ollie knocked on the screen door just as they were about to start cooking the big barbecue breakfast feast.

'Merry Christmas,' Hadley said, her morning brightening, and she wondered when this new butterfly feeling each time she saw him would fade. It showed no signs of diminishing yet.

'Merry Christmas.' He lowered his head for a deep kiss.

'Aww, gross,' Griffin called out, earning an elbow in the ribs from Olivia and a glare from his mother.

'Come on,' Hadley said, rolling her eyes at her brother.

'Leave the door open,' her father called behind them as they went down the hallway towards her bedroom.

'I feel like I'm fifteen again,' Hadley groaned in mortification.

'I'm not sure he's actually joking,' Ollie said, pointedly making sure the bedroom door was open.

'Don't get too excited, this is only where your present is.'

'That sounds promising,' he said, sliding his arms around her hips and pulling her close against him.

After quite some time, she gently eased back to look up at him. 'I seriously didn't bring you in here just to get you alone.'

'I'm not complaining.'

'Here,' she said, leaning across him to pick up a brightly wrapped parcel.

She watched as he lifted out the T-shirt and held it up and read: *Farming: the art of losing money while working 400 hours a month to feed people who think you're trying to kill them.*

'I thought it quite appropriate in the current climate.'

There was a jeweller's box beneath the T-shirt. He opened it and stared quietly for a minute before looking over at her.

'I'm pretty sure even you can't break that one.' She nodded down at the lethal-looking black watch in the stainless-steel case. 'It tells you barometric pressure and has sensors to show your altitude,' she listed off. 'And most importantly, a scratch-resistant triple-coated sapphire crystal face.'

'This must have set you back a fortune,' he said doubtfully.

'Nah, I had Linc source it. He knows a guy,' she shrugged. Despite the generous mates' rate, it had still cost more than she'd realised a watch could cost.

He strapped it on his wrist and turned his arm to get a better look at it from each angle. 'It's awesome,' he said with a grin, before leaning down to kiss her and pull a slim, rectangular box from his pocket.

Hadley opened it to find a rose gold chain with a small compass pendant hanging from it. She gently picked it up and saw there was a set of numbers engraved on it. 'Are these coordinates?'

'That's the longitude and latitude of Stringybark Creek,' he said, lowering his voice, 'so you'll always be able to find your way home no matter where you go.'

Hadley's throat instantly closed up tight as she stared down at the delicate necklace. Her gaze blurred as tears welled and spilled over.

'You don't like it?' she heard him ask, sounding devastated.

'No. No, I love it,' she said quickly, sniffing and wiping her eyes with her fingertips. 'It's beautiful.' And it was. She was so touched by the sheer thoughtfulness of the gift. She'd been expecting maybe chocolates or a gift voucher to the beauty spa next door, not something this meaningful. He seriously couldn't have touched her any more deeply if he'd tried. 'It's perfect.'

'Are you sure?'

She lifted her gaze and smiled. 'I love it. Thank you.'

She saw relief filter through his expression and his shoulders lost some of their tension. 'I wasn't sure if it was too soppy. It's just . . .' he started and then paused, shifting uncomfortably. 'Look, I know you've always said we have to see where this goes, and I get that you can't be here forever . . . I just thought that your job takes you all over the world, and this place can't compare to that kind of excitement, but maybe, when you wear that, you'll carry this place with you.'

She swallowed hard. How did he always seem to pick up on what she was thinking and feeling? She'd never mentioned it to anyone, but the last year or so she'd often found herself sitting in some of the most iconic locations around the world and, instead of sitting in awe, she'd found herself thinking of home. She'd never been one to get homesick. She'd always been too busy trying to get her story and making sure she didn't get herself killed, but lately that had changed. Leaning forwards, she kissed him, trying to put the words she couldn't find into the kiss.

'Well? Did he propose?' Gran asked as they walked back into the family room.

'Oh my God, Gran,' Hadley groaned, feeling all eyes turn to them expectantly. 'No,' she added incredulously when they continued to wait. Her family seriously had no shame.

'You want to hurry up,' the older woman said with a scowl, eyeing all her grandchildren. 'I won't be here forever.'

'No pressure or anything,' Griff murmured, earning himself an elbow to the ribs from Olivia.

'Linc and Cash should be the ones you're hounding, Gran,' Hadley pointed out. 'They've had a baby and they're not even married yet.'

'Oh, nice. Throw me under the bus, why don't ya?' Linc scoffed.

'Come on, Gran. You're gonna outlive all of us,' Griffin said, handing his grandmother a glass of eggnog, which seemed to pacify her somewhat. 'Cash? Eggnog?' Griff asked, lifting an eyebrow.

'Funny, Griff,' Cash muttered, eyeing the drink warily, no doubt recalling her first Christmas experience with Gran's famous recipe. It was much like Gran herself—deceptively sweet and innocent, but packing an unexpected punch.

'Finally. Here's your sister,' Lavinia said with a note of relief as a car pulled up outside. Hadley suspected her mother had been worried her eldest daughter might not show up today.

As usual at any mention of her sister, Hadley felt a mix of anger, disappointment and sadness wash through her. It was a cocktail of emotions she wished would go away. Would she ever be able to look at her again without this heaviness hanging over her heart? She hoped so, but it wouldn't be any time soon.

'Merry Christmas, darling,' Lavinia called as she met her daughter at the top of the stairs.

'Sorry, we're late,' Hadley heard Harmony say, before her mother hugged her as she entered the room, squashing the bags she carried between them.

'Holder, Merry Christmas,' her mother called, releasing Harmony as Hadley's nephew appeared. 'Where's your sister . . . Oh!' Lavinia's surprise caused everyone to turn their heads towards the staircase.

'Payton,' Lavinia said weakly. 'You've changed your hair.'

'Changed your hair' was an understatement, Hadley thought as her niece appeared, her once long dark hair now cut short, with one side shaved completely and the other dyed bright blue.

Bob came out, spotting his daughter. 'Well, it's about time,' he started jovially, before letting out an almost breathless, 'Christ Almighty.'

'Robert,' Lavinia reprimanded faintly.

'What the hell have you done to your hair?' Bob continued, ignoring his wife's weak protest to shush.

'I got it coloured,' Payton said defensively.

'You look like a flaming peacock.' Bob shook his head, his expression flabbergasted. 'You let her do this to herself?' he asked, looking over at Harmony with a frown.

'It's what she wanted for Christmas,' Harmony said wearily and Hadley saw her shoulders sag slightly. Hadley felt some of her anger shift. Her sister looked close to tears. She couldn't recall her ever looking so defeated before.

'I guess we should be grateful she didn't want to put a bloody stick through her nose like some New Guinea highlander then,' Bob said sarcastically.

'It'll grow back,' Harmony said, heading for the kitchen.

'I think short hair suits you, Payton,' Cash said, coming to the rescue and breaking the awkward silence that followed the shocked reactions.

This was the ice-breaker everyone seemed to need to snap out of their stunned silence and there was a murmur of compliments before Linc brought over the presents and started handing them out, creating a timely distraction.

Hadley gave Ollie a quick kiss on the cheek and told him she'd be right back, then followed her sister into the kitchen. She wasn't sure what she was going to say once she got in there; she wasn't even sure why she felt a need to check on her, only that their father *had* been pretty harsh in his opinions and she hated seeing anyone upset.

She found Harmony standing at the sink, her hands braced on the edge and her head hanging low. She straightened immediately, hearing someone enter the room, and Hadley knew once she turned around there would be no sign of her earlier vulnerability.

'Are you okay?' Hadley asked.

'Oh, just wonderful. I love nothing better than to be attacked by my family and have to defend my child's appearance.'

'Come on, Harmony. Even you have to admit that's some statement Payton's making.'

'Yes, well, maybe she's entitled to have a moment of rebellion. Things haven't exactly been easy for either of them lately with a divorce and their father leaving.'

'Admittedly, I'm no parent, and I imagine a teenager would be a handful, but I think what's worrying Mum and Dad is that, as her mother, you probably could have stopped her from being so . . . extreme.'

'You're right. You aren't a parent and you have no idea what it's like. So you and your condescending, smug opinions can bugger off!'

'I wasn't trying to be condescending *or* smug. I'm just trying to explain Mum and Dad's reaction.'

'It's really none of your business.'

'It is my business. I was worried about you.'

'Since when? Come on, Hadley. You don't have to go to all this trouble just to get in Mum and Dad's good books. You're already the favourite child. You can do no wrong. We all know who the villain is here.'

'Whose fault is that?' Hadley snapped, then instantly regretted her remark. Every time she tried to put all this behind her, she ended up saying something snarky. Maybe it was still too soon.

'Mine, Hadley,' Harmony sighed sarcastically. 'It's always my fault.'

'Here you are,' Lavinia said, coming into the kitchen. 'We're giving out the presents, come out and join in.'

'Sure, Mum. I'll be right there,' Harmony smiled vaguely. 'Just bracing myself for another blast of Dad's disapproval.'

'It just took us by surprise. He'll come around.'

'Well, we'll only be here for lunch. We're heading off to Sydney later for a few days.'

'Sydney? Why?' Lavinia asked, frowning.

'I thought it might be nice to take the kids away for a break. We'll stay with a friend and play tourist for a few days. It'll do us all good to get out of town for a bit.'

Hadley had a fair idea who the friend was, but she didn't look at her sister. She already heard the note of self-justification and she could imagine her sister's defensive glint as she dared Hadley to comment. God, she was so sick of all this crap. She just wished everything was already out in the open once and for all. Actually, she wished this was a few years down the track and they'd all moved on. That wasn't about to happen any time soon, so meanwhile here they were, all stuck in this horrible holding pattern, waiting for everything to fall apart.

Eighteen

Hadley leaned back in the lounge chair and groaned. She couldn't believe the amount of food they'd just consumed. Why did she do this to herself every year? Because it was her mother's cooking, that's why. She and Linc used to joke that they'd gorge themselves at Christmas to make up for the rest of the year when they were away from home.

'So what's your plan, Hads?' Linc asked now as they recovered from the afternoon's overeating.

'My plan is to lie here until I can move without feeling like I'm going to explode.'

'That's not what I meant. Although it sounds like a good plan,' he nodded. 'I was wondering when you're going to stop hiding.'

'I'm not hiding.'

He lifted an eyebrow and she gave an irritated grunt. 'I am lying low, which is completely different.'

'Hey, I'm not saying I wouldn't do the same thing. You did the right thing by coming back here and staying as far away from those media vultures as you can. But does this mean you're giving up the foreign correspondent job?'

'No. I mean, it was kind of a mutual agreement with my boss that I take some time away when everything was set to blow up, but I was already coming home for Christmas anyway, so technically I'm just on annual leave at the moment.'

'Do you think you'll be able to make a relationship with Ollie work once you go back? I mean, it would put a bit of strain on things when you're away all the time.'

'It's not that much different to a lot of other jobs. Yours for instance ... the military ... fly-in fly-out work,' she shrugged. 'We'll make it work.'

'The success rates with relationships in all those fields aren't great.'

'What do you suggest I do? Give it up and become a stay-at-home mum?'

'Not at all. I think you've worked hard to get where you are. I'm proud of you, kiddo,' he said with a smile that slightly mollified her growing irritation. 'But I guess what I am saying is this thing with Ollie could be the real deal and maybe changing your direction might not be such a bad thing. And before you jump down my throat,' he said, putting up a hand, 'I've gotta tell you, if I'd met Cash when I was still in the service, I'd be rethinking my career too.

I don't think I'd have stayed in. When you find a relationship that works, a job just isn't worth the sacrifice.'

'I'm just not sure I'm ready to give up my career yet.'

'You might not have to do that. Look at me. I may have gotten out of the military, but I'm still using all my skills and training, just in a different environment. It's the same with you. There'd be any number of different ways you could use your skills without having to leave everyone you love behind for months on end.'

Her brother hadn't said anything she hadn't been thinking herself, but she hadn't realised just how much the rest of her family had been worrying about her. She knew it asked a lot of them, her line of work. Like Linc's career in the army had, it took her to some of the most dangerous parts of the world at some of the most perilous times—after earthquakes, lava flows, political unrest. She accepted the risk because she believed people's stories needed to be told. Would she be able to give that up? A year ago the question would have horrified her. Today though, she hesitated. There was only so much you could compartmentalise and there were some things that you simply couldn't forget or push to the back of your mind. Some images haunted you forever; for her it was faces of hurt children and grieving mothers. Over the years she'd learned how to tell the story and move on, but you never truly forgot those faces. They stayed with you.

Yes, she'd miss reporting on world events from out in the field, but there'd been times recently when she'd felt burnt out and disillusioned. She'd become cynical, and that had always been her greatest fear.

When she'd started out as a foreign correspondent, she'd sat next to an American journalist in an airport bar. She'd only been a few weeks in her official position and was full of excitement and burning with determination. After listening to the veteran reporter for the better part of an hour, she'd come away from the encounter vowing that if she ever became that jaded and bitter, she'd leave the job. There'd been something empty in his eyes as he'd given her sage advice and then begun telling her war stories. There was no life in his voice. He'd gone through three marriages and had kids he didn't even know. He was looking at retiring soon and Hadley suspected that terrified him more than any conflict he'd reported on or dangerous situation he'd found himself in. He had no life beyond his career. He had no real home and no one to miss him if he stayed away too long. It was sad.

A few years later she'd heard that he'd been killed in a plane crash somewhere up in the Amazon rainforest.

'Hey,' Ollie said later as he and Hadley lay in bed. 'What are you thinking about?' It crossed his mind that once upon a time he'd have laughed if anyone had told him he'd be willingly initiating a deep and meaningful conversation after sex, but it just went to show that when you found the one . . .

'Lots of things,' Hadley's reply interrupted his train of thought.

'Like?' he prodded, gently tracing a pattern along her arm as they lay comfortably entwined. God, he could lie like this forever and never get sick of it.

'My job,' she said after a long while, and turned slightly in his arms to look up at him. 'I want to go back, Ollie.'

His stomach dropped and disappointment, no, it was much more than that—gut-wrenching anguish—twisted his insides. There was no way he could cover up what he was feeling, not when she'd sprung it on him without warning like this.

'Wait, I haven't finished.' Clearly from the distraught look on her face, his dismay had been obvious.

He couldn't bring himself to get his hopes up, he was still hearing her tell him she wanted to go back. That she wanted to leave.

'I want to finish out my contract. I've got eight more months,' she said calmly. Too calmly? Was this a sign that maybe their relationship wasn't the biggest mistake of her life? 'Ollie?'

'Yeah. I'm listening. I'm just trying to digest it.' She was leaving him for eight months. The longest they'd been apart lately had been twenty-four hours and that had felt like a lifetime.

'I need time to plan what I'm going to do next. I've got some ideas—I really love the freelance work I've been doing and I have an editor who wants to talk about a permanent arrangement—but I need to take my time and consider all my options. I've worked too hard to get where I am to just give it all up without a plan. You know?'

He saw the searching look she gave him and took comfort in the fact that she hadn't given up on them completely. If she had, wouldn't she have just said she was going back and it was over? 'I get it.' *But eight freakin' months?*

'I know it seems like a long time.'

No shit. Eight months!

'But I'll be back and forth a lot and maybe we can have some time in Sydney together if you can get away.'

He tried to feel relieved that she wanted to make this work, but he couldn't stop thinking that a hell of a lot could happen in eight months. He knew she believed right now that she was ready to walk away from her job once her contract was finished, but what if she realised how dull life was here compared to the plane-hopping international one she was going back to?

It wasn't the happy-ever-after he'd been hoping for. Although he wasn't sure he'd ever believed, deep down, that she would give up her career, he'd been holding on to a wild hope.

'Ollie?'

'Yeah. No, of course you can't give up your job. I'll do whatever it takes,' he said, forcing a smile to his lips.

'You don't look very sure,' she said and he hated the worry he read in her eyes.

'I am. You just caught me off guard. I thought we had more time before we got to this bit.'

'I don't like leaving things till the last minute,' she told him and added a look that said, *You should know that by now*. And he did. 'I want to make sure we have a plan.'

'I like plans,' he said, coaxing her back into his arms again.

'You do?' she asked, and a small smile soon smoothed the tension from around her eyes.

'Absolutely. For instance, the plan I have for the rest of the night is one of my best.'

'Oh, really? And are you going to tell me what this plan is?'

'I think I'd rather show you,' he told her, leaning down to kiss her, effectively putting an end to any more making plans. At least until he had time to process the humdinger of a one she'd just dropped in his lap.

∞

Hadley sat cradling her coffee the next day, the remainder of its contents forgotten as she watched Cash nursing her baby.

'Hey, you okay?' Olivia asked, dragging her attention from mother and child.

'I'm fine,' Hadley said. 'Just tired. I had a late night.'

'Oh, I can only imagine,' Cash teased, looking up from her child's sleeping face.

'Gross, I'm trying not to imagine that,' Olivia said.

'Oh, come on, Liv. It's romantic,' Cash said wistfully. 'I remember hot sex . . . before babies,' she added.

'Eww. Gross. That's *my* brother,' Hadley said with mock indignation.

'It's impossible to have a conversation with anyone in this family,' Cash said, rolling her eyes.

'But seriously, Hads. What's going on?' Olivia prodded, and Hadley's hope that she'd dodged a bullet disappeared.

'I told Ollie I was going back to work.'

'Oh.' Olivia exchanged a glance with Cash.

'Oh, what?' Hadley demanded, eyeing the women.

'It's just that we were wondering what was going to happen,' Cash told her gently.

'And when,' Olivia added.

'It's not like it was unexpected,' Hadley pointed out.

'No,' Olivia agreed slowly.

'But?' Hadley prompted.

'I don't know. Maybe it's because he's my brother and I thought there might somehow be a miraculous happy ending.'

'I don't want to give up my job, Liv. I thought you of all people would get that.'

'I do,' she said quickly. 'And you shouldn't give up your job. I just want you both to be happy.'

'What is it that you really want, Hadley?' Cash asked quietly.

'What do I want?' she repeated. 'I *don't* want to give up my career that I've worked hard for.'

'I didn't ask what you didn't want . . . Don't think. Just say the first thing that comes to mind. What do you *want*?'

Ollie. It was Ollie that came to mind, and there was a flash of regret when she also saw an image of the two of them huddled together over a sleeping baby. She blinked quickly and swallowed past a tightening throat. Why was she thinking about that? Okay fine, so maybe that was what she wanted someday, but that didn't mean it was what she wanted now.

'What I want is to finish out my contract and find the perfect job to move on to. And don't look at each other like that,' she groaned.

'Like what?' Olivia protested.

'Like it's a big cop-out or something. I don't want to just hand my job over to someone like bloody Amber Latoy.'

'Who?' Cash asked, screwing up her nose.

'Never mind,' Hadley said. 'The point is, I want to finish what I've started. I do want to be with Ollie, and we've talked about it. We have the next eight months to get through and then we'll have a permanent solution.'

'And he's fine with this?' Olivia asked doubtfully.

'Yes, he is,' Hadley said firmly.

∞

'And you're okay with this?' Griffin asked Ollie as they shot a game of pool at the pub.

'It's not like I have much choice, is it. She's going back.'

'Eight months is a long-arse time to be apart,' Griff added doubtfully.

'It's doable,' Linc corrected his younger brother, looking pointedly at Ollie. 'It can be done.'

'Yeah,' Ollie said, taking his shot and sinking the ball. 'It's not so much the time away.' He lined up his next shot. 'I just don't know if she can give it up—the whole danger thing, you know?' He glanced across at Linc. If anyone knew about the adrenalin-rush career it was this guy.

'She never told Mitch she'd finish up her contract and leave the game,' Linc pointed out, taking a sip of his beer.

That was true.

'Look, there comes a time in everyone's life when they re-evaluate,' Linc continued. 'I think if Hadley's sayin' she's finishin' up in eight months, then you should take her word for it.'

'Maybe this whole Mitch scandal did you a favour,' Griff said, patting Ollie on the shoulder in mock sympathy as he missed the next shot.

'How do you figure that?'

'It forced Hads to lie low out here. I didn't think I'd ever see her hang around this long.'

Also true.

'So you two got the buck's night sorted?' Griff asked, changing the subject.

'What? We're supposed to throw you a buck's night?' Linc said, reaching for his beer. 'I didn't get the memo.'

'No one told me.' Ollie shook his head as he watched Griff set up the next shot.

'You better be throwing me a buck's night,' Griff warned.

'I'm pretty sure your lovely fiancée told us, quote, if anyone throws Griffin a buck's night, they will lose their nuts. Unquote. As I'm fairly partial to mine, I can safely say it won't be me who throws you a buck's night,' Linc said.

'Hey! She's getting a hen's night. I heard her talking to Hadley about it.'

'Why don't we just go to that then?' Ollie suggested.

'That's not a bad idea,' Linc said, straightening from his shot and considering the idea thoughtfully.

'I don't bloody think so,' Griff said, staring at them as though they'd both lost their minds. 'Oh, hang on. I see where this is goin',' he said slowly, eyeing them shrewdly. 'You're just yankin' my chain. Good one,' he slapped his brother on the shoulder but his grin faded a little as he looked between the two men uncertainly. 'You are, right?'

'Sure,' Linc said, returning to the table.

'You bastards better be sortin' something out.'

'It's your shout, Griff,' Linc grinned and his brother eyed them both narrowly and headed to the bar.

'So have you organised anything yet?' Ollie asked once the two of them were alone.

'Nope. You?'

'Nope, but I suppose we should,' Ollie sighed.

'Yeah. I guess so. But we'll let him stew a bit before we tell him.'

'He'd do no less for us,' Ollie agreed.

'Speaking of which. When are you gonna propose to my sister?'

The question surprised him. 'I don't know. I'm not actually sure she wants to get married again. The last time was a bit of a fizzer.'

'You talked to her about her it?'

'Not in so many words.'

'Don't let this whole disaster with Mitch throw you off. I know my little sister tends to put out this big, independent woman-of-the-world vibe, but I also know that family is important to her.'

If he thought proposing to Hadley would change her mind about going, he'd do it in a heartbeat, but he knew it wouldn't change anything. Besides, he wanted to wait until it was just them. No drama about Mitch and Harmony looming over them; no media speculation that would try and turn it all into a headline. If he was willing to wait eight months for Hadley, he could wait for the right time to ask her the most important question of their lives. He chuckled to himself as Kenny Rogers' 'The Gambler' came on the jukebox. Maybe it was an omen. He'd know when the time was right.

New Year's Eve came around too fast and Hadley felt a wave of melancholy fill her as she stood in front of the mirror putting in a pair of earrings. The end of a year always made her feel a little sad. As though she was saying goodbye forever to something. It hadn't been the best year by any stretch of the imagination, but she was still sad to see it go.

Cash and Linc were leaving for Brisbane the next day. Christmas was always officially over once everyone started going home. Usually she'd have been going home too—if she hadn't already left. This was strange, her being the one waving the others off.

The five siblings were heading to the pub and by the time they arrived the place was packed. It had taken Cash and

Linc a significant amount of time to go over the mile-long list of instructions for Lavinia, who was babysitting Mia for a few hours.

The evening sped past. Hadley caught up with old schoolfriends and thought back to the evenings out she'd had with Mitch. None of them had involved a pub with a live band playing 'Run to Paradise'. She tried to imagine Mitch standing here with her as she laughed with people she'd spent her childhood with, but couldn't. He'd never have come with her in the first place. This wasn't his world any more than the red carpet and glamorous opening nights was hers. She glanced across at Ollie who was talking with some other people nearby and caught his eye. She loved that they could share a smile and it felt as though there was no one else in the room with them. Her heart did a little flip and she almost groaned at how pathetically sappy she'd become.

'You look happy,' Ashley commented as she walked past, picking up glasses. Hadley gave her a weak smile, unsure if she was being sarcastic or not. It was hard to tell with Ashley. 'I mean it,' she said, giving Hadley a shy kind of grin. 'I know we don't really know each other well, I mean I was only with Griff for a bit of fun,' she said, before waving a hand impatiently, 'but I remember that Christmas, just before your wedding ... You didn't look as happy as you do now. That's all.'

'I am happy,' Hadley said and felt her smile widen.

'Ollie's a good fella. I'm kind of disappointed I never managed to bag him though. Now I know why,' she said shrewdly, before picking up her tray and flashing a bright smile, 'Oh, well. Plenty more fish in the sea as they say. Hooroo.'

Hadley was still trying to work out if she should be offended or relieved by Ashley's off-hand remark when Ollie came up to hand her another drink.

'What's up?'

'Nothing,' she chuckled. 'But I was thinking of bringing in the new year . . . naked,' she said and saw his interest pique instantly.

'Really? Not that I'm trying to be a killjoy, but that might get us kicked out of this joint.'

'Then we probably should go somewhere else.'

'Just to be on the safe side,' he agreed. 'Let's go.'

'You can think it over if you like,' she told him dryly.

'No need. I'm on board.'

'You're so easy, Dawson. Seriously.'

'Easy? Who said I won't make you work for it once we get home?'

'Really?' she asked doubtfully.

'Probably not.'

Later, in the early hours of the brand-new year, Hadley lay with one of Ollie's heavy arms across her side as she drifted off in a peaceful sleep. Now *that* was the way to send off the old year and see in the new. Maybe she'd look forward to New Year's Eve a lot more in the future.

Nineteen

The day of the fundraising high tea arrived and Hadley found herself immersed in an ocean of tulle and lace and crockery.

Her mother and the other ladies of the CWA had organised to bring in whatever fancy crockery they had. There were lots of heirloom tea sets and fine bone china and Hadley was a nervous wreck. How many of these beautiful cups would get broken today?

'You can't have a high tea without Royal Doulton,' her mother had said when she'd voiced her concerns. 'Besides, if we don't use them, they're going to sit in a cupboard gathering dust. Everyone was excited for an excuse to bring along their favourite cups. Speaking of which, has Griffin dropped in that box I forgot earlier?'

'What box?'

'The box of extra cups that were on the bench.'

'I haven't seen him, but I'll keep an eye out,' she said before Lavinia was called away to sort out another mini crisis.

Hadley looked around at the inside of the hall. Already it was looking amazing. They'd set up long rows of tables covered with white tablecloths and draped pink tulle across the backs of the chairs. More tulle and fairy lights had been draped from the roof to form a canopy and the lights twinkled prettily.

The kitchen was a hive of activity with women organising the delicious array of high tea delicacies to be served to the guests who'd paid to attend today's fundraiser.

'Darling, can you give them a hand in the kitchen?' her mother said, brushing past and giving out instructions like the seasoned general she was. Hadley placed the last dessert fork on the table she'd been setting and headed for the kitchen. She'd no sooner walked in than she was handed a plate of bread and a knife and told to find a spot and start buttering bread. As she scanned the available real estate at the long bench she discovered, to her inner dismay, that the only vacant place was between Harmony and Mavis Goodwin.

She forced a cheery face and set herself up.

'You have to butter right to the edges,' Harmony said as Hadley stacked her first two slices on the plate in front of them.

'They cut off the crusts anyway,' Hadley shot back. 'I'm saving butter.'

'I'm sure they'll appreciate that saving of point two of a gram of butter.'

'That's not the point though, is it,' Hadley forced through a brittle smile.

Mavis shot a quick glance between them and Hadley released her clenched jaw slightly for a more believable smile.

'Here, give me some of your pile and I'll help,' Harmony said, moving to take some of Hadley's bread.

'No,' Hadley snapped, causing Mavis to whip her head up in alarm. 'Thanks, but I can manage.'

'Oh, for goodness sake, Hadley, I've almost finished my pile. Let me help.'

'You've helped enough, thanks.'

She heard her sister's irritated sigh and continued to butter her bread, stopping short of the crust just because she knew Harmony would be watching and it would annoy her.

'Your mother mentioned you've been away for a few days,' Mavis said, glancing over at Harmony, no doubt trying to smooth things over.

'The children and I spent a few days in the city.'

Hadley was sure Mavis wasn't missing the increased tension.

'That must have been nice. Where did you stay?'

Hadley lifted an eyebrow as she waited for Harmony to answer. Her sister shifted slightly and concentrated with far more focus than was warranted to butter bread. 'Just with a friend . . . an old friend,' she quickly added.

'Oh? From school? Who was that then?' Mavis asked, clearly expecting to know the family—the woman knew literally everyone there was to know in the entire region.

'No, not from school,' Harmony said briskly.

'Oh.' Mavis looked confused, clearly wondering how she had missed Harmony somehow having made other friends at some point in her life, considering she'd never left town to go to university or to work between leaving school and getting married.

'So how did that visit go?' Hadley asked sweetly. 'I haven't seen you since you got back. You weren't gone very long.'

'It was fine,' Harmony said, although her smile, no doubt for Mavis's benefit, looked forced. 'I had to be back to help out here,' she added.

'Such a thoughtful girl,' Mavis said, nodding her approval.

'Selfless even,' Hadley added with a dramatic simper, which was apparently lost on Mavis as her head bobbed even faster in agreement.

'Well, that's my lot finished,' Harmony said briskly. 'I'll see what else Mum needs help with.'

'I don't know how she does it, raising a family, volunteering on all the committees . . . Harmony's so much like your mother that way,' Mavis said.

Hadley didn't trust herself to speak, so she simply smiled and continued buttering.

'Oh, heavens, dear. You might want to try not pressing the knife so hard.'

Hadley glanced down at the bread and saw she'd managed to rip the slice down the middle.

'Don't worry,' Mavis said sympathetically, 'your sister's had a lot more practice at this than you. You'll get there.'

Hadley counted to ten, slowly, and tried not to picture her sister's face on the next slice of bread she reached for. It was going to be a very long day.

∽

Hours later, the hall was like an episode of a *My Kitchen Rules* sudden death cook-off. She watched the seconds ticking down and frantically placed the finishing touches on plates and tables. With barely moments before the first of the guests arrived, she took one final look around and gave a relieved sigh.

Hadley could barely contain her delight as people began flowing into the room. Tables started to fill up and conversation soon became a dull roar as people caught up with friends they hadn't seen in a while and relaxed into what was proving to be a lovely afternoon. More importantly, Hadley was mentally adding up the money they were raising and knew this would be a very successful event.

Across the room, Hadley noticed Olivia trying to catch her eye. She was standing with Gran and a group of elderly ladies. Hadley sent her a confused look, but Liv's expression only grew more urgent, even though she was smiling and nodding at the women chatting around her. Hadley made her way across to her friend and followed Olivia's gaze as it darted pointedly to the woman beside her. Hadley had no idea what she was on about.

Olivia didn't say anything but continued to signal urgently towards the three ladies deeply immersed in conversation. Clearly something was wrong, and it was something Olivia couldn't say aloud . . . but what?

Hadley smiled at each of the women as Gran held out a hand to clasp hers gently. The other two women, Mary and Esther, greeted Hadley warmly, commenting on what a beautiful event it was. Hadley thanked them for coming along, her smile faltering slightly as she glanced down, and something familiar caught her eye.

Her startled gaze flew to Olivia who sent her a look back of, *I know! Do something!*

Hadley fought an impulse to close her eyes and pray it was an optical illusion. This was no illusion, though. It was really happening. The fine bone china the women sipped their coffee from had come from the box of cups Griffin had dropped off earlier. Only they weren't her mother's cups . . . they were *her* Christmas cups, from Linc and Cash.

'I just need to borrow Olivia for a moment,' Hadley said, grabbing hold of Liv's arm and moving away from the small group.

'How the hell did they end up here?' she whispered frantically.

'I have no idea.'

'We have to get rid of them,' Hadley whispered back desperately.

'Let's see if they need a refill,' Olivia suggested.

'Good idea,' Hadley said, relieved. They turned back to the women and Hadley forced her face into a serene smile. This was just perfect: a fancy high tea with all the prominent dignitaries in attendance and profanities written across the teacups.

'How about we get you all a nice refill,' Liv said, reaching for Mary's cup.

'Oh, no, I'm still going, thank you,' she said, moving the cup out of reach.

'I'm fine too,' Esther said. 'I do like this cup. Aren't there some gorgeous ones around nowadays?'

The other two women nodded in agreement and Gran turned hers around to examine the front. 'Just so delicate and pretty,' she said.

So delicate, Hadley thought faintly, thinking the words on the cup her gran held had never been more apt. *Fuckity, fuck, fuck!*

'I wish I'd brought my wretched reading glasses,' Gran continued. 'I can't read anything without them.'

Oh. Thank. God.

Hadley held her breath as the other two women squinted at theirs. 'I didn't bother with mine either,' Mary said. 'Never mind, they're very pretty.'

'New plan,' Hadley said under her breath to Olivia. 'We wait here until they finish, then confiscate the evidence.'

'Yep. Plan B it is,' Olivia sighed. 'Thank God for reading glasses,' she added, and they shared a small grin, but no sooner had they breathed a sigh of relief when a chirpy voice from behind called out, 'Big smiles, ladies.'

Hadley turned her head and watched in horror as the journalist from the local newspaper waved them all in closer. 'Let's hold those cups up high and say cheese,' she instructed.

The last thing Hadley heard before the click was Olivia echoing her own thoughts in a harsh whisper at the camera. '*Fuuuuuuuuuck.*'

Twenty

Ollie was wiping his eyes as he listened to his sister retelling the whole ordeal later that evening when the siblings were gathered at Griff and Olivia's house for dinner. 'So it's going to be in the paper?' he asked.

'Not if I can help it,' Hadley said eyeing him without amusement. 'I've left a message with Debbie, the journo, and as soon as she gets back to me I'll ask her to make sure she doesn't print the photo. This is all your fault.' Hadley glared at her brother, who was grinning at her.

'Don't blame me. I just picked up the box of cups Mum asked for.'

'Oh, and these just happened to be in there?' she said, holding up one of the cups they'd finally managed to wrestle off the women.

'Apparently,' Griff shrugged, leaning back in his chair.

'Yeah, right. This is exactly the kind of thing you'd do, thinking it would be funny, *Griffin*,' Hadley snapped.

'Uh-oh. *Griffin*,' Ollie mimicked. 'You're in trouble, mate.'

'Hads, I swear I had nothing to do with it,' he said, shaking his head. 'But I wish I had.'

'Look, it's done now,' Olivia said, always the diplomat. 'Debbie will see the funny side of it and delete the photo, and everything will be fine. You know how crazy things get when big social events happen around here. I know Mum goes into lunatic mode and she's the most sensible woman I know,' Liv said. 'If you weren't looking at them closely, you wouldn't even notice what the teacups said. She probably just ran around looking for suitable cups, saw these and put them in the box along with the others.'

It made sense, but Hadley was still mortified.

'Dinner's ready. Let's eat,' Olivia said, giving Hadley a sideways hug.

'Hads, don't worry about it,' Ollie said, taking her hands to make her look up at him. 'The day was a huge success. We raised heaps. Thank you.'

Maybe Ollie was right, maybe she needed to stop focusing on the one thing that went wrong and remember that a whole lot had actually gone right. They'd raised a lot of money today, and it was all going to the Royal Flying Doctors mental health unit, whose teams of clinicians offered twenty-four-hour tele-health services, as well as visits from mental health professionals to remote towns and properties. Those were the kinds of services that rural towns like theirs needed.

She and Ollie had spent a lot of time researching which charity would be the best fit for the money raised in Luke's honour. The information they'd uncovered had been startling. On average, people in rural and remote Australia died from suicide at twice the rate of those in the city yet were only able to access mental health services at a fifth of the rate of their city counterparts. Farmers, young men and Aboriginal people were among the most at risk of suicide, partly because of the lack of access to services and early intervention. It seemed a no-brainer that this was the charity they needed to help promote.

The coffee cup debacle was unfortunate but, Ollie was right, overall the day had been a huge success and she was very glad that it was over. She didn't know how her mother managed to make these fundraising events look so simple—they were exhausting.

Hadley made her way out of the bedroom to the kitchen, rubbing her eyes. The phone had woken her earlier, and as she reached the kitchen it was ringing again. Her mother answered. She glanced at her watch. It was an early start for whatever crisis the community hotline was sharing this morning.

Her father walked into the kitchen as she was reaching for the coffee, but she paused mid yawn when she saw his face.

'I have to go. Yes, he's just got back from town now. I'll call you later,' her mother was saying as she hung up.

'What's going on?' Hadley asked as her mum crossed the room, foregoing the usual morning greeting and grabbing the local paper from the bench.

'Oh, dear God,' her mother breathed, covering her mouth with one hand.

'What?' Hadley repeated, but suddenly she had a terrible feeling. She went across to stand beside her mother and saw the front-page story about the high tea. *NAUGHTY HAUGHTY HIGH TEA* was written above the photo of the three elderly, well-respected members of the community smiling happily at the camera. They were holding up teacups with words no respectable little old lady would ever be caught saying in public.

'The phone's been ringing all morning. Everyone's demanding to know what's going on,' Lavinia said. 'Hadley, do you know anything about this?'

She wasn't in the photo; she and Liv had been cropped out of it. Clearly a photo of three old ladies proudly holding up cups with profanities scrawled across them was what Debbie had wanted. *The conniving witch.*

Profani-tea anyone? the article began. *We are not amused! Local reporter, Debbie Winfellow, investigates the seedy underbelly of the high tea revolution.*

'Investigates, my arse,' Hadley muttered.

One would have to ask what kind of event would promote the use of foul language at a function attended by the Riverina elite. Where's the digni-tea in that?

Hadley rolled her eyes.

Could this augur the fall of the High Tea?

Hadley was furious. The article wasn't even about the fundraiser. It didn't mention how much money they had raised or why they were raising it. The whole point of the high tea had been to increase community awareness of mental health struggles. But, no, Debbie had decided she wanted to make fun of three old darlings who weren't even aware of what the stupid cups even said. Instead of talking about what a success the day had been, she'd written a scathing report of how a room full of women had spent the afternoon gossiping while gorging themselves on pastries, cake and profanity.

'Hadley!' her mother snapped.

'No, I didn't have anything to do with it . . . not intentionally,' she amended, and flinched when her mother narrowed her gaze. 'Somehow my Christmas gift cups got mixed up with the ones in the box from the house. I had no idea they were in there, and Griff swears it wasn't a practical joke. I don't know how it happened.'

'*That's* what was written on your cups?' her mother asked incredulously.

'Linc thought they'd be funny.'

'Oh, no,' Lavinia rubbed her temple with her fingertips then sighed. 'It's my fault. I was worried we didn't have enough cups, and I remembered your lovely ones from Christmas, so I put them in as extras in case we needed them. I forgot all about telling you once I got to the hall.'

'It wasn't your fault,' Hadley said, putting an arm around her mother's shoulders. 'You didn't know what was on them.'

'What was Linc thinking?' she demanded.

'It was just a joke. I'm sure Linc would be devastated if he knew something like this had happened. Look,' Hadley said, deciding to take charge of the situation, 'the only person to blame here is Debbie. I specifically told her *not* to run that photo. I explained what had happened, and she lied to me. She said she'd delete it and instead she ran a piece on it. She already had her nose out of joint because I refused to give her an exclusive interview before the wedding. I should have realised I couldn't trust her.'

'You let me deal with Debbie. Her editor is the husband of the vice president of the View Club. She's soon going to realise she's bitten off more than she can chew,' her mother vowed, stalking from the room.

Hadley was glad she wasn't the one on the end of that hardened glare.

✍

Hadley fumed as she waited on hold a few minutes later. Who the hell did this Debbie woman think she was? There was no talking her mother out of dealing with the situation in her own way, but Hadley intended to confront this head on.

'Hello, Debbie Winfellow speaking.'

'Debbie. Hadley Callahan.'

'Hadley, good morning,' Debbie answered, sounding remarkably calm.

'Is it, Debbie? Because my morning hasn't started out all that great.'

'Oh?'

'Why on earth would you publish that photo after I specifically asked you to delete it? Not to mention making a mockery of our fundraising efforts.'

'What can I say? It made a great story.'

'You've humiliated those women and have done who knows how much damage to the cause we're trying to promote.'

'Oh, come on, it was funny.'

'I'm not seeing it.'

'Admit it, this will get more people talking about your high tea than some run-of-the-mill recap. So, you're welcome,' she said smugly. 'I'm sorry, but I'm late for an appointment. Lovely chatting, talk soon.' And she hung up, leaving Hadley speechless on the other end.

She put the phone down and braced her hands on the kitchen bench. It frustrated her to admit, but maybe, just maybe, Debbie had a point. Hadley eyed the phone thoughtfully. They needed to turn this negative into a positive, but they had to act quickly.

She grabbed her phone and called Ollie.

'Hey, it's me. Can you come over later? I need to show you something.'

∞

Ollie had plenty of work to do, but he'd detected the strain in Hadley's voice and knew he wouldn't be able to wait until he'd finished work before he went over to make sure she was okay.

He had a bit of an idea what it was about—he'd already heard from his mother that the shit had well and truly hit the proverbial fan over the teacup scandal.

He climbed the steps of the Callahan house and found Hadley sitting at her computer on the verandah.

'Hey,' he said, loving the way the morning sun caught the tips of her hair.

'Hey. I didn't mean you had to drop everything and come over now. I hope you weren't doing anything important.'

'Nothing that won't keep. What's up?'

'I take it you've heard about the newspaper?'

'Yeah. Listen, Hads, it's going to be okay.'

'Oh, yeah, no . . . I know. That's not why I asked you to come over,' she said, waving a hand dismissively.

'Okay,' he said slowly, eyeing the way she was cracking her fingers nervously.

'So, I was thinking we need to turn this newspaper disaster around to work *for* us. We need to pounce on the publicity and use it to our advantage.'

'And how are we going to do that?'

'By taking this thing in a different direction.' He watched her get up and begin pacing. 'It's like you said earlier, having the community support things like the high tea is fine—it's better than fine, it's really awesome—but we need to think bigger than this. I think we need to aim this at a younger audience.'

'Any ideas on how we're going to do that?' he asked. He saw her nervousness fade and excitement replace it.

'I'm glad you asked,' she said, sending him a tentative smile. 'I think you need to be the face of the campaign.'

'Me?' he laughed, waiting for her to tell him she was kidding. When she didn't, his amusement turned to wariness.

'Okay, so you remember the photos I took a couple weeks ago? In the chaser bin.'

'Yeah.' His unease was growing by the minute. 'Hadley. What did you do?' Warning lights began flashing as she gave a small wince and turned her computer around to face him. He looked down at the screen and saw a Facebook page . . . along with a photo of himself reclining back in a bin full of lentils.

'You put it up on Facebook?' he yelped.

'I asked you about using it yesterday,' she said defensively, holding his alarmed stare. 'Before we hung up,' she added, as though to prompt his memory.

'You asked if you could put a photo of me on Facebook,' he agreed, 'but I didn't know you were talking about *that* photo.' She'd been taking photos the whole time she'd been home; he figured she was posting a photo of them *together*.

'You've got a hat covering your face, and I haven't used your name anywhere,' she reasoned. 'But before you freak out too much, look at this,' she said, coming out of her chair to stand beside him and point to the screen.

He followed her finger to a number at the bottom of the post. Two hundred shares and five thousand likes.

'I only posted this a little over five hours ago.'

'That's how many people have seen me naked?'

'That's how many people have interacted with this photo on social media. That's how many people have clicked on that photo. If we tie in this photo, *more* of these photos, with a message, with some kind of way to get people to talk about rural suicide . . . can you imagine the reach we'd have?'

'You want to use porn to get attention?'

'It's not porn,' she said rolling her eyes. 'You're strategic-ally covered. But let's face it, a calendar of naked . . . well, *anything* really, will always sell more copies than photos of landscapes. Naked farmers? Rural suicide awareness?' She held up her hands, weighing the words. 'They go together. It's marketing genius. We need to cause controversy in order to get people to notice us. Once we have their attention, we can start the conversation. You wanted to do something positive, Ollie . . . well, this is your chance. You need to be the face of this campaign. *You* need to drive this.'

'I don't know anything about marketing and campaigns.'

'You don't have to. I can do that part, but you have the passion and the drive. You're the soul of this whole thing and people will relate to you.'

He shook his head; this was crazy. She'd posted the damn photo on the internet! But part of him was kinda chuffed that he seemed to be getting a lot of likes. He reached out and scrolled through the comments and gave an embarrassed grunt as he read through them. Then he looked at the page itself. 'You made a page for it?'

Dare to Bare was written in big letters across the banner.

'We can change it to whatever you like. I was just experimenting with this to see what would happen. This is your baby, Ollie.'

'So we just post a heap of semi-naked photos?'

'At first maybe, but I was thinking we could get everyone we know to do similar photos, get a whole bunch and make a calendar to sell. All that research you were doing, all those places you found online to get help, we could list them in the calendar, and put a whole heap of other useful info in there. The photos are a bit of fun; they're a way to get people to have a bit of a laugh, then we can open up conversation about rural suicide.'

'I don't know about the photo thing, Hads. I mean, that was just muckin' around. I don't know if I wanna put myself out there like that.'

'We could open it up online, get other rural communities involved. Come on, you know what it's like out here, if one bloke does it, everyone else will want to do one even better. It'd be huge.'

Ollie considered her words silently for a few moments. 'It would be kinda cool, I guess.'

He smiled as she clapped her hands excitedly and beamed up at him. 'This is so exciting, so first we need to . . .'

He lost track of what she was saying. He'd just agreed to be the face—or rather, bare arse—of a campaign to bring awareness to rural suicide. All she'd had to do was turn those big blue eyes on him and he'd caved. Hell, who was he kidding? He'd run buck naked down the main street if she asked him to. There was very little Hadley Callahan could ask of him that he'd refuse. He was putty in her hands. Suddenly the thought of being in her hands began setting off a whole other train of thought and he had to pull on the brakes in order to listen to what she was saying. It was not an easy ask.

Twenty-one

'You're doing what?' Olivia asked, staring at him open-mouthed. She glanced at the Facebook page with her almost naked brother lying in a truck of lentils.

'Making a calendar.'

'I'm in,' Griff said immediately.

'What?' Olivia asked, almost giving herself whiplash as she turned to look at her fiancé.

'I'll do it. Come on, Liv, it's funny as hell. Naked farmers? Jeez, we used to do this stuff on a weekend just for entertainment.'

'As kids. Not as grown men,' she reminded him dryly.

'It's for a good cause,' Ollie told his sister.

'Yeah, I suppose it is,' she admitted grudgingly.

'Who else is in?' Griff asked.

'You're the first person I've told about it. I thought we could split up a list of names and call a few of the local lads. Hadley's doin' up an online request, so I reckon we should get at least the dozen we need for the calendar.'

'You know, I reckon Luke would have been the first one to put up his hand for something like this,' Griff said.

'I wish we'd decided to do this earlier. Maybe it'd have made a difference,' Ollie muttered.

'You think so?' Griff asked quietly.

'I have to believe it. Otherwise what's the point?' The three of them sat quietly for a few moments. 'Until Hadley brought all this up, I'd been feeling useless. You know?' He glanced up briefly then looked away. 'He was our mate. I thought we were always there for each other. I mean, we *are* always there for each other—look at how everyone pulled together when Dad had his accident. Blokes came from everywhere to lend a hand . . . we all do it, we help each other out. But when it comes to stuff like this, you know, emotional shit, it's like no one thinks anyone wants to hear about it. I keep thinkin' how desperate he must have been at the end. And how we could have stopped it . . . maybe . . . if he'd said something to someone. It's gotta change,' Ollie said and he hated how his voice shook a little, but that, too, was part of the problem. Being afraid what people might think if you showed any kind of emotion other than sarcasm or humour. Hell, even anger and swearing were acceptable in men, but other emotions, like sadness and fear, they were for women.

'I was thinking only last night,' Ollie continued, 'that we've made an art form out of insulting each other. Look how we always greet someone when we see them: "Hey, dickhead. Jeez, ya packin' on the weight".' Ollie gave a self-deprecating grunt. 'No wonder these backpackers look at us weird when they first come here. Who speaks to their *mates* like that?'

'Yeah, but come on, Ollie, that's the whole point. They're your mates. The meaner the insult, the more you like 'em.'

'That's what I mean. It's become a culture of putting each other down. You're supposed to be tough enough—thick-skinned enough—to take the worst insult anyone can throw at ya. Only what about when you're feeling really crappy? That night I saw Luke at the pub, the last time I saw him, I could tell he wasn't himself. But he couldn't have sat down and brought up whatever was goin' on with a tableful of blokes who would have called him a pussy and handed him another beer till he got over his mood. It's not good enough.'

A thoughtful silence followed and Ollie realised it felt good to get that out in the open.

'Maybe you've got a point,' Griffin said slowly. 'I've been guilty in the past of brushin' off someone who's down in the mouth as feelin' sorry for themselves.' He shrugged. 'I suppose we could take it a bit easier on the ribbin'.'

'Like you said, it's how it's always been. It's going to take time to change the way we do things.'

'Well, I'm proud of both my boys,' Olivia said, leaning over to kiss her fiancé, before smiling at Ollie. 'If anyone can make a difference it's you two.'

Ollie sat back, later that night, stretching his hands over his head. It'd been a long day, but he'd managed to achieve a lot. Hadley had released a few more of the photos she'd taken and interest in the Facebook page was growing at an alarming rate. For the first time since he'd heard about Luke's death, he felt the helplessness that had been twisting around inside his gut begin to loosen. If they could change the world for just one person, if they could get one person to ask for help, then it'd make all this worthwhile. He had to believe it would.

Over the next few days Hadley and Olivia, who had been dragged on board to help, were inundated with interest about the Dare to Bare Facebook page. Photos came pouring in, more than they could ever possibly use, and the media had begun to take notice. The high-tea fiasco had faded into oblivion as this new, even more outrageous story came to light.

Hadley bit back a grin as she passed some older women in town who were in the middle of expressing their outrage at the photos of *that Dawson boy*. She felt the heavy weight of their combined stares on her back, but she didn't turn around.

'So when do we get a copy of this famous nudie calendar I saw on Facebook last night?' asked Peg, the woman working the cash register in the local store.

'As soon as we can get them designed and printed,' Hadley smiled. 'Actually, I wanted to ask if you'd be interested in selling a few for us in here at the shop?'

'Happy to. I really like what you're all doing . . . the naked men are just an added bonus.'

'Well, they're not all going to be men. We have some pretty impressive women farmers sending in their photos too.'

'Hmm, maybe I should throw my hat in the ring then,' Peg said with a deep chuckle that shook her ample bosom.

'Anyone can contribute,' Hadley said, unsure if Peg was serious or not and deciding to cover her bases by being noncommittal.

'Put me down for three calendars and feel free to bring in a stack for the shop. Actually, have Ollie Dawson bring them in . . . I'd like my copy signed,' she said with a wink.

Ollie was going to really love that. Hadley decided not to tell him about his new-found local celebrity status. The poor guy wouldn't set foot in town ever again if he knew. Oh, well, she'd deal with that problem later. Right now she was excited that their cause was getting exposure. This was what Ollie had been hoping for—to make a real change. Behind the humour was a very serious topic, and she knew that this was a good approach to get people talking. Telling people to access help didn't work. Communication had to happen in a friendly, familiar environment. These people were a hard-working, tough breed. They didn't want to be reminded that they sometimes couldn't handle everything life threw at them. It had to be spoken about in a way that showed them they weren't the only ones finding life hard. If that meant showing a bunch of farmers in the nude, then so be it. Country people were down to earth and didn't much stand on ceremony. This was relatable. Humour was relatable. If it broke the ice, then maybe it would help. Their community couldn't continue to grieve year after year for the loss of their brothers, friends and husbands. Enough was bloody enough.

Ollie sat in front of his laptop and scrolled through his newsfeed. He should have been in bed, but he'd given in to the temptation to take a quick look at the Facebook page. *Dare to Bare*. He still chuckled when he saw the name. It was pretty awesome. His smile faded into an incredulous gape. The likes had gone through the roof, but what was even more remarkable were the comments.

There were hundreds of comments from people—people just like him, like his mates, his sister, his family. Everyday people who had been hurting as much as he had. Even more humbling were the comments from people like Luke. People who were afraid and lost and lonely and too scared to speak up . . . until now. He read through a few and felt his throat tighten; then his heart lifted as people—complete strangers—responded to these posts and begged them to open up and talk freely . . . which they did! He was gobsmacked. Literally. He was sitting at his computer in the middle of the night watching a miracle unfold before his eyes.

From the initial, heart-wrenching post to the final optimistic comment, he saw time and again people's transformation through the words of strangers. People poured out their problems and their grief and then others responded and gave them hope. Would this have saved Luke? If he'd found a place where he could unload his worry and despair, would it have changed his mind about going through with suicide?

He blinked and wiped at his eyes, realising with surprise that his face was wet.

He jumped slightly when Hadley spoke from the shadows behind the dim light of his computer screen.

'Couldn't sleep?' she asked, coming across and sliding onto his lap. 'What is it?' she asked, sitting up straighter as he swiped a hand across his face.

'Nothing.'

He saw her turn her attention to the screen and read through the page he had up, before lifting her gaze to his once more. 'It's working,' she said simply, placing her hands either side of his face gently.

'Yeah. It is.' Christ, where the hell had these bloody tears come from? He couldn't seem to stop them. It just felt so good to see some kind of light at the end of what had been a very long tunnel since losing his mate.

He saw the slow smile transform her face and he gently wiped his thumb under her eye to catch the tears that had spilled over. 'Thank you.'

'You knew something had to be done. This was all you, Ollie.'

'I couldn't have done it without you.'

'It's only just started. This is your baby now,' she said softly, kissing him gently. 'It's important, and there's a lot more work to be done.'

He had no idea what they were going to do with it now that they had this explosion of interest, but she was right, he'd been the one doing all the talking about needing a change of approach, and now that it was here, he was beginning to worry. 'I'm just a farmer. What do I know about any of this stuff?'

'Just a farmer?' she said and frowned. 'Would you stop it!'

'I'm being serious, Hads. What the hell do I know about mental health and counselling?'

'Firstly, you're not here to provide mental health care or counselling. We need to leave that to the professionals. This is like the pub. People feel free to come in and pull up a chair, have a chat, have a laugh at the photos, all the while, I might add, thinking to themselves, that would take a lot of guts to get naked like that and put the photo up for the entire world to see,' she said, scrolling through the Facebook page. 'But that gets the wheels turning. It starts opening people's minds to this stuff. Then someone says something in a comment that might resonate with them, and that might make them like the post,' she said. 'Maybe next time they come on they actually write a comment on someone's post, and then maybe they move on to write their own. It's taking that first step. Opening up lines of communication—everything you've talked about that was missing from Luke's situation. He might have been too embarrassed to talk with you or anyone else—maybe he needed a stranger, someone he thought might not judge him.'

'That's the point, though—I wouldn't have judged him if he'd talked to me.'

'Maybe not,' Hadley agreed gently, 'but maybe at the time, if you weren't aware of his mental state, if he covered it up in public, then you may have brushed off what he said as a joke or something. I think some of the problem with this whole thing is we're not a people who often open up. It's not something that we've seen our parents or grandparents do, and it's going to take time to change that pattern. Being able to talk to strangers online—connect with other people who might be struggling—it's a really positive start.'

'But what if that's not enough?'

'Then we make sure we're promoting places that people can go to. We pump the page with numbers of helplines. Places to find professionals, that kind of thing, so people can choose to reach out in their own time.'

Ollie nodded. Then a thought occurred to him. 'What about setting up pub nights?' he said slowly. 'Like casual kinda get-togethers in a place that isn't too daunting. I mean, most blokes I know would have to be dragged to a counsellor's office or a doctor's surgery, but it might be different if they knew it was in a familiar place, like a pub. Maybe down the track we could even get mental health workers to come along and talk to us there?'

'You're amazing, Oliver Dawson,' Hadley said softly, and when he glanced down at her, he felt his heart fill with so much gratitude and . . . love. The realisation took his breath away. He'd always thought he was in love with this woman, but it wasn't until this very moment that the actual meaning of the word hit home. The emotion flooded every cell, every inch of him, until he felt as though it threatened to explode from his body.

'I love you,' he said simply. 'I always have.'

He saw her eyes widen in surprise, moments before they filled with more tears. 'I love you too.'

He had doubts about a lot of things in his life right now, but the one thing there was absolutely no doubt about was his feelings for the woman he held in his arms. As long as he had her, he knew he could fumble his way through anything.

Hadley reached over to her bedside table and searched blindly for the source of the insistent noise that had woken her from a deep sleep. Grasping the phone, she managed to open her eyes and focus her blurry gaze on the lit-up screen as she swiped the answer button.

'Mitch? What the hell?' It probably wasn't the politest greeting, but it was her ex, so she wasn't going to feel guilty.

'Hadley, they're running the story about me and Harmony.'

'Who are?' she managed to get out once his words registered.

'Everyone. Morning TV. Newspapers. Radio.'

Hadley wasn't sure if she swore aloud or inside her head, but she didn't waste any time thinking about it. She tossed back the covers and disconnected the call, heading out her bedroom door. This was going to be a disaster. She could already hear movement in the kitchen and the chatter of the radio. She knew her parents would be up and about, despite the fact it was still dark outside.

As she entered the kitchen she saw both her parents listening intently to the radio, both wearing frowns, and her heart sank as she caught the last part of the news story.

'Hadley?' her mother said, turning towards her.

'I don't know how they found out.'

'It's true? What they're saying?' her father cut in abruptly.

'They shouldn't have broken the story like this.'

'They're saying Harmony and Mitch . . .'

'I know.'

'But . . . I don't understand,' her mother said dully.

'Harmony and Mitch have been having an affair. I wanted to tell you, but I didn't know how.'

'So instead we're finding out on national TV?'

'It was never supposed to get out this way. They were supposed to have their publicist handling it.'

'I can't believe you would keep us in the dark like this,' her mother snapped.

'I'm sorry, Mum,' Hadley said quietly. Damn it, this was not her fault. And yet she knew she could have broken the news to her parents at any point since she'd returned home. But it wasn't her place. Hadley clenched her teeth and focused on letting out a slow breath.

'You've known? All this time?' her father said, looking haggard.

'Yes.'

'I can't believe Harmony, of all people, would do this. Not after her own husband cheated on her.'

'They say they're in love, Mum,' she shrugged helplessly. 'I don't know. Maybe they are.'

'I can't believe she wouldn't tell us.'

The morning TV program came back from an ad break, and the first topic up for discussion was TV's golden boy and the leaked weekend footage about his mystery woman.

'*A reliable source has come forward to reveal the dirt on Mitch Samuals and the reason behind his recent marriage break-up to foreign correspondent Hadley Callahan. You remember all the hype over the wedding and the guest list—it was a who's who of Australian celebrities, and then the bombshell break-up not even a year afterwards,*' said the blonde gossip magazine editor, called in by the show as a supposed expert. The woman's eyes lit up with mischievous glee. '*Well, we now know the reason behind the split was because Mitch was having an affair,*' the editor revealed. '*And to make things even worse for the network's most highly paid and respectable current affairs personality, the woman he chose to have an affair with was Hadley Callahan's own sister,*' she said, eliciting mock gasps from the other two people on the panel.

'*Will there be any ramifications from this, do you think?*' the morning show host asked.

'*Let's face it, the channel executives have invested a significant amount of money here. There was that massive bidding war between the two TV networks for Mitch Samuals. And he's the highest paid presenter on Australian TV. He's had this reputation for being a clean-cut wholesome guy who's worked his way up the ladder through sheer talent and hard work. That good guy reputation will be taking a huge hit from this. He cheated on his wife with her sister,'* the woman stressed again. *'That's a pretty low act for anyone, but if your reputation is based on being a trusted, respected face of the news, then it's going to really cause an outrage.'*

'Is his career finished?' the host asked bluntly.

'I don't know if it will be career-ending, but it's certainly not going to go down well with his employers and I wouldn't be surprised if they pull him off the show for a while until this all passes. But they've invested too much money in him to sack him. So I'm guessing he won't lose too much face over this in the long run. Unlike his wife. Can you imagine how betrayed Hadley Callahan would be feeling right now?'

Hadley's dad stabbed at the remote and turned off the TV. 'Bloody vultures.'

'Oh, darling, I'm sorry,' her mum said, standing up to cross to her side. 'It was such a shock. I didn't stop to think . . .'

'I'm okay. I guess I've had time to come to terms with it. But I *am* sorry I didn't tell you what was going on. I really didn't want you to find out like this. I was just worried about how you'd take it. And there's Harmony . . . I felt as though it was her responsibility to tell you . . .'

'Yes. She should have said something. I knew she'd been going through a lot lately, but I never imagined anything like this.'

The house phone rang and Hadley's father stood up to answer it.

'No, Dad,' Hadley said quickly. 'Don't. It'll be reporters. Don't answer any calls today.'

'I'm calling Harmony,' her mother said, reaching for her mobile.

Hadley left them to it. She had enough problems of her own to deal with. She knew her phone would be going off its brain back in her room and she didn't even want to think about how full her inbox would be.

She avoided her phone and got dressed, pulling on jeans and a T-shirt before calling out to her parents that she was going next door. She didn't want to think about reporters and interview requests and old friends calling in favours for an exclusive. She just needed to find a decent cup of coffee and a sympathetic ear.

As she drove along the track that led to the Dawsons', a plume of dust up ahead alerted her to an approaching vehicle. She pulled her car over to the side as a familiar car came into sight.

'Hey. I was on my way over to your place,' Ollie said, climbing out of his four-wheel drive. He wore a concerned frown and her heart gave a kick.

'I guess you've heard,' she said dryly.

'Yeah. How does this crap make national news?'

'Don't you know? People love a juicy fall-from-grace story. Tall poppy syndrome and all that.'

'I don't give a toss about anyone tearin' down Samuals, but they're draggin' you through it all too.'

'Yeah, I know. I'd hoped things had died down and it'd just go away, but I should have known better. It's Mum and Dad I'm worried about. I'm so angry at Harmony for not telling them. I knew I should have followed through on my threat but, damn it, why should I be the one to do their dirty work?' Hadley gave a frustrated groan as she rested against the front of her car, tipping her head back and closing her eyes wearily.

'They must be in shock,' Ollie said, after settling beside her.

'They are, I think. The phone calls have already started. I feel so bad. They must be dreading having to face everyone.'

'It's not your fault. You weren't the one who did this. Harmony needs to step up and take responsibility.'

'I still should have realised it was inevitable. They should have been prepared.'

'Your parents have handled worse situations than this. They'll be okay. Besides, they have all of us to help deflect some of the scrutiny.'

He gathered her into his arms and for the briefest of moments Hadley felt safe from the world. She knew it was only a fantasy—no one was ever really safe from the world, and it could be a cruel place—but right here, in this instant, she allowed herself to believe it.

Twenty-two

'Is it true?' Linc's voice on the other end of the phone sounded deceptively calm. She knew her brother well and could imagine him sitting at his office, fist and jaw clenched tightly, waiting to hear confirmation. He wouldn't take gossip on TV as gospel; he'd wait and get it straight from the source.

'Yes,' she said quietly. 'It's true.'

The silence that followed reminded her how dangerous her brother's training had made him. This was not laid-back Linc. 'You knew about this at Christmas?'

'Yes,' she said.

'Why the hell didn't you tell me?'

'Because I didn't want drama to take over at Christmas time and ruin everything.'

'You could have told *me*, Hadley,' he said, and she heard the hurt in his tone.

It was true. Of all her siblings, Linc was the one she was closest to. Maybe it had to do with the fact they shared similar hobbies, like war zones and long absences from home. Or maybe it was just because he was her eldest brother and she'd always looked up to him. She understood why he was feeling a little hurt. 'I could have,' she said softly, 'but trust me, it hasn't been any kind of picnic knowing all this time.'

'I can't believe she'd do this. How long has it been going on?'

'A while. At least since your visit home when you announced Cash was pregnant.'

She heard him let out a long, slow expletive and could picture him running a hand through his short hair in a mixture of disbelief and frustration. 'You've kept it quiet *that* long? Christ, Hads, you didn't have to go through this alone.'

She didn't want to hurt him further by telling him that Ollie, Griff and Olivia knew. 'I wanted to tell everyone, in case something like this happened, but I just couldn't bring myself to do it. Christmas would have been ruined. Mum and Dad would have been devastated. It just wouldn't have been fair to everyone.'

'I can't believe Harmony would even consider doing something like this. I mean, I wouldn't have put it past Mitch . . . but Harmony? I know she can be selfish and self-centred at times, but I never thought she'd stoop this low.'

'I can't say it didn't hurt . . . it did—does. But I think it is more because it shows how far apart we've grown as sisters. And I don't know how it got this bad.'

'I don't think it's just you,' he said after a short sigh. 'Harmony's been unhappy for a long time and she's been distancing herself from all of us. I've been worried about her for a while. I should have sat her down and made her tell me what was going on. If I had, who knows, maybe she and Mitch might not have got together.'

'If it hadn't been her, it would have been someone else. Mitch and I haven't been much of a couple for a while now. I'm not sure we were ever really right for each other, and since his career took off, we've been even less compatible. You saw what it was like at the wedding. It was a circus—I hated what our life was becoming, but I let it go on. I knew I didn't want to be in the spotlight, dressing up for stupid black-tie events. He thrived in that kind of environment and I avoided it like the plague. It was always going to become an issue eventually.'

'I really look forward to seeing him again,' Linc grated.

'I don't think that's going to happen for a while yet.'

'How the hell do they even think this is gonna work? Surely Harmony doesn't believe she can just leave her family behind?'

'I don't know.' Hadley suddenly felt sad and weary. 'It's all a big ugly mess right now. I'm more worried about Mum and Dad. Linc, you should have seen the looks on their faces.' She stopped as hot tears pricked her eyes. It killed her to see them so hurt.

'I'm coming home.'

'What? You can't. You only just got back to work.'

'This is family. I'm booking a flight. I'll call you back when I have the details.'

He didn't give her time to reply, disconnecting the call without a goodbye. She'd been worrying for so long about how this would all pan out and it was turning out to be every bit as horrible as she'd imagined.

How was the family going to put all the pieces back together after this? Her heart ached for the damage that had been done and she wished she could go back in time and change everything. If only she hadn't been so stubborn and listened to what her gut was telling her before the wedding. If she hadn't gone through with the marriage, then none of this would have happened.

Would she have ended up with Ollie? Would she have finally seen him for who he really was? Or would it have been just like every other time she'd come home for Christmas—a quick visit and back into the next story? Who could say? But why was it that to get to the good things in life you usually had to go through a whole lot of pain first? Whoever made up those rules really needed to rethink things.

∽

The next day felt like a repeat of Christmas, only the opposite. If Christmas had a depressed twin, this would be it. Griffin arrived home after driving to Griffith to pick up Cash, Linc and Mia from the airport, and although the baby brought a smile to Lavinia's face, an overwhelming sadness hovered beneath that smile.

The phone wasn't ringing as much as it had yesterday, but there were reports of a camera crew hanging around town. Mitch wasn't faring quite as well, with a brief glimpse of him on the afternoon news angrily gesturing at photographers camped across the road from his apartment block. Luckily Harmony wasn't in Sydney, having left as soon as the news had broken.

Hadley noticed her mother was even quieter than before but was suddenly very busy in the kitchen.

'Can I help with something, Mum?'

'No, I've got it all under control,' she said, flashing her a distracted smile and making quick work of the remaining potatoes in the sink.

'You don't need to go to all this trouble for dinner, Mum.'

'It's no trouble. Just a roast.'

Hadley watched her mother with growing suspicion, which only strengthened when she noticed the dining room table had been set. Usually when everyone was home they ate out on the verandah. The dining room was only used for formal events. 'Why are we eating in here tonight?'

'Because I think we need to have a family dinner,' Lavinia said briskly. 'All the family.'

'Mum,' Hadley groaned, 'can we not do this tonight?'

'We need to get this out in the open. The way it should have been handled in the first place,' she added firmly.

There was nothing she could say to that.

'So Harmony's coming?' she asked doubtfully. It was hard to imagine her sister agreeing to a family crisis meeting.

'She'll be here,' Lavinia said briskly.

Hadley knew that tone. *Or else.* It didn't matter how old you got, when your mother used that particular tone, you were five years old again and not game to talk back. Hadley saw the strain on her mum's face and felt an equal mix of anger and guilt. She was furious that her husband and sister had put them all in this position to start with, but she knew she had to take some responsibility for the hurt they were suffering now.

'I'm sorry, Mum. I know I should have told you.'

'Hadley, I'm just so—' she stopped abruptly, and shook her head '—disappointed.' She finished. 'I'm not even sure who I'm more disappointed in: Harmony or Mitch. And I feel stupid.'

'Mum, no. Why would you feel like that? This was nothing you could have known about.'

'I've been furious at this other woman Mitch left you for, thinking terrible things and wondering how her parents could have raised a child who would even consider breaking up a marriage . . . and all this time I was the parent. I was the mother of this woman,' she said and looked up at Hadley tearfully. 'Only I'm so confused. I'm devastated for you, and I'm ashamed of Harmony, and yet I know her. I know that deep down she must truly believe she loves Mitch because the Harmony I raised has a good heart. She had such a terrible first marriage and I've been praying for her to find a good man, a man she could have a happy marriage with . . . I'm torn. I'm so incredibly angry at her, and my heart breaks for you, but at the same time, the feelings I had towards the woman who did this, the one I didn't know, I just can't feel that towards my own child.'

'Oh, Mum.' Hadley hugged her mother tight. This was exactly why she hadn't been able to bring herself to tell them the whole truth and why she felt so bad now. Maybe part of her had wanted to hang on to knowing how much her parents despised the faceless woman involved in the whole drama. Maybe this was her way of getting a tiny bit of smug satisfaction. But it had come at a cost and there was no pleasure in any of it. Just a whole lot of pain.

The sound of a car outside made Lavinia pull away and quickly wipe at her eyes. 'I'd better finish getting this ready. Your father's outside—why don't you go and freshen up and come out when you're ready?'

Hadley was hesitant to leave her mother, but she realised her parents probably wanted some time alone with Harmony. She didn't have to be asked twice—she wasn't in any great hurry for tonight's intervention, Callahan style.

'Do you want me to come over?' Ollie asked when she called him from her bedroom.

'I think Mum and Dad want it to be a closed discussion. But thanks anyway.'

'No worries. Let me know how it goes.'

'Will do.' She hung up and chewed the inside of her lip thoughtfully as she stared at the bedroom door. *Just get it over and done with*, she told herself firmly. Getting everything out in the open would be a good thing. As she walked down the hallway she could hear the murmur of voices coming from the verandah.

Swallowing over a sudden attack of nerves, she forced one foot in front of the other until she reached a spare chair. Her mother reached out and touched her hand as she passed by, giving her a small, encouraging smile as she took her seat.

Her father looked tired. The lines around his eyes, created by long hours working outdoors and squinting against the sun and wind and dust, seemed more pronounced than ever. Hadley sent a quick look across at her sister. Although her clothes were as fashionably chic as usual, there was a sense of disarray about her. She'd always appeared so confident and poised, but tonight she seemed vulnerable. Her eyes were pink-rimmed from recent tears and her usually immaculate makeup had all but washed away. She looked older and more drained than Hadley had ever seen her before.

Griff was across from Hadley, and Linc was sitting beside him, arms crossed and silent. She couldn't hold the concerned look she saw in his eyes, not if she wanted to keep her emotions in check and get through this with some shred of dignity.

'I'm glad you're all here,' Lavinia started, sounding far more in control than her saddened expression suggested. 'You know how important family is to us, and now more than ever I think we need to remember that we *are* a family. This has been a terrible shock to all of us,' she

261

said, looking between her two daughters. 'Hadley, we've spoken to Harmony. There were things I felt your father and I had a right to express to her. Now that we've had our say, we won't be speaking any more on the subject. You children and your happiness are the most important things to us. We celebrate all your successes and we feel all your disappointments,' she said slowly, holding each of her children's eyes as she swept around the circle, 'and if you've fallen along the way we've always been there to make sure you got back up on your feet again. This is no different.'

Hadley felt, more than saw, Griffin shuffle in his seat, clearly wanting to disagree but wisely keeping his mouth shut.

'Yes,' their mother conceded quickly, 'it's a very complicated issue, and as parents it's put us in a very difficult and heartbreaking position. But your father and I want you to know that we will always be there for *all* our children. If any of you need us, we will be here for you. Nothing you can ever do will change that. Having said that, I realise this is going to take a bit of effort to get through, but it's important that we make that effort. We are family.'

'How are we going to do that, Mum?' Griff finally spoke up. 'How's it all going to work? Family dinners will have Mitch sitting at the table with Harmony, right across from Hadley. Throwin' it all in her face.'

'Sitting across from Hadley and Ollie,' Harmony pointed out with a sharp glance at her youngest brother.

'That's not the point.'

'It *is* the point,' Harmony snapped. 'Mitch and Hadley didn't work. They've both moved on. Why can't you just be happy that we've all found the right person? You should be over the moon Hadley's finally with Ollie. He *is* your best friend, after all.'

The comment seemed to render Griff speechless.

'None of you wanted Hadley to marry Mitch to begin with, remember?' Harmony pointed out. 'So don't you think it's a bit hypocritical now to be jumping up and down about it?' She sat back in her chair calmly.

'I don't think it's the break-up that's the issue,' Linc put in, breaking his watchful silence. 'What we're having trouble accepting is the way in which it was done.'

Hadley saw her sister shift a little at that, but her jaw tilted forwards ever so slightly, almost as though she were preparing for attack. 'I'm not perfect, I'll be the first to admit that, but I dare any of you to stand up and say that you are,' she said lifting a perfectly shaped eyebrow in challenge.

Outwardly, her sister put on a good show, but Hadley knew she wasn't as tough as she was making out. Hadley had always hated watching anyone standing alone, and right now her older sister was facing her entire family on her own. Hadley couldn't help but feel sorry for her.

'There's a difference between not being perfect and sleeping with your sister's husband,' Griff said in a low growl.

'Okay,' Hadley said, stepping in before her siblings' anger threatened to ignite into all-out war. 'I get that everyone has a right to vent their feelings about this, and I know that it affects all of us to some degree, but at the end of the day what's happened is really between Mitch, Harmony and me. Yes, I was incredibly hurt by it and, yes, I felt betrayed by both Harmony and Mitch, but it's not entirely fair to blame it all on Harmony. Mitch was a willing partner in it all, and clearly, if he felt a need to become involved with someone else, then he wasn't happy with me. No,' Hadley said, holding her hand up to stop Griffin arguing. 'Sitting here and pointing fingers isn't going to do anything except cause even more stress for everyone. I don't know how things are going to go if Mitch comes to family gatherings. It's most likely going to be very weird and uncomfortable, but the honest truth is Mitch and I weren't happy and we were probably going to break up sooner or later. We're all just going to have to play it by ear and see how it goes.'

'So, how serious is it?' Linc asked Harmony, after a few moments of silence.

Harmony eyed her older brother warily, as if deciding whether he was genuinely interested or if it was another launching pad for an attack. 'It's serious. I'm planning on moving down to Sydney in the next few months.'

'What?' her parents asked in unison.

'I'm putting the house on the market. Mitch is going to drive out to help me pack up.'

'What about the kids? What do they think about that?' Lavinia asked.

'The children will finish out the school year here and then we'll move them down to live with us permanently.'

Hadley felt a surge of betrayal wash through her anew. Mitch had always been so vocal about how much of an inconvenience kids were. He'd often pointed out how lucky they were not to have to worry about finding a babysitter if they wanted a night out together, or to be able sleep in on weekends when their friend were up at the crack of dawn with their children. Clearly he'd had a change of heart somewhere along the line. Although teenagers probably valued sleep even more than he did, so that was no doubt a factor in their favour.

'So they know all about it?' Bob asked, frowning.

'They know.'

'And how did you explain that?' Griffin asked dryly.

'Unlike you, my children actually grasped the complexity of the situation remarkably well,' Harmony told Griff dismissively. 'They quite like Mitch and they're excited about moving to the city.'

They all looked over as Lavinia stood up abruptly.

'Mum?' Linc said, half rising from his seat.

'I need to check on dinner. I'll be right back,' she said without looking at anyone and walking briskly to the kitchen door.

'It's all been a bit of a shock,' Bob said gruffly as the rest of them exchanged worried glances.

'I'll go and talk to her,' Harmony said, surprising Hadley. She paused, turning back slightly to face them. 'I know what I've done is hard for everyone to understand. I'm truly sorry for the hurt it's caused you, Hadley,' she said, her voice thickening slightly. 'I don't expect you to forgive me, but I do hope that one day, when things have settled down, you'll see that Mitch and I really do love each other and we just want a chance to have a happy life together. I'll check on Mum and let her know I won't be staying for dinner.'

Hadley swallowed hard over the lump in her own throat as she watched her sister head inside. And judging by the sudden silence from the rest of the family, it appeared Harmony's words had caught them off guard too.

Hadley looked up as her father's big hand gently covered her own. She gave him a weak smile. A few minutes later they heard the sound of a car starting up and driving away and their mother called them in for dinner.

The meal was a sombre one, but at least everything was now out in the open and there were no more secrets. She only wished she didn't feel so torn inside each time she looked up and saw the grief in her mother's eyes.

Twenty-three

While so many things seemed to be falling apart around her, the Dare to Bare Facebook page was not one of them. Calendar sales were going through the roof; they'd already had to do a second run and that wasn't looking like it would last too long either. The mail orders were a full-time job on their own, and they were now working out of Ollie's house and Griff's, both of which were wall-to-wall with boxes of calendars.

'You know this is crazy, right?' Olivia said, shaking her head at Hadley after sealing the last envelope containing a calendar and adding it to the stack on the table ready to take to the post office later that afternoon.

'It's insane,' Hadley agreed.

'We're going to have to get some help in here. I have to get back to work and you can't handle all this alone,' Olivia said, looking at the stacked boxes worriedly.

'Mum said she'll give me a hand tomorrow, and I'm sure she can rope in a few volunteers if we're struggling.'

'I can't believe how fast this thing has taken off.'

Hadley was torn between excitement and dismay. Ollie had only done a few radio interviews before the orders for calendars had started pouring in. Over the next few days the local news network was scheduled to do an interview, and Hadley's freelance pieces were due to come out within the next few weeks.

'How's your mum doing?' Olivia asked. '*Really* doing,' she added. 'I know she tells everyone she's fine, but ... well ... you know your mother, keep busy and all that.'

She knew exactly what Liv meant. Her mum had practically invented the whole stress-cleaning thing—if she was worried, she cleaned; if she was angry, she cleaned; if her family was falling apart at the seams, she went through the entire house and cleaned it from top to bottom. 'I tried to talk to her but I think it only makes it worse.'

'I can't see why it would. This is not your fault, Hads.'

'I know, and it's not that she blames me, it's more that she gets so upset about everything all over again. Dad says to give her some space—which is pretty much what he's been doing—and she'll come good, but I don't know ... maybe he's right. It has been a huge shock. It took me time to get *my* head straight.' The two women shared a lopsided grin. 'I'm really sorry, Liv. I was a shitty friend taking it out on you the way I did.'

'Don't start that again,' Olivia warned, shaking her head. She'd been the one to discover Mitch and Harmony's affair. It hadn't been one of Hadley's finer moments, the day Liv had told her what she'd seen.

'I'm only going to say this one more time then we'll never speak of it again, okay?' Hadley said, waiting for her friend to look up from the box she'd just finished packing. 'I get it. I really get how hard it must have been for you to come and tell me about Mitch and Harmony. I'm so sorry I didn't believe you at first.'

'You were in shock. Just like your parents are now,' Olivia said. 'I knew it was hard for you and, besides, there was a whole heap of other stuff going on at the time. I knew you just needed some time to process it.'

'Yeah, but I couldn't even bring myself to tell Mum and Dad. I wimped out.'

'Well, if you recall, your annoying brother pretty much frogmarched me over here, so it's not like I had much choice. And don't be too hard on yourself for not telling them. Who knows when I would have told you—I mean, I was waiting for the *right time* too, and it may never have come. So Griff probably did us both a favour.'

'I just wish everything was back to normal. You know what Mum's like . . . it's going to kill her if Harmony and the kids stop coming around. Their leaving town is going to be hard enough on her, but it'll break her heart if the whole family isn't ever together anymore.'

'Just give it time. Underneath that ice queen exterior, we both know Harmony has a heart. It may be buried down pretty deep,' she admitted, 'but she's a Callahan and family matters. She won't let anything come between that.'

Hadley gave a small smile. She hoped Liv was right.

'And what about you? How are you coping with it all now?'

'Mitch and Harmony?' She saw Olivia nod and thought about it for a moment. 'You know, I actually feel sorry for them. I know it sounds dumb, but they're doing it tough with all the media attention at the moment. If this thing between them is real, then I can only imagine the stress it must be putting on them. I seriously wouldn't wish that on anyone.'

'Have you forgiven them?'

'I don't know if I'd call it forgiveness,' Hadley said slowly. 'I was hurt that Harmony didn't have the decency to make Mitch end our marriage before they started anything, but I'm not hurt because Mitch and I are getting a divorce. I don't think it was ever really love between us. Not if it isn't hurting that it's over.'

A sudden realisation hit her. She knew without a doubt that if she and Ollie ended this, even after only a month or so of being together, she'd be devastated. The thought both sobered her and reinforced something. She was in love with Ollie and she knew that was something special. Something she couldn't throw away.

Could she really leave him for eight months to finish her contract? Once she would have been certain she could.

Her job meant everything to her. But now she wasn't so sure. Damn it. Just when she thought she had everything figured out, love went and messed up her plans.

∽

Hadley disconnected the call and put the phone down on the table, swearing silently. She'd had pitches turned down before—not often, but it still happened now and again. However, having the pitch she'd just made to her network's morning show turned down was somewhat of a shock. What the hell? Admittedly she'd never worked with the morning show's editor before, but it wasn't as though Hadley was some rookie journalist. She'd been doing them a favour, for crying out loud, in approaching them to do a story on the Dare to Bare calendar. All they had to do was send out a crew.

Something felt off about it. She didn't like jumping to conclusions, but the most obvious reason behind the rejection was that the network didn't want to risk giving Hadley any kind of airtime while they were trying to keep a lid on the whole divorce scandal. What did they think she'd do? Have a rant live on air? That's probably exactly what they feared, she conceded with a small grunt. They were circling the wagons to protect their wholesome, clean-cut poster boy or, more realistically, their investment.

It made her feel . . . expendable. The more Hadley thought about it the angrier she got. She snatched up the phone and scrolled through her phone contacts, her thumb hovering over a number. She chewed her bottom lip as she considered the implications of this decision, then let out a resigned sigh and pressed the number. Listening to it connect in her ear, she barely had time to go over what she was going to say before a crisp, businesslike voice answered: 'Hillary speaking.'

'Hi, Vanessa. It's Hadley Callahan.'

There was a brief pause on the other end of the line before Vanessa Hillary, producer of her network's rival morning show, gave a surprised chuckle. 'Hadley. What a lovely surprise. To what do I owe the pleasure of your call?'

Hadley could practically hear the woman's mind ticking over as she tried to work out an angle. 'I was hoping you might be interested in covering an exciting new campaign aimed at rural suicide prevention. It centres around a calendar featuring naked farmers.'

'Naked farmers?'

'It's all done very tastefully, but the underlying message is very serious. The rate of suicide in rural Australia is fifty per cent higher than in capital cities. Also, numbers of male deaths by suicide are three times greater than female deaths. With these facts in mind, it's become apparent that there needs to be some kind of change in how and who we target in a campaign to try to improve those figures.' Hadley paused to take a breath. 'There's a group of farmers who've come up with an idea to change the approach around mental health conversations.'

'By getting naked?' Vanessa asked doubtfully.

'By *using* getting naked to catch the attention of younger farmers and people in rural Australia. Suicide is a very hard subject to talk about—especially when so many people are touched by it in some way. Every rural town across Australia has a heartbreaking story to tell about young people taking their lives. It's destroying whole communities. We have to break the cycle and this is as good an idea as anything. If it's approached from a more larrikin angle, it might have a better chance of getting through to people.'

'I wasn't expecting a pitch quite like this from you.'

'It's a little left field,' she agreed, determined not to be the one who brought up anything to do with Mitch or the divorce.

'So how exactly are you involved in all this?'

'It was started by a group of young farmers in my home town. I'd like to see them succeed. I'm hoping you might send someone out to do a feature on them.'

On the other end of the line, Hadley heard Vanessa give a drawn-out sigh and braced herself. 'I don't know, Hadley.'

'Oh, come on Vanessa. Hot, naked young farmers in a calendar . . . it's a ratings shoe-in.'

'And why would you be bringing it to us instead of your network?' Hadley could almost picture the woman's eyes narrowing shrewdly.

'They didn't want it,' she said simply. She was too tired to play any more games.

'I see.' There was a wealth of meaning behind those two little words. 'I agree it certainly has merit,' she finally admitted when Hadley remained silent. 'But I may need something a bit more substantial . . . for my boss to agree.'

She understood all right. An image of a piranha flashed before her eyes. 'Really? Like what?'

'An interview. About your divorce. You know, just so people can hear your side of it. I think many people feel invested in your relationship after so much publicity around your wedding. The viewers feel as though they know you. I'm sure they'd want to see that you're all right. It would give them closure, so to speak.'

'You want to give the public closure . . . on my failed marriage?'

'Come on, Hadley. You know how it works. Unless of course you've been slapped with a no-talk order?'

Hadley glanced down at her hand and realised it was clenched. Tightly. She forced herself to release it, letting out a slow breath. 'I do not have any kind of order on me,' she said, striving for a calmness she was far from feeling. Mitch's request was not an order, she reminded herself firmly. She chose to go along with remaining silent out of respect for her family—not because her bosses told her to.

'Oh. Well, in that case, there's nothing stopping you from telling your side of the story, is there.'

Only common decency, she thought bitterly. Something no one in this business apparently thought much of. 'I'm not going to talk about my marriage, Vanessa.'

'I understand,' the other woman said. She couldn't have sounded any more fake if she'd tried. 'Unfortunately I don't think your farmer story will suit our line-up at the moment. I'm very sorry.'

Faker. 'That is a shame. I know that a lot of your viewers live in rural Australia, so they'll be very disappointed to hear that your show doesn't consider something that concerns them important enough for a story. Still, thanks for your time, Vanessa.'

'If you change your mind about that interview, we might be able to reconsider,' Vanessa slipped in before Hadley had the satisfaction of hanging up on her. She didn't bother responding, but pressed the disconnect button on her phone a little harder than was necessary.

Where was a decent sweary teacup when you needed one?

∽

Ollie grinned as he got down from his tractor and walked across to Hadley, loving the feel of her body pressed tightly up against his own as she greeted him with a kiss. 'I could get used to this,' he said, then frowned a little as she went still. Damn it. He hadn't meant to say it aloud. Despite the moment they'd had a few nights ago, the future was still a touchy subject and one that had a bad habit of ruining perfectly good moments. 'What are you doing here?' he asked, ignoring any awkwardness.

'I came out to show you this,' she said, moving out of his embrace to hand him her phone.

He looked down at the screen and read the email, then looked up at her in alarm. 'What? Are you serious?'

'Yep,' she said with a calm smile. 'They want to come out and do a live interview with you.'

'On TV?' He knew what he'd just read, but somehow his brain was feeling completely overwhelmed by the idea.

'On breakfast TV,' she added, sounding far too impressed by the news.

'I don't know about that,' he hedged, handing back the phone. He hadn't even wanted his photo taken, let alone to be on national television.

'Come on, Ollie. You're the face of this campaign. You have to take the helm.'

'It wasn't exactly my face that caught everyone's attention, if you recall,' he added dryly. The initial photo in the lentils had been swiftly followed by one of him climbing down the side of the chaser bin. He still cringed a little at the thought of his naked arse being posted and shared on social media more times than he cared to think about, despite the fact you couldn't really tell who it was.

'Oh, trust me, the face didn't hurt. You've got women everywhere swooning.'

'I don't want women everywhere,' he said, slipping his arms around her waist and lowering his head to nuzzle her neck. 'I just want one woman in particular.'

'And that woman is very relieved to hear it,' she murmured, and he grinned when he heard the slightly slurred reply, knowing he'd found her weak spot. 'However,' she said, recovering slightly, 'we need the publicity and we need to jump on this now.'

'I don't know anything about being interviewed on TV.'

'There's nothing to it. We'll get them to run you through the questions they'll be asking so you know what you want to say and it'll be over in a few minutes. Quick and painless,' she said.

'That's not something a guy should ever feel proud of.

Just sayin'.' He grinned as she rolled her eyes. 'I'm about to finish up. You hanging around?'

'I need to get back and help with dinner. You do remember it's Cash and Linc's farewell dinner tonight, didn't you?'

'How many farewells do they get? Didn't we just do one of those?' he joked. Where the Callahans were concerned, there was no such thing as too many family dinners.

'They keep coming back,' Hadley shrugged.

He gathered her close again as a sudden thought caught him off guard. The next farewell dinner would be for Hadley. Christ, how many of those had he endured over the years? Too bloody many. It should feel different this time, only it didn't. Not really. His gut dropped to his feet just like it always had when he thought of her leaving, only this time it was even worse. This time she was so much more than Hadley, sister of his best friend, long-time neighbour. This time she had his whole heart—his very future—packed up in her bag. Every time he tried to imagine her gone, he came up against a wall. His mind refused to even picture daily life without her nearby. Deep down, he still hoped, somehow, she'd change her mind about going back. There was still time to help her change it. He just had to figure out how.

Twenty-four

Less than forty-eight hours later, Ollie stared at the scene before him with a mixture of horror and trepidation. He'd gone to check on the cattle he'd moved up to the top paddock yesterday, and when he came back, it was to find a cluster of cameras and lights and a heap of other paraphernalia he had no idea about set up on his parents' front yard. And where the hell had all these people come from? He watched them running about like ants, carrying stuff and checking equipment.

A woman he instantly recognised from the TV was talking to Hadley but stopped speaking as she spotted him. 'You must be Ollie,' she said, her gaze roaming the length of him before adding in a low throaty purr, 'I recognise you from the photo. I'm Cynthia Rivers.'

He was never going to live down that bloody photo. 'Yeah. Hi. Nice to meet you.'

'The pleasure's all mine. So,' she said abruptly, clapping her hands, 'we thought we'd start with you, Hadley.'

Ollie glanced over at Hadley and caught the slight grimace on her face before she gave a quick nod. That was weird. He'd tried to get out of all this initially, hoping she'd do the interview, given she was the one with experience in front of a camera, but he'd conceded that the risk they'd bring up her divorce was too great. She hadn't mentioned she'd changed her mind.

'This won't take long,' Cynthia said, placing a long, slender hand on Ollie's arm. 'Then we'll get to you and we can talk about your new venture.'

His gaze swivelled once more to Hadley. She sent him a smile that didn't reach her eyes and he instantly had a bad feeling. Something was not right here. 'Hadley,' he said, reaching out to stop her turning away. 'Excuse us for a moment,' Ollie said to a surprised Cynthia. 'I just need a word.'

He moved Hadley far enough away to have some privacy before looking down at her. 'What's going on?'

'Nothing. It's just a thing I said I'd do.'

'A thing?'

'Look, it's no big deal. They agreed to come out here and do a segment on Dare to Bare if I gave them a quick interview.'

'About Mitch?' he prodded, frowning. This was exactly what she'd been avoiding the press about. What the hell was going on?

'It's fine.'

'It's not fine.' She looked miserable. 'Was this the only way they'd do the story?'

'We need this exposure, Ollie.'

'Not if it means you have to talk about Mitch when you don't want to.'

'I can handle Cynthia. I won't say anything I don't want to.'

He had no doubt that Hadley could handle herself, but this was a live interview. He didn't know a lot about the TV industry, but he knew that being interviewed live would make it a lot harder to dodge invasive questions. 'No,' he said abruptly, 'I don't want you to do this. I know you don't want to either.'

'Ollie, it's the only way they're going to do the story on Dare to Bare. It's important.'

'You should have told me they had terms, Hadley.' There was no way he would have agreed to blackmail.

'And we would have missed out on this opportunity,' she told him pointedly.

'Well, screw 'em. I won't do it.'

'You *will* do it,' she told him firmly.

He went to open his mouth to argue, only to realise she had that steely glint in her eye that he recognised from their years growing up together; he knew they'd be here all day if he started anything. Letting out a long breath, he took a mental step back. 'I don't want you to do this,' he said simply. 'I hate feeling like some pawn in a game they're playing. I *know* you don't want to do it either.'

His softer tone seemed to diffuse her own anger and he saw her shoulders drop slightly. 'Do you remember after Luke's funeral? Remember how badly you wanted to do something? To stop it happening to other people?'

A brief, sharp pain stabbed his chest at the memory. 'Of course I do.'

'This is your chance. This is what will help make that change. We are not going to let a stupid, insignificant thing ruin this opportunity.'

Damn it. He knew she was right, but . . . damn it. 'Okay,' he said after a few moments. 'So here's what we do. We'll tell them you'll give a statement, not an interview.'

'She's not going to accept that.'

'She won't have a choice. Look, they're here now and they're set up. It'd be stupid to have come all this way without doing the interview with Dare to Bare. Plus,' he said, taking out his phone, 'I'll show her the number of likes the page has got in the last twenty-four hours. They'd be crazy not to do the story on us.'

∽

Hadley dropped her head. He was right. They probably wouldn't pull up and leave if she refused to talk to them . . . It wasn't as though she'd accepted any money for the interview or signed a contract to do it. She could give a statement, but things were going to get extremely messy and awkward.

'Is everything all right over here?' Cynthia asked, picking her way carefully across the yard.

'Everything's fine. Just a change of plans,' Ollie answered before Hadley could open her mouth. 'Hadley won't be doing an interview. She's prepared to give a statement, but there won't be a live interview.'

'That wasn't our deal,' Cynthia pointed out, her fake smile threatening to crack like glass at the slightest movement.

'If I'd known there *was* a deal, you can bet your sweet ar—'

'I'm happy to release a statement, Cynthia,' Hadley cut in quickly.

'I was sent here to get an interview,' the other woman said tightly.

Hadley suddenly found herself back in control. 'You'll be the only network that's managed to secure a statement. I haven't even given my own network one, so take it or leave it.'

The woman was not happy, that was more than obvious; however, after taking it to her producer and having an impromptu phone conference, she came back and reluctantly announced they would accept the statement. And thanks to the interruption, they were now rapidly approaching the time slot scheduled for the live cross to interview Ollie for Dare to Bare, so any further drama was cut short.

The interview went better than Hadley could have imagined. Ollie was a natural on camera—he told his story briefly, yet with so much heart that when he spoke about Luke's death, she noticed she wasn't the only one who had to blink away tears. Quite a few of the TV crew also seemed to have something in their eye that needed to be quickly wiped away. Everyone other than Cynthia, of course. Nothing seemed to crack that cool, sophisticated shell.

After the live cross was over, Cynthia sent her assistant over to inform her she'd be waiting for Hadley to give her statement.

'Want me to come with you?' Ollie asked, taking the bottle of water she offered and downing it quickly. Off camera he wasn't as calm, cool and collected as he'd seemed.

'No, I'll be fine. You were great.'

He sent her a doubtful glance before finishing the last of the water and screwing the lid back on the bottle. 'Yeah, I don't know. I'm not sure this is my thing.'

'It'll get easier,' she promised, kissing him softly before heading off to find Cynthia.

'Just for the record, Hadley, I'm not impressed with this little stunt. I'm sure you can imagine the flak I'm going to get once I get back to the office. I'd always thought you were a professional,' the woman said as Hadley took a seat.

'I am a professional, Cynthia, when it comes to my job. This is my private life and that's not on the table for you and everyone else to take a slice of.'

'Come on, Hadley. You knew what you were getting into when you married Mitch. It goes with the territory. It's the trade-off for all the glitz and glamour and the big pay cheque.'

'Selling my soul was not what I signed up for. That's Mitch's problem.'

Cynthia eased back in the chair, her long legs crossed with a feminine grace Hadley had never been able to master. She eyed Hadley shrewdly. 'It has to be hard being kept on a chain like you are,' she said in mock sympathy. 'I mean, you're an independent woman, a veteran in your field, and yet you're being gagged by your network who, let's face it, will probably be dumping both you and Mitch after this scandal, to distance themselves from any public humiliation . . .'

'I think you're clutching at straws now, Cynthia. You know,' Hadley added coolly when she saw the flicker of annoyance in the other woman's eyes, 'there was a time when you were above this kind of tabloid reporting. It's sad that this is where your network thinks you belong.'

'Cynthia, we need to pack up and get on the road,' a young production assistant announced, having approached the women timidly.

Hadley didn't like hitting below the belt, but right now it seemed all gloves were off—she was just grateful that she could escape after delivering her statement.

On her way back across to Ollie she caught the last of his conversation with one of the producers. She chuckled at the look of dismay on Ollie's face.

'So we'll hang around and do a bit more filming, grab some stuff for the story. We'll interview a few people around town, get some nice stills of the place, that kinda thing. We'll need you to do a sit-down interview a bit later. You can be available?'

'I've got work to do, mate.' Ollie wasn't looking thrilled by the whole idea.

'I'm sure we can work something out,' Hadley said, stepping in. 'Why don't you let me know when you'll need him and I'll take care of it.'

The young woman's worried face relaxed significantly as she turned to face Hadley. 'They absolutely loved him back at the studio and we really want to do a feature story on Dare to Bare. We'll air it later in the week.'

Hadley turned a bright smile onto Ollie after the woman left. 'How good's that?'

'Yeah. Fantastic,' he said dryly. 'When am I supposed to get any of my actual work done?'

'It's just a day, Ollie. I'm sure we can get someone to help out. This is huge. Everyone can benefit from it. Your parents' paddock-to-plate business will get a mention; they'll film in the town and give Rankins Springs a bit of exposure, and best of all, they'll be talking about the whole issue of rural suicide,' she pointed out gently. 'Remember? The actual reason we're doing all of this?' Hadley moved into his arms and hugged him. 'Do it for Luke, Ollie.'

She felt his long sigh against her and closed her eyes briefly. Standing here, like this, with Ollie's arms around her, she felt as though she had everything she would ever need. This felt like home.

'Okay,' he finally said, and she eased back to look up at him.

'I'm so proud of you.'

'So this is all I had to do to win you over? Get on morning TV and look like a goose? If I'd known that, I would have done it years ago.'

'You didn't look like a goose,' she grinned. 'In fact you looked pretty damn sexy.'

'Oh yeah?' He kinked an eyebrow and Hadley wiggled hers back.

As Hadley drove home, her thoughts returned to the exchange she'd just had with Cynthia.

Now that everyone knew the truth, was there anything holding her back from doing an interview? It couldn't hurt her parents any more than they were hurting now. There was nothing to lose, she supposed, except her own principles. What would telling her side of the story on national television achieve? She didn't want anyone else knowing about her private life. She couldn't think of anything worse than sitting in front of a camera and answering questions from someone like Cynthia Rivers.

Twenty-five

Ollie pulled up outside the main house and noticed a familiar car parked there. He heard low voices coming from the kitchen and braced himself as he walked in.

'Here he is,' his mother said, sending him a reassuring smile. He switched his gaze to the visitors seated at the table with his parents. 'Alice and Terry came out for a cuppa.'

'Workin' hard?' Terry asked, leaning forwards to shake Ollie's hand in greeting.

'Someone around here has to,' he said, then had a weird sensation at the familiar exchange. For the briefest of moments it was as though life had gone back to the way it used to be. This was their standard greeting—the one they'd always used when Luke was still alive—and he was torn between relief and sadness.

'We wanted to come out and tell you we saw the TV segment,' Alice said after they'd exchanged small talk about the weather and the local footy team's chances that weekend.

Ollie fought the urge to squirm in his seat. 'Oh. Yeah. That.' He'd spoken to them briefly the day before the interview, not wanting to spring it on them without any warning, but hadn't gone into too much detail. Now he eyed his mate's mother warily, unsure if he'd upset them.

'It's a really terrific thing you're doing, Ollie,' Alice said softly.

Their approval hit him harder than he'd expected. He took a minute before he trusted his voice. 'Hadley's the one who lined everything up. I just got thrown in front of the camera.'

'You did a great job and I think this is a wonderful idea.'

'Wish we'd done it sooner,' Ollie said quietly.

'It's like anything important—it always takes something painful to bring about change. Loss and love are two of the world's greatest motivators,' she said sadly. 'I know you feel like you should have done something to stop Luke,' Alice said, surprising him by reaching across the table to put her hand on his, 'but you're not the only one. We feel it too,' she said, turning back to her husband. They shared a long look full of pain and heartache.

'No one could have known Luke was going to do what he did,' she said more firmly, now holding Ollie's reluctant gaze. 'Not even us—and we knew him better than anyone. So you have to stop blaming yourself.'

He swallowed hard over his tightening throat.

'What you're doing is great, Ollie. It needs to be done. For us . . . for you . . . for anyone else who's ever lost someone to this horrendous thing. It's too late once someone decides that's what they need to do—so we need to stop it reaching that point.'

He saw the tears that ran down Alice's face and his heart broke, but it was the tears in Luke's father's eyes—one of the toughest men he'd ever known—that hit him harder than any tackle ever could. He felt out of his depth, confronted with so much emotion, but something held him in his seat. They had to stop running from everything. You couldn't keep all this pain inside, hidden. Letting it out sure as shit didn't feel much better, in his opinion, but if Terry could sit there and let someone see his pain, then surely that had to mean something? This was what needed to change—there had to be hard conversations and uncomfortable moments around kitchen tables. This was what he'd been talking about and it sucked big time to feel this raw and exposed, but at the same time he felt better. His grief was still there, but some of the guilt had gone. These were the first tentative steps and they gave him hope.

The following few days sent the Dare to Bare team into a frenzy of packing orders and promotional opportunities. Ollie felt like he was struggling to keep his head above water. It'd been such a sudden rise that there had been no time to prepare for it. He hadn't factored in all the things that went hand in hand with the calendar idea, like the media interviews and the time it was taking away from farming. He was beginning to feel more than a little inundated. There was new pressure on him too. Luke's parents' visit had been a turning point for him. He knew that what he was doing was important for other people now, and while that was validation that he was on the right track, it was also an added responsibility. He watched Hadley across the room, writing on envelopes and posting off the orders that had been flooding in since the TV interview had gone to air. She looked as exhausted as he was feeling.

'Do you want to go to the pub for dinner tonight?' he asked.

'I've got another box of these to get ready to post yet,' she said, shaking her head.

'Leave it.'

'I can't leave it. People have paid for them,' she said, looking up at him, and he felt bad for suggesting it. 'What's the matter?'

'Nothing,' he said, opening another box.

'You should go in to town and kick back for a while, you've earned it.'

'I'm not leaving you here to do all this alone.'

'Ollie, we took this on together, remember? You've been working as well as doing Dare to Bare stuff. If you don't ease up when you get a chance, you'll burn out.'

'I'm not sure I'm cut out for this, Hads.'

He watched her put the pen down and walk across to him. 'I know it must feel as though it's got out of control,' she said, coming to a stop in front of him. 'But Ollie, you are such a natural at talking to reporters. You come across so honest and real. People can relate to you and that's important.'

'I just don't know how I'm gonna juggle it all if . . . I mean, when you go,' he said, feeling helpless. He didn't want to talk about when she would leave—they'd been doing so well at avoiding it. But he feared this whole project would crumble once she wasn't here to hold it up. It was Hadley who ran everything behind the scenes.

'I've been thinking about that too.'

'Are you sure you have to go? I mean, I know this isn't your job, and it doesn't actually pay a wage,' he added, and the more he spoke the more he heard how ridiculous the idea was. Of course she wouldn't want to stay and run this thing. What the hell was he thinking?

'I can still do a lot of it even when I'm not here. I can organise the media stuff and run the Facebook page from pretty much anywhere as long as I have my computer and wifi,' she said gently. 'Both our mums have agreed to come on board and they're happy to take calendars to the post, so you won't be stuck doing this at night. Everything will continue just like it has been.'

'Except you won't be here,' he said.

'It's only eight months.'

'It feels like forever already and you haven't even left yet.'

'I know. I've tried not to think about it either, but it's getting closer and I think we need to talk.'

'There's nothing to talk about, is there. I mean, you're going and that's that.'

'I thought you were okay with it?'

Ollie gave a harsh sigh and rubbed his face. 'I am. It's just, it's almost here and I feel as though we've let all these bloody interviews and photo shoots get in the way of the time we've got left. I'm not sure I can do all this alone.'

He felt a lurch in his chest as she slid into his arms and held him tightly. 'You won't be doing this alone. We're in this together.' She pulled back a little to look up at him. 'Think of this as how we'll stay connected while I'm away. We'll still talk every day, we can video chat, so we'll still see each other.' She lowered her voice, 'We might even be able to do some kinky video sexting . . .'

He grinned down at her. 'Is that a thing? I think it's called making a sex tape.'

'Whatever it is, if it makes you smile, I'm up for it.'

'With our luck, someone will hack your computer and put it up on the bloody internet.'

'Yeah, maybe you're right, I think we've had enough scandal. But, seriously, it's going to fly. You'll be busy with all this,' she said, waving an arm around the crowded room. 'And I'll be back before we know it.'

'What if something happens to you? I know it's not the cool, feminist thing to say, but I hate that your job puts you in danger. I really wish you worked in an office.'

'You know, statistically, farming is far more dangerous than reporting news. Farming comes in at number seventeen and journalism doesn't even rate in the top fifty.'

'You just happened to know this off the top of your head?' he asked doubtfully.

'I may have anticipated you bringing this up at some point,' she answered sheepishly when he raised an eyebrow.

'I can't even remember life here without you now,' he said after a few moments of just holding each other. It was true. He'd lived all this time without her, and now he wasn't sure he knew how to go back to being that old Ollie.

'It's the first time in my entire career that I'm actually questioning everything,' she said, pulling back a little. 'I've never done that before. Nothing has ever made me rethink my future, until you came along,' she told him softly. 'I need to finish out my contract, but after that, I want us to work out our future . . . together.'

Nothing had ever sounded so good. He'd hate every second of the time they were apart, but he could wait. He was a patient man when he had to be, and Hadley Callahan was worth waiting for.

∽

The late afternoon shadows were falling across the road as she turned into Stringybark and headed towards the house. She'd been sorting out the last-minute things she needed to do before she flew out to London next week, where her next assignment would take her. How had it come around so fast? Usually she was couldn't wait to get back to work, but so much had happened since she'd arrived home before Christmas. It was hard to believe the changes her life had undergone in such a short stretch of time. She'd had no idea as she'd driven down this very road back then, disheartened and betrayed, that she'd be now driving down it excited by the prospect of a future with a man she'd known all her life.

As she climbed the steps she dug out her mobile, which had unhelpfully run out of charge, and headed into the kitchen to plug it into her charger. Instantly the phone lit up and began pinging with message after message.

What the hell? Hadley picked up the phone and frowned as the screen filled up with missed calls and messages from her sister. She scrolled through them until she found the first ones.

Hadley. Answer your phone it's urgent.

For God's sake, Hadley! Answer your phone!

Hadley put the phone down and called out, 'Hello? Mum? Dad?'

'We're out the back,' her mother called and Hadley stuck her head out the door, seeing her parents and grandmother seemingly relaxed and having an afternoon drink together.

'Is everything okay?' Hadley asked casually.

'I think so,' Lavinia said, eyeing her daughter curiously. 'Why?'

'No reason,' Hadley smiled, relieved that at least there didn't seem to be any major crisis unfolding. Clearly Harmony was having some kind of meltdown; about what, she had no idea.

Hadley couldn't be bothered reading the rest of the messages, so she hit redial and waited for her sister to answer the phone.

'Thank God! Hadley.'

'What's going on?' Hadley had never heard her sister sound so relieved to hear from her. Like . . . ever.

'I tried to stop him, but he won't listen to me.'

'What? Who?'

'Mitch. He's on his way out to you.'

'Out . . . *here*? ' Hadley asked, ending with a disbelieving shriek.

'Yes. You have to make sure Dad and Griff don't do anything to him.'

Hadley had never heard her sister sound so panicked before. 'Why on earth is he coming out here?'

'I don't know. He called me from the car and told me he was heading there to see you about something and he'd tell me about it when he got to my place. Hadley, Griff . . . Dad . . . they'll kill him.'

Hadley did actually roll her eyes at that. 'Harmony, they won't *kill* him.' Maybe they'd maim him a little . . . 'Stop being so melodramatic.' God, the last thing she felt like was seeing Mitch face to face now . . . or pretty much any time in the near future to be honest.

'I'm not being dramatic,' Harmony screeched and Hadley pulled the phone away from her ear. 'I'm on my way out there. Just make sure no one does anything before I arrive.'

Can we do something after you get here? she was tempted to ask, not sure if she could be trusted not to do Mitch some bodily harm herself. The dogs' barking alerted her to the arrival of a car and Hadley was at least grateful her sister had warned her of Mitch's arrival. 'He's here.'

'Oh, God,' Harmony said, sounding as though she needed to breathe into a brown paper bag.

'Calm down.' She was liable to have a damn accident at the rate she was going. 'It'll be fine.'

'I'm twenty minutes away.'

'I wonder who that is?' Lavinia said, coming through into the kitchen to look out the window.

'It's Mitch,' Hadley said dryly. 'I just got off the phone with Harmony. She's convinced Dad will tear him apart. She's on her way.'

'Hmm,' her mother said, eyes narrowing as she watched the tall well-dressed man unfold from his flashy gold Audi. 'I'm not sure it's your father Harmony should be worried about,' she said pointedly, and Hadley bit back a grin. 'What does he want?'

'I have no idea.'

'You don't have to speak to him alone.'

'I'd rather not cause a scene. The sooner he gets whatever it is off his chest, the sooner he can leave.'

'Are you sure?'

'I'll be fine,' she said, turning to walk away before pausing, 'but maybe keep Dad occupied, just to be on the safe side.'

'I can't make any promises,' she heard her mother mutter, and shared her annoyance, although her curiosity was well and truly piqued by his sudden appearance. This was not like Mitch and that alone made her uneasy.

Mitch reached the bottom of the outdoor steps. 'Hadley,' he greeted in the smooth, deep voice that was his trademark.

Audiences trusted a voice like his. They believed whatever he said, which was important for someone reporting the news. The network needed people to believe the news.

'What are you doing here, Mitch?' she asked, forgoing any polite greeting and staying at the top of the stairs.

'I tried calling you,' he said, and she bristled at the slight accusation in his tone.

'My phone was off.'

'Is there somewhere we can talk?'

'I thought that's what we were doing.'

'Inside?' he prompted.

'What is it you want, Mitch? You can't just turn up like this without any kind of warning.'

'I wouldn't have come all this way if it wasn't important.'

'Well?' she said, crossing her arms, refusing to budge.

Mitch gave a frustrated sigh, before planting his hands on his hips and looking down at the ground, seemingly composing his thoughts. 'The network wants to do an interview.'

Hadley's eyes narrowed dangerously.

'The thing is,' he said and bit his bottom lip briefly, before looking up at her, 'they want the three of us to do an interview.'

'The three of us?' she said dryly.

'You, me and Harmony.'

'Are you freaking kidding me?'

'They want us to show everyone that it's been an amicable decision. That it's not the scandal everyone's trying to make it out to be.'

'You've lost your mind.'

'Just hear me out,' he said, climbing the stairs and taking hold of her arm.

'Oi! What the hell do you think you're doing?' Hadley saw Griffin storming towards them. 'Get your hands off my sister!'

'Griff, it's all right,' Hadley said, realising this had the potential to turn very ugly very quickly.

'What the hell is he even doing here?'

'Griffin, this is between your sister and me,' Mitch said calmly.

'You've got a bloody hide showin' your face out here.'

'Hadley, can we go somewhere private to talk about this, please?' Mitch asked impatiently.

The sound of an engine signalled the arrival of even more drama—Hadley spotted Harmony's car approaching. *All she'd wanted was a nice hot shower and a glass of wine. Was that really too much to ask for?*

'What the hell is going on out here?' her dad's gruff voice bellowed from the front doorway. 'You?' he all but roared as he spotted Mitch and charged across the verandah towards them.

'Dad, *no!*' Harmony cried as she ran from the car and threw herself between Mitch and her father theatrically.

'Oh. Dear. God.' Hadley groaned under her breath. This was more painful than a bad soapie.

'Harmony, sweetheart, I told you I could handle this,' Mitch said gently, trying to unlatch her hands from his arms. 'We're all civilised adults here. I'm sure your father and brother understand that I'm here to speak to Hadley—not to do anyone any harm.'

'Not do anyone any harm?' Lavinia repeated in disbelief, pushing past her husband to march up to her son-in-law. 'Mitchell, I am so unbelievably disappointed in you right now. I thought you were better than this, I really did.'

Mitch lost a little of his arrogance once faced with Lavinia Callahan—and it was almost comical to watch this celebrity, who had managed to charm presidents of foreign countries and warlords from Africa, lower his head in shame before a housewife from Rankins Springs.

'Lavinia, I'm sorry—'

'Not as sorry as I am. We welcomed you into our family. We treated you as our son from the very first moment Hadley brought you home, and this is what you do? I am not excusing Harmony in any of this, but we've already had that conversation—a conversation, I might add, that you should have been present for. The least you could have done was support Harmony instead of letting her come out here alone to face the family.'

'You're right,' Mitch said soberly, nodding his head. 'I'm not proud of the way I've handled things, but I intend to change all of that. Which is why I'm out here,' he added, looking over at Hadley. 'I want to stand beside Harmony now and tell the world our story. I want to explain to people how we fell in love.'

Hadley almost laughed. He was such a pro at manipulation. He could turn any situation around to suit him and he usually did. Like now. Yep, the guy knew how to sweet-talk his way out of pretty much anything.

'That's why I'm here, Hadley. We need you to be there. We need to show people that this is real. They won't believe us if you're not part of the interview.'

Harmony send a swift glance to Hadley, and gave a shake of her head. 'Mitch, I don't think that's a very good idea. Hadley doesn't want to get involved in all of this.'

Hadley did a double-take. It almost sounded as though Harmony was trying to help.

'If she doesn't, I could lose my job, Harmony,' he said, the stress in his voice making it sound husky and low.

She saw Harmony's eyes widen slightly at that, before she seemed to brace herself and take a calming breath. 'If it comes to that, we'll deal with the situation together.'

'Harmony, this is my career we're talking about,' Mitch all but pleaded.

'You're Mitch Samuals,' she said firmly. 'If this network is crazy enough to fire you over something like this, then they'll regret it when another one scoops you up. We don't need to put Hadley through this. She's been through enough.'

Hadley stared at Harmony, a little dazed that her sister was sticking up for her.

'But—' Mitch protested.

'No, Mitch. If they want an interview, we'll do it, but we're leaving Hadley out of this. They can take it or leave it.'

Right at that very moment Hadley could have honestly said she'd never loved her sister more.

'Finally. Someone with a bit of common decency,' Bob put in with a glare at his ex son-in-law . . . potentially, one day, *new* son-in-law.

'Go ahead and set up a time,' Hadley said wearily. She couldn't believe she was doing this.

'What?' everyone asked in varying tones of disbelief.

'Mitch's right. His career will be over. No other network's going to pick him up if he gets fired,' she told them bluntly. Mitch may have deserved it, but she couldn't do that to her sister after she'd turned her life upside-down for this man. For all his faults, somehow Harmony really loved him.

'You don't have to do this, Hadley,' Harmony said firmly.

'I know,' she shrugged.

'Thank you, Hadley,' Mitch said, making to move towards her again, before she sent him a look that halted him in his tracks.

'I'm not doing this for you,' she said coldly.

'Hadley, I don't understand. We agreed that things weren't working out between us. I thought we'd parted on good terms?' He actually looked confused, which would have amused her had she not been so angry at him.

'You know, I always knew you were self-centred and ambitious, but I had no idea just how much of an arsehole you really were until all of this media attention began to unfold. Not once have you *ever* given a damn about how anyone else has been affected by all of this. It's always been you and the network spinning it however it works best for *you*. I couldn't care less if you were dumped by them,' she added and took satisfaction from the shocked expression on his face. 'But I do care about my sister and her children and they're the *only* reason I'm agreeing to do this stupid interview.' Well, that and the fact that once it was done, there'd be no more hounding from the rival networks to give an exclusive.

She turned away. She was done. If she stood there a minute longer she'd quite possibly give in to the temptation to smack that dumbfounded look from his handsome face. God, the man infuriated her. Did he seriously believe that, after everything that had happened, she'd fall over herself to make sure he didn't lose his job? That everything was fine between them? Harmony could have him and good riddance.

Twenty-six

The phone was ringing as she walked into the house.

'Are you okay?' Ollie asked before she could get in a hello.

'I'm fine.'

'Is the bastard still there?'

'How did you know he was here?'

'Griff called.'

Of course he did. 'It's fine. Everything's under control.'

'What did he want?'

'An interview. It's all good. I'll do it and then it'll be over.'

'You're *doing* it?' he said, his voice rising.

'Yes. I'm doing it. Harmony, Mitch and me.'

'Because *that's* completely normal. You don't think sitting there with your ex-husband and your sister, who he cheated on you with, feels like some kind of reality show gone wrong?'

'It won't be like that. They'll bring out someone with all the right credentials to turn it into a story.' No doubt they'd bring in some other current affairs big name to lend credibility to the whole thing, she thought cynically.

'That guy either has balls the size of rockmelons or he's the biggest piece of sh—'

'Safe to say, it's not the first option. Look, I'm doing it for Harmony. I know she hasn't been easy to get on with lately, but I think she's really trying to fix things. If Mitch loses his job and it ends his career . . . she's selling her house and moving her kids to another town . . . new schools. It'd be a huge mess. Who knows? He may *still* lose his job, but if sitting through a few minutes of questions is all it takes to help him keep it, then I'll at least be able to say I did what I could.'

She heard an irritated hiss of breath get released on the other end of the line and knew he wasn't happy with her decision. 'Did your dad at least hit him? Give me some good news.'

Hadley chuckled despite herself. 'Actually, I thought Mum was going to be the one we had to hold back.'

'You should have let her at him. Want me to come over?'

'You've got pool on tonight. I'm fine. It's all over now.'

'I wish it was, but somehow it always seems to flare up again.'

She had to agree with him: every time she thought she was free of Mitch and Harmony, something always seemed to drag her back in. Well, not this time. After this she was done. No more Mrs Nice Guy.

∽

'Drink?' Hadley asked her parents as they came inside. She held up the bottle of wine she'd just opened.

'Are you sure you want to do this interview?' her mother asked, taking a seat across from her.

'It's such a dumb idea,' she laughed wearily. 'But if they think the three of us sitting in front of a camera and not killing each other is what it's going to take to end this thing once and for all, then I'll do it. I just want it over.'

'It feels like you've been doing a lot of the sacrificing in this whole bloody mess,' her father said, leaning against the kitchen bench.

Hadley shook her head sadly. 'I'm not the victim in all this, Dad. Not really. I don't think they should have gone about it the way they did, but now that I see how shallow Mitch has become, I'm just glad he's out of my life,' she said, then looked at her parents helplessly. 'But I feel bad that he's part of Harmony's. I just don't understand how she's fine with him putting his career before everything.'

'Harmony's not you,' her mother said simply. 'She's always seen the bigger picture in things. She took that old house and created a masterpiece,' she pointed out. 'She was always trying to push Don into bigger and better things. That's just the way she's always been. I think Harmony and Mitch see something of themselves in one another. If she's happy, then all we can do is support her.'

She supposed her mother was right. She usually was.

'And what about you? Are you happy? It's been so lovely

having you here for longer than a week, not hurrying off someplace for a story. Are you sure you want to go back?'

'I do want to go back to my job, Mum. I love it,' she said honestly. 'I also love Ollie,' she smiled and her mother's eyes lit up hopefully. 'I need to go back and finish my contract for my *own* peace of mind. I want to make sure I use the time I have left to make a difference. Then I can come back and know that I'm ready for a new challenge. We still haven't worked it out yet and that's fine,' she told her parents, who still looked a little doubtful. 'It's an adventure,' she shrugged. 'One I can't wait to start.'

'See how lucky you are to have me, Mum and Dad?' Griff said from the doorway. 'Aren't you glad you were blessed with *one* uncomplicated *normal* kid.'

'Normal?' Hadley scoffed.

'There's a lot to be said for low-maintenance kids. We just plod along and keep the place moving while all the drama unfolds.'

'Oh, because you're *so* low maintenance,' Olivia said, stepping into the room. 'I missed the excitement apparently.'

'Drama,' Griff put in pointedly as he took an apple from the fruit bowl.

'It was pretty uneventful, so you didn't miss much,' Hadley said, ignoring her brother.

'And no one decked Mitch?' Olivia asked.

'Nope. All very civil,' Hadley said, leaning back in her chair.

'What a shame. I was looking forward to that.'

'Hey! You were the one who told me I wasn't allowed to touch him!' Griff protested.

'Since when do you ever listen to me?'

'Because all we need is a new twist in the whole sorry saga when Mitch sues his in-laws for assault,' Hadley pointed out.

'Still,' Olivia said wistfully. 'Bet Ollie's spewing,' she added. 'He would have loved to be here and had an excuse to punch Mitch Samuals in his handsome, two-timing face.'

'Hey,' Griff frowned at Liv, raising an eyebrow.

'Well, he *is* very good-looking,' she admitted, before eyeing the rest of the family, who were watching her with varying shades of curiosity, 'in a completely cheating, arsehole kinda way, of course.'

Hadley grinned and shook her head. 'Of course.'

Ollie watched the filming of the interview from behind the cameras set up in Harmony's lounge room. He'd had his own reservations about the whole thing, but Hadley had been adamant this was what she wanted to do. He had refused to let her talk him out of coming along though. He was still annoyed that he'd missed being there when Mitch had arrived out of the blue. That would have been his one and only opportunity to deck the guy with Bob and Griffin's blessing.

As he watched Mitch now, dressed in a business shirt and pants, complete with shiny shoes and *makeup,* for

Christ's sake, Ollie wanted to hit him just for dressin' like a complete knob.

He switched his gaze across to Hadley, who sat on a chair just to one side of her sister and ex-husband. Initially the producer had attempted to place her in the middle of them until Hadley had sent the man a glare that quickly made him change his mind. So far it seemed to be going well. Mitch was doing most of the talking—naturally—and exchanging sickeningly sweet glances with Harmony. The questions had all been straightforward, and since they'd all been written by Samuals, there were no nasty surprises.

'And Hadley,' the interviewer said, turning away from Mitch, 'what was your reaction to all this? Your husband and your sister? I think anyone would find that extremely hard to accept.'

'It was a shock,' Hadley said, nodding. 'I had no idea. I suppose at first things were a little strained between us all,' she said, playing it down considerably. 'But Mitch is right, we were better at being friends than we were at being husband and wife.'

'And Hadley's job didn't help matters,' Mitch added quickly, 'She was away for months at a time on occasion . . . that really wasn't any way to make a marriage work,' he said, shaking his head sadly.

Ollie's fists clenched by his sides as he listened. The slimy bastard was deliberately making Hadley out to be the bad guy.

'Well, it takes two to make a marriage work . . . and, let's face it, in ours there was three,' Hadley answered swiftly. 'Myself, Mitch and Mitch's ego,' she said with a helpful smile.

'Ha,' Mitch gave a nervous chuckle, before adding, 'that was always our little in-joke, but the truth was that our marriage had been over for quite some time before Harmony and I started seeing each other.'

'Over, but not divorced?' the interviewer commented, 'You don't deny that you *were* still married when you began seeing Harmony?'

Mitch's confident, suave exterior faltered slightly as the questions went rogue. 'For all intents and purposes, it was over,' he said, 'and we've all remained very good friends. We'll always be family,' he added, taking Harmony's hand in his and bringing it to his lips to kiss, as he steered the questions back on track.

The interviewer threw in a few more questions before the opportunity to announce a brand new special Mitch was going to be hosting later in the year. Then, finally, it was done.

'Thank God, that's over,' Hadley said as she reached his side a few minutes later.

'He's the biggest coc—'

'Head into town for a celebratory drink later?' Mitch asked, cutting in on his way past. Clearly feeling generous now that his career seemed to have been saved.

'We have plans,' Hadley told him.

'We do?' Ollie asked after they'd left.

'We sure do,' she said, sliding her hands up his chest slowly. 'We have a motel room booked for the whole night.'

Inside he was jumble of emotions. He knew this would be one of the last times they'd have together. She was leaving in three days' time to head back to Sydney and sort out her last-minute things before flying to London and back to her real life.

He didn't want to spoil the time they had left by moping about, even though that's exactly what he felt like doing. It was hard to ignore the fact she was leaving and he hated it. And yet he knew that if he begged her to stay, told her he couldn't bear to let her go, she'd probably cave. He knew she hated the thought of leaving as much as he did, but it was important to her to see out her contract. When it came down to it, he couldn't ask her not to do that. He'd just have to suck it up and be patient.

They spent the night lapping up the luxury of the newly opened apartments in town and spent far too much time in the spa bath before making love long into the night. It was perfect. And it was over all too soon.

Ollie watched the sun rise, holding Hadley in his arms, torn between watching her sleep and wanting to spend every waking moment touching her. *She's coming back,* he told himself. He knew it was true, but he also knew that life could change in the blink of an eye. What if he lost her? What if something happened to her while she was working in some remote hellhole and he couldn't do a damn thing to save her?

'Stop it,' Hadley's sleepy murmur made him jump slightly.

'Stop what?'

'Worrying. I can hear that mind ticking over. It woke me up,' she smiled gently.

'I can't help it.'

She lifted a hand and traced the side of his face. 'I love you, Ollie. I'm coming home.'

He stared into her sleepy blue eyes and felt himself drowning. He wished they could stay here, like this, forever. Block out the rest of the world and just lie here.

'I love you too. More than you'll ever know.'

She smiled before pushing herself up on her elbows and kissing him slowly.

The sky outside the window began to lighten, filling the room with a gentle light. He couldn't stop the new day dawning and he couldn't change the world. All he could do was show the woman he loved how much he adored her and trust that she was right—that she'd be back in his arms again and their life together could finally start.

⁂

Hadley looked around her bedroom one last time and let out a small sigh. It was always hard leaving, but this time it was excruciating.

She carried her suitcase out and her father came forward and took it from her to put in the car. 'Thanks, Dad,' she said, kissing his cheek. She knew he hated goodbyes even more than she did, the big old softy. They wouldn't be making eye contact when it was time for goodbyes. That would just set everyone off and she wasn't sure she'd be able to go through with leaving if they all started crying.

Her mum was already sniffling. 'I packed you some morning tea,' she said, handing over a bag. Hadley knew what would be inside. A sandwich, wrapped in plastic wrap; some homemade biscuits, usually jam drops, which were Hadley's favourite; and an apple. It was always the same and she loved that, even as an adult, she was clearly not too old to have her mother pack her a care parcel for her car trip home.

Griff and Liv had come over and were hanging out in the kitchen.

'You're not going to let anything get in the way of you coming back for the wedding, are you?' Liv asked when the two women hugged goodbye.

'Of course not. I put in for the time off last year.'

'Not even if there's a tsunami? Or a royal birth?'

'I promise. Nothing will make me miss this wedding.'

It was only a few months away and that had been her bargaining chip when it came to saying goodbye to everyone . . . she'd be back home before the end of her contract for the wedding.

She gave her parents and brother one last hug and opened the car door. It was almost over. She really hated goodbyes. Thank goodness she and Ollie had said theirs last night. A distant sound made her glance up and her heart dropped briefly before soaring once again as she made out Ollie's ute heading towards them.

She tried to blink away the tears but they began swelling, and by the time he pulled up they were falling unchecked down her face.

'I know you said you didn't want to say goodbye today, but there's no way I'm letting you leave without doing this,' he said. He kissed her, his arms holding her so tightly that she wasn't sure she could take a breath, but she really didn't care at this point. When he pulled away she didn't bother holding back the sobs. 'I'm not sure I can do this, Ollie. I love you.'

'I love you too. You *can* do it. You won't be happy if you don't. So go get this bloody eight months over and done with so you can come home,' he said, his voice husky with his own failed attempt at keeping up a brave face, a trail of tears running down his cheeks.

'You're so pushy,' she said, wiping her eyes and straightening up.

'It's annoying, huh?' he grinned as they swapped a long glance. 'Be careful.'

'I will.' She took a deep breath and slid into the driver's seat, sending one last look up at the man she'd fallen so deeply in love with.

She drove the car down the long driveway, heading away from Ollie, and somehow, despite this, she felt that she was driving towards him. Their future was ahead of her, not behind. It didn't stop her looking back through her rear-vision mirror and smiling through her tears. She wasn't leaving. This wasn't the end. It was the start of the rest of their lives.

Epilogue

Hadley looked around at the people gathered and her heart swelled with gratitude and love. She'd missed everyone so much in the time she'd been away. She'd had a week back home for Olivia and Griff's wedding, but other than that there'd only been a few weekends here and there and brief stops on her way through to assignments.

She and Ollie had spoken almost every day, either on Facetime or by phone, but it hadn't made up for the fact she wasn't with him. She'd been homesick over the years when she'd been away too long, but it had never been like that.

If her time away proved nothing else, it at least wiped away any doubts she may have had about leaving her job. There was no way after this last stint that she could or *would* go through that again. Things were different this time around. *She* was different. Before, she did her work and went home, grateful for her comfy bed and some civilisation; now, she pined only for Ollie. She'd never pined for anything before . . . except maybe indoor plumbing and a decent coffee now and again, but she'd felt such an aching loneliness for Ollie. She still did her job and focused on the stories, but in the down times—long hours of travelling and waiting in airports—her thoughts were always of how much she missed him. She had never really understood when colleagues had moaned about how much time they spent away from their partners on assignment. After all, she'd never really felt disappointed if she'd had to stay away longer than originally planned. She'd known Mitch would be fine with her absence, and she hadn't missed him overly. *Now*, she got it though.

Dare to Bare had gone from strength to strength during her time away. Ollie's idea to bring 'The Next Shout' sessions to pubs throughout rural communities had become a big success. Teaming up with a group of volunteer counsellors, he'd taken the concept on tour, and the response had been incredible. It was a great start. It was never going to be a quick fix. After all, the walls built to enforce resilience in a hard country had taken generations to install, but they were chipping away at them and eventually change would come. She was so incredibly proud of Ollie for dedicating himself to his promise to ensure Luke would be remembered.

Her gaze moved to the back of the room and rested on a couple sitting close together, a matching pair dressed in expensive designer outfits, looking like a power couple even at a relaxed family gathering. Harmony held her gaze, but Hadley detected a shadow of reservation. While she'd been overseas, Hadley had thought a lot about her sister and their relationship. Over the years she'd judged Harmony, maybe unfairly, for how perfect her life had always seemed. With the revelation of her affair with Mitch, and the benefit of a little distance and time for the wounds to heal, Hadley had realised some of the blame in their strained relationship was her fault. If she'd taken the time to ask Harmony what was going on in her life—really taken the time, instead of looking in from the outside and making assumptions—maybe their relationship would have been stronger. Maybe Harmony would have seen Hadley as a friend instead of some stranger and maybe . . . well, you could talk yourself in circles . . . but maybe things might have turned out differently.

One particularly lonely night Hadley had reached for her phone and dialled her sister's number. She hadn't allowed herself to think about it, she'd just done it. 'Hi, Harmony. It's me,' she'd said, feeling more nervous than she had in a long time.

'How are you?' Harmony said after a brief pause.

'I'm okay. In France, waiting at the airport.'

'Yes, I saw your piece on the riots. Are you safe?'

Her sister's concern surprised her. 'Yeah, we're fine here. That was further north. Things seemed to have quietened down a bit.'

'That's good then.'

'How are the kids settling in to the big smoke?'

'They're loving it actually. I think it was the right move. Griffith was feeling a little stifling.'

'I'm glad everyone's happy.' Hadley closed her eyes briefly at how awkward the conversation felt. It was wrong. This was her sister. It shouldn't be like this. 'Look, Harmony, I just wanted to say that I'm sorry.'

'Sorry? For what?'

'I've been doing a lot of thinking lately. I've been a really crappy sister to you and I want things to be different.'

'*You've* been a crappy sister to *me*?' she repeated dryly.

'I have actually. I should have been there for you. I should have realised you were unhappy. I'm your sister and I should have forced you to tell me what was going on with your marriage, but instead I was intimidated by how perfect I thought your life was.'

'I probably wouldn't have admitted it to you anyway.'

'It should never have gotten to that point. If we'd been closer, we would have talked more.'

Neither woman spoke for a few moments as the words settled between them.

'Maybe we can start now?' Harmony said softly.

'I'd like that,' Hadley answered, and from then on the two sisters had spoken to each other every week. The conversations weren't exactly deep and meaningful; they stuck to easy subjects—the kids, Hadley's latest story. They didn't talk about Mitch or the past—this wasn't about him, it was about two sisters trying to forge a new relationship, and it meant a lot to Hadley that they were trying.

She smiled and it was a genuine smile, one that said how much it meant to her that Harmony was here, and she saw her sister's smile lift and the shadow of uncertainty disappear.

Beside her, Olivia gave a small sniff and Hadley sent her a rueful grin. Hormones were playing havoc with her best friend lately. Five months earlier, Olivia had finally made an honest man out of Griffin and the wedding had been beautiful. Hadley had been maid of honour, and that brief week of being home had been both a curse and a blessing. It had broken up the eight-month stint, but it had made it near impossible to leave again.

Griff and Liv hadn't messed around, with Liv announcing only a few weeks later that they were expecting . . . twins. Griff couldn't be happier and it was a welcome relief to have something positive to celebrate again in the family.

She saw Linc with not-so-baby Mia on his lap, seated beside a radiant-looking Cash, resting one hand on her basketball-sized belly that held their second child, due within a few weeks. If anyone had said a couple of years ago that she'd give up being a foreign correspondent and Lincoln Callahan—her big, tough, ex-commando brother—would be happily playing peekaboo and attending prenatal classes, she'd never have been able to imagine it. And yet here they were. She held Linc's gaze and read the silent message. *We made it.* And they had. He'd had his demons and she'd had hers. Of course, they'd taken the hardest, longest way around, but they'd finally reached their destination.

Her parents and Gran looked happy, and Hadley was relieved there was no sign of the stress and sadness that had been weighing them all down before she'd left.

She smiled at the man on the other side of her and felt a sudden rush of overwhelming gratitude flow through her, causing a sting in her eyes. She blinked furiously to stop them falling. Hormones were a bugger of a thing. She could relate to Liv's struggle, since that brief catch-up in May had resulted in a surprise of her own. Luckily at five months' pregnant she was hardly showing, much to Olivia's disgust, given she had a noticeable bump.

Ollie smiled down at her and her heart lurched. He was so handsome.

'I now pronounce you husband and wife,' said the celebrant, and the tears she'd almost managed to control spilled over as the loud applause from their family and friends filled her ears and Ollie stepped closer to kiss her.

'I love you,' he said softly, against her lips.

'I love *you*,' she said back, and smiled as he wiped the tears from her face.

They'd come full circle. All her family together, at her wedding—even the original groom, she conceded dryly with an internal shake of her head. Only this time, even he'd finally found the woman he was meant to be with, and Hadley was with the man who'd been there, right under her nose, her entire life.

And now there was a new generation of Callahans coming into the world and the circle would continue to turn once more on Stringybark Creek.

Acknowledgements

The idea for this story was sparked when I read an article about a real-life Ollie named Ben Brooksby and the site he'd started called The Naked Farmer.

The work Ben and his co-founder partner, Emma, have done to raise money for rural mental health through the Royal Flying Doctor Service is a credit to them both. They started the original Naked Farmer calendar and travelled around the country, visiting rural Australia to interview and document some of the stories behind the farmers on their calendars in an effort to raise awareness of rural mental health.

I hope you've enjoyed this series, The Callahans of Stringybark Creek, as much as I've enjoyed writing it.

Thank you to all my friends in Rankins Springs and surrounds who gave me the inspiration to write this series and helped me out with questions. If you haven't been out to the Riverina area, put it on your bucket list—it's a beautiful part of our country to visit.

Thank you as always to my readers, many of whom have become friends and who always lend a hand when I put out a call for help!

∽

If you or someone you know is struggling with a mental health issue, you can call the Royal Flying Doctor Service mental health unit on 1300 887 678 twenty-four hours, seven days a week. Also available are:

Lifeline on tel: 13 1114

Beyond Blue on tel: 1300 224 636

Calendars and merchandise to help fundraising for The Naked Farmer are available from thenakedfarmerco.com.au. Please support this initiative if you can.

Something Like This

KARLY LANE

Jason Weaver just wants to be left alone. It was a tough transition from his army days to civilian life, so when he buys an isolated fixer-upper property on the outskirts of Ben Tirran in the New England mountains, he's looking forward to some peace and quiet.

Tilly Hollis is working two jobs to save for her dream career: running an equine therapy program from her farm in Ben Tirran. It's not the most glamorous life—as her New York fashion designer sister would agree—but Tilly loves her horses more than anything, and after losing her husband and business partner just a few years earlier, she's determined to make it work on her own.

When Jason walks into the cafe where Tilly works, his plans for a quiet, solitary life quickly evaporate. They're drawn to one another immediately, but they both have walls up and aren't afraid to tell it like it is. They've both been alone for too long, but can they overcome their pasts to build a future together?

ISBN 978 1 76052 925 3

One

Jason Weaver stood out on the verandah, cradling his coffee cup in his hand as he watched the sun slowly poke its head above the horizon. There was a crispness in the air, a signal that winter was on its way, but it wasn't as cold as other places he'd been, and he liked that sharp slap to the face from an early-morning rise. It reminded him that he was still alive.

He'd never heard of the township of Ben Tirran before he'd stumbled upon the house and land in an online real-estate search. Nestled in the New England mountains, it was a world away from the Hawkesbury region where he'd grown up.

He loved the bushland that surrounded his new home. Thick eucalypt forests full of brush box, Sydney blue gum and tallow-wood stood towering over the gullies and mountains that he looked out on from his back yard. Jason breathed in a lungful of clean mountain air as he rested his cup on the huge round strainer post that supported the fence. He let his gaze follow the high ridges that rolled, like a set of waves, one hill after another as far as the eye could see. His property overlooked a valley, the farmland of paddocks like a patchwork in varying shades of green and brown as it unfolded over the hills into the distance.

Jason had arrived just two days earlier, and the place could only be described as a fixer-upper, but that was okay because that's what he'd been looking for. It wasn't a cutesy little farmhouse with wide verandahs; it was more of a boxy, tired-looking dwelling that had been added to over the years by previous owners—none seemingly particular about improving the aesthetics. Despite that, the old girl had good bones and would come up a treat with a little tender loving care. He could already see the finished product in his mind.

As a builder, Jason was more than capable of constructing a new house from scratch, but he didn't want something new. New houses lacked character. He wanted something rustic; something he could put a bit of his own personality into. And most of all, he wanted peace and quiet.

It had been a rough transition from his army days. He'd had a lot to adjust to: coming back home, fitting into the civilian world again and adjusting to life with a disability. That had been the hardest challenge. It wasn't only that he'd lost part of his leg, it was that somewhere along the way he'd lost a part of what had made him . . . *him*. The army had given him purpose and stability. He'd planned on it being his career, and then one day he'd woken up in a hospital bed, with half a leg missing. At thirty-two years old, he suddenly had no idea what he was going to do with the rest of his life.

He'd been lost for a long time after returning home from the Middle East—trying to work out where he fitted in. He wasn't particularly pleasant to be around for the first six months, but he was lucky to have a mum who refused to let him wallow in drink and self-pity for too long, and friends and a community who supported him when he started up his own handyman business.

He'd grown up in Lochway. All Jason's childhood memories were filled with the small town, but after his mother had passed away from a long illness, he knew there wasn't anything left for him there. He needed something new. A place he could put his own stamp on, and get away from the memories and constant reminders of the life he hadn't even realised he'd wanted until he couldn't have it.

Jason tipped the last mouthful of coffee down his throat and turned away from the view. There would be plenty of time to sit around and head down memory lane. Now, he had a house to rebuild.

❧

Tilly Hollis rested her arm across the long neck of the horse which was nudging impatiently through the bucket of feed at her feet. 'Anyone would think you're starving,' she said, shaking her head. 'Nothing could be further from the truth, could it, boy?' Her old brumby, Denny, who technically hadn't been a brumby for almost fifteen years, ate on, oblivious to her gentle mocking.

Denny was her star—he was the horse she taught beginner riders on and used in demonstrations. He loved kids and would stand as docile as a statue while they climbed about on his back. He'd been seven when he was caught wild in the Guy Fawkes National Park, and was the first horse she had ever trained. Tilly had bought him when she'd first moved to Toowoomba, and then when she had returned to the family farm, Brumby Creek, of course he had come too. David used to joke that he came second to a horse in their marriage. In all fairness, Denny *had* been there first, and Tilly *had* warned David about what he was getting himself into. A familiar pang of grief touched her lightly at the thought. It wasn't as painful now, not like it had been for the first year or so, but it was still there, lurking in the shadows. She gently pushed the sadness away and breathed deeply against the horse's neck.

Denny was a buckskin, a creamy tan coat, with dark legs and mane, the same colouring as the iconic horse from *The Man from Snowy River*—Tilly's favourite movie of all time.

That film had shaped her life, from her love of horses to her very name. She blamed her mother for the latter, but it was her Pop who had instilled the passion for brumbies. It was family folklore that her mother's side of the family were related to Banjo Paterson, the great Australian poet, though no one had gone back that far in their family history to prove it, but her Pop took great pride in the Paterson name.

Her mother, growing up with the Paterson surname and family pride, had fallen in love with the movie inspired from Banjo's famous poem. She had named Tilly, Matilda after the main character's young mother from the story; Tilly's older sister was named Jessica after the lead character, and her brother was named Jim. Tilly hadn't thought it strange, until she'd got older and realised that perhaps her family's obsession went a little too far with their cats being named Mrs Bailey and Rosemary, and their dogs Spur and Harrison.

Her mother never thought it a problem. 'There's nothing wrong with being quirky and passionate about something, Tilly,' she'd said on more than one occasion. If you looked up quirky and passionate in the dictionary, there was probably a photo of her mother there—possibly her sister as well.

With a reluctant last pat of her trusty steed, she trudged back up the hill to the house. She wished she had time to just hang with the horses. Maybe if she won the lotto, but in the meantime in order to keep her horses fed and her bills paid, she had to go off to her day job.

The cafe wasn't exactly her dream job, but it helped put food on the table while allowing her time to build up her business. She was a veterinary nurse by trade and would have still been doing that if there'd been a local vet close enough to make working in a practice practical. But the truth was that Tilly had grown weary of the job she'd once loved. Her passion lay in horses—it always had—and now her dream to build up an equine therapy business to one day become her main revenue earner was getting closer.

∽

'Morning,' Tilly called as she walked in through the back door of the cafe.

Allie glanced up from her chopping board and gave her a bright smile. 'Morning, Tilly.'

Tilly loved her workmates. Allie, the chef, was a single mum who had moved back to Ben Tirran a year ago with her three teenage sons after a divorce. It was hard to imagine that she was old enough to be the mother of teenagers. She always had a smile on her face and her long dark hair was usually pulled back in a ponytail, giving her a youthful appearance. Tilly knew Allie had married quite young and then had her first two children. She didn't like to talk about her second marriage, which had recently ended, but Tilly knew from the little things she had said over the past twelve months that Allie felt a little ashamed that she had two failed marriages and two different fathers for her three children. It didn't seem to matter that Tilly always pointed out it wasn't a big deal; it remained a touchy subject.

'Morning, Paul,' Tilly said as she put her handbag away and picked up her notepad and pen.

'Mornin'.' Paul was the least likely person you could imagine owning a cafe. His surname was Searle; Searle by name and surly by nature was how he was known. But the Cafe-inated was his pride and joy. Coffee was not only his business, it was his passion. He had an intense dislike for the yuppie modern barista—the 'man-bun–wearin' hipster freaks givin' the coffee industry a bad name'. You would no sooner see a man-bun on Paul than a pink tutu on a construction worker. But he did make the best coffee Tilly had ever tasted.

'Morning, girls,' a bouncy blonde greeted them cheerily as she burst through the back door a few minutes later wearing the cafe uniform. Today Josie's T-shirt read: *May your coffee be strong and your Monday be short*. For a grump, their boss had a very weird sense of humour, which he took very seriously when it came to sourcing their coffee-related T-shirt slogans.

'Morning, Pauly,' Josie added as he walked from the front of the shop to stand in the doorway.

'You're late,' he said, mid scowl. 'Again.'

'No, I'm not. Look,' she replied, holding her wrist up in front of the big man's face.

Paul pointed at the clock on the wall. 'We go off that time. You're late.'

'Oh, come on, five minutes. If that. It takes time to get this pretty. Beauty doesn't just happen like magic, you know,' she pouted, crossing her arms over her ample chest.

Tilly and Allie exchanged glances. Josie used her feminine wiles on men all the time, and much to Tilly's disbelief, it usually worked. Paul was no exception; it seemed Josie's heaving breasts were even too much for Surly Searle to fight.

'Set your watch to that,' he said, throwing a nod at the wall clock before turning back to the front of the store—but not before Tilly caught a creeping redness begin to make its way up the back of his neck.

'I will. I promise,' Josie cooed after him.

'Really?' Tilly said, sending the other girl a dry glance.

'What?' Josie shrugged.

'One day he's not going to be blinded by those boobs and then what are you going to do?'

'We both know that day will never come, *Matilda*,' Josie said sweetly, before sashaying from the kitchen.

Sometimes Tilly wished she could dislike the woman, but she was actually quite likeable. It was hard to understand—usually the Josies of the world were very annoying. Tilly couldn't think of anything worse than acting helpless just to attract the attention of a man, and yet Josie did it on a daily basis. At twenty, she was younger than the other two women, and Tilly suspected most of her behaviour came from sheer boredom. Tilly and Allie had been encouraging her to find a job out of town, somewhere with more opportunities than Ben Tirran. Tilly was a firm believer in broadening one's horizons, and if anyone needed their horizons broadened, it was Josie.

'Morning, Tilly dear,' the older woman seated at the window said as she came over.

'Good morning, Vera. It's nice to see you up and about.'

'I wanted to thank you for dropping my groceries off to me the other day. You're a good girl,' she said, patting Tilly's hand.

'That's okay, I have to drive past on my way home anyway.'

Tilly smiled. Vera Loveday had been a dear friend of her grandmother's and had been a godsend during her mother's illness, often staying with her so Tilly could come in to work.

Vera gave a small, somewhat annoyed sniff. 'It saved a visit from my son anyway—he's still trying to talk me into selling the house.'

Tilly knew Vera's family were worried about her living alone in the house she and her husband had bought as newlyweds almost sixty years ago. She was getting on and had recently had a small operation, but as far as Tilly could tell she seemed to be capable enough. She came into the cafe at least twice a week to meet up with friends and was still an active bowler. She drove herself around wherever she needed to go and even took her own bins out each week. It seemed a little unfair that her son and daughter-in-law continued to hound her about giving up her independence as often as they did.

'It's no trouble, Vera. Honestly. You make sure you call me anytime you want me to do it again.'

'I should be fine, thanks, sweetheart. But it's always good to know there are people about who I can rely on if I need them.'

'Always, you know that. Now what can I get you today?' As Tilly took the order out the back, she smiled a little sadly, remembering how kind so many people had been when she'd needed help with her mother. There were a lot of good folk in this town and she valued the close-knit community more than they'd ever know.

Tilly heard the door of the cafe open and glanced up, noting with a touch of surprise that she didn't know the man who was walking in. She watched him move across to a table in the far back of the cafe, absently observing he had a limp, but waited until he was settled before she approached him to take his order.

'Good morning,' Tilly said pleasantly.

'I'll have a coffee and a bacon-and-egg roll,' the newcomer said.

'Please,' Tilly tacked on dryly. Rude people annoyed her, but she hated even more that she'd wasted a perfectly cheery 'good morning' on this particular one.

'What?' The man looked up at her with a slight crease between his eyes.

'You forgot to say please,' she said, taking the menu from him.

'Please,' he replied a little stiltedly, a somewhat guarded frown on his face.

'Not a problem. I'll have that brought out to you as soon as possible.' She plastered on an extra wide smile just for him, before turning away from the table.

'Who's the new bloke?' Paul asked, craning his neck for a better look out into the cafe.

'I have no idea. He's not exactly the chatty kind.'

'Send Josie out, she'll get the info out of him,' Paul said with a grunt, before getting busy with the order Tilly gave him.

'I should,' she said with a hint of malicious glee. He looked like the kind of man who would welcome a bubbly blonde chattering away in his ear first thing in the morning . . . not.

At this time of the morning the cafe was frequented mostly by locals dropping in for their morning coffee, and Tilly saw them darting quick glances over at the nearby table, talking quietly, more than likely trying to work out who the stranger was.

When Paul had finished making the coffee, Tilly carried it across, placing it carefully on the table before him. 'There you go. Your roll won't be long.'

'Thanks,' he said, almost reluctantly, but when Tilly looked up at him, she noticed that he wasn't wearing the petulant expression she was expecting. In fact, she was rather surprised by the level look he gave her, his hazel eyes watching her curiously.

'You're welcome.' She moved away from the table, slightly confused. What on earth was that? He was a jerk a few minutes ago, and now he was turning those smouldering eyes on her. She wasn't even sure she wanted to admit they *were* smouldering . . . Clearly, she needed some quality horse time to realign her whatever-the-hell that was out of kilter.

Horses could fix anything—well, if not fix, at least help break down barriers, which could lead to ways to fix things. That's what Healing Hooves was going to do. Tilly had volunteered in a horses-for-therapy centre when she was younger and had seen first-hand the difference animals could make. Having horses in her life had certainly helped her work through her grief over the past two years.

It had always been her and David's dream to create such a place, right here in Ben Tirran on her grandparents' property. She wanted to make a difference to the world.

'Order up,' Paul called, snapping her from thoughts of horses and her wish that she could be home with them right now.

Tilly braced herself as she made her way to the stranger sitting alone and placed his food in front of him. 'Enjoy.'

'Thank you,' he said, and this time there was less hesitation in his voice.

Tilly smiled to herself as she walked away. She had done her good deed for the day—given a grump a lesson in manners and hopefully turned his day around.

The door opened and the cafe began to fill with a busload of elderly residents from a nursing home on a day out from the coast, arriving ready for morning tea. She was kept busy taking orders and helping with seating arrangements, and when she glanced up later, she found the table at the back empty. Tilly told herself it was fine that he hadn't said goodbye. Why would she even care? He was probably some guy passing through, who she would never see again. It happened every day, people came and went. Well, maybe not every day—this was Ben Tirran, after all. She had far more important things to think about, though, like trying to remember what was on the shopping list she'd left on her kitchen bench. She was pretty sure there wasn't even milk left in the fridge to have on cereal for dinner tonight.